IRISH KNIT MURDER

Bettina had been staring bleakly at the unadorned tombstone. Now she stared bleakly at Pamela. "What shall we do?" she asked.

"Go back home?" Pamela shrugged.

"It might be here, somewhere," Bettina said. "It might have blown away."

"But the point of your photo was going to be that someone placed it on Isobel's grave. If it's just lying in the grass, far from the grave, the connection with the Isobel Lister story is lost."

Pamela's words were wasted. Bettina was off again, scurrying toward a path that led up a slight incline. Pamela followed, but at some remove. The incline leveled off to a plateau bordering a wooded area that marked the cemetery's eastern boundary. Ancient tombstones worn to shapelessness by wind and weather shared the space with a few gnarled trees. Then the grass gave way to land claimed by a dense thicket of trees.

"I think I see something white," Bettina cried, plunging among the trees.

From the thicket came a wordless shriek.

"Bettina! What happened?" Pamela called. "Are you okay?"

"I am," Bettina called back. "But somebody isn't."

Stepping into the thicket, Pamela caught sight of Bettina kneeling near the base of an especially large tree. A twisted swath of white, like a knitted scarf or shawl, trailed over the composted leaves, but it was tethered at one end to the neck of a recumbent body . . .

IRISH KNIT MURDER

A Knit & Nibble Mystery

PEGGY EHRHART

Kensington Publishing Corp.
www.kensingtonbooks.com

KENSINGTON BOOKS are published by

Kensington Publishing Corp.
119 West 40th Street
New York, NY 10018

Copyright © 2023 by Peggy Ehrhart

All Kensington titles, imprints, and distributed lines are available at special quantity discounts for bulk purchases for sales promotion, premiums, fund-raising, educational, or institutional use.

Special book excerpts or customized printings can also be created to fit specific needs. For details, write or phone the office of the Kensington Sales Manager: Attn.: Sales Department. Kensington Publishing Corp., 119 West 40th Street, New York, NY 10018. Phone: 1-800-221-2647.

The K and Teapot logo is a trademark of Kensington Publishing Corp.

First Printing: March 2023
ISBN: 978-1-4967-3885-1

ISBN: 978-1-4967-3887-5 (ebook)

10 9 8 7 6 5 4 3 2 1

Printed in the United States of America

In memory of my father, Matthew Nicholas Ehrhart
(1918 – 2021)

ACKNOWLEDGMENTS

Abundant thanks to my agent, Evan Marshall, and to my editor at Kensington Books, John Scognamiglio.

CHAPTER 1

Bettina Fraser's amiable features usually radiated cheer, but at the moment her expression revealed that her feelings had been hurt.

"The *Advocate* may be a weekly," she said, raising her voice to be heard over the many conversations echoing in the large room, "but many people—*most* people—in Arborville appreciate a newspaper that focuses exclusively on their own town."

"Of course they do." Pamela Paterson reached an arm around her friend's shoulders and gave her a quick squeeze. "I don't see the *County Register*'s Marcy Brewer here to cover the senior center's St. Patrick's Day luncheon."

"She wouldn't come to a thing like this. She thinks she's too important." Bettina's head drooped forward, and the scarlet tendrils of her carefully styled hair quivered. The scarlet coiffure offered a striking contrast to the bright Kelly green of her ensemble, a silky blouse and tailored wool pants in the same shade.

Pamela had overheard the offending comment too. A woman sitting at a nearby table had nudged her companion, pointed at Bettina, and remarked that she was a reporter for the *Arborville Advocate*—whereupon her companion had replied, making no effort to keep her voice down, "Oh, that silly thing. Nobody takes it seriously or even reads it."

"Anyway," Pamela added, with another squeeze, "they're coming around with coffee and dessert now, and the entertainment is about to start."

The luncheon menu had been a very appropriate corned beef and cabbage, with boiled potatoes and Irish soda bread still warm from the oven. As Pamela spoke, a server whisked away the plates bearing the luncheon remains, and a few moments later dishes of chocolate ice cream appeared, as well as a platter of cookies the shape and color of shamrocks. Another server circled the large table filling coffee cups.

Cheered by the sight of the cookies, the ice cream, and the steaming cup of coffee, Bettina seemed happy to nod and agree when a woman across the table, sixty-ish and cheerful, began to praise Meg Norton, who had organized the event. "The volunteers from the high school too," she added, "cooking and serving all this delicious food."

"Too bad about the flower delivery though," observed a gray-haired woman who had acknowledged the holiday by looping a bright green scarf around her neck.

"Flowers? I don't see flowers." This was uttered by a woman who had heretofore been focused more on her dessert than on the topic at hand.

"You don't see them because they weren't appropriate," said the gray-haired woman. "Not appropriate at all!"

"What was wrong with them?" Bettina inquired, postponing the bite of cookie she was about to take.

"They were all white," the gray-haired woman explained. "Lilies and things, mournful things, not like something for a party—and worst of all, there was a card that read 'In deepest sympathy for your loss.' Meg was horrified, but by the time she saw the card, the delivery man had gone."

But that conversation was cut short when a lively run of notes drew their attention to the piano near the back wall of the room—Arborville's spacious rec center had been pressed into service because the senior center was too small for an event like this. A man no less dashing for being well into middle age had just launched a melody that Pamela, after a moment of thought, recognized as "When Irish Eyes Are Smiling."

He paused after a few verses and swiveled around to acknowledge the sprinkling of applause with a nod. Then he advanced toward a microphone on a stand a few yards from the piano and flung an arm out toward a doorway in the back wall. Into the doorway stepped a statuesque woman smiling a bright, lipsticky smile. The undulating waves of her blonde hair evoked the Hollywood of decades past, but her sleek leggings and stiletto heels brought a more up-to-date glamour to the look. The ensemble was completed by a form-fitting green sweater in a shade that was more Day-Glo than Kelly.

"Isobel Lister!" the man exclaimed, arm still extended. "Let's hear a big welcome for Arborville's own Isobel Lister!"

The woman took his place at the microphone after an inaudible but flirtatious exchange with him, and he returned to the piano. In a moment Isobel Lister's amplified voice, husky but pleasant, rang out in celebration of "Whiskey in the Jar." As she sang, she scanned the room, bestowing a teasing wink here and an insinuating smile there, particularly at the piano player. Meanwhile, the fingers of her right hand snapped in time to the rhythm, and her feet—impractical shoes notwithstanding—hopped about in a kind of jig.

The applause that followed the song was hearty and well-earned. When it had died down enough to make conversation possible, the gray-haired woman in the bright green scarf leaned forward.

"She's over seventy, you know," the woman said. "I don't know how she does it. *I* couldn't wear those shoes."

But there wasn't time to explore the topic further. After brushing her hand across her forehead and exclaiming, "Whew! That was fun," Isobel turned toward her accompanist. "Hey, Mr. Piano Man," she said, "how about 'Molly Malone'?"

And she launched into a raucous version of that familiar tune, complete with a hint of Irish brogue.

Bettina had rummaged in her handbag for her phone as soon as Isobel started to sing. Now she left her seat and moved to the side of the room, where she could angle for good shots without obstructing other people's views of the performance. Pamela found herself tapping her foot in time to the music, cookies and coffee forgotten. The women facing her across the table had rotated their chairs to face the makeshift stage. Pamela couldn't see their expressions, but their bobbing heads suggested they were as caught up in the lively rhythms as was Pamela herself.

"Here's a classic one," Isobel said, as the applause for "Molly Malone" trailed off. Turning toward her accompanist, she added, "We'll slow things down a bit . . . and try not to cry. 'Danny Boy'!" She closed her eyes, tossed her head back, and sang the opening line, "Oh, Danny Boy . . ." with a hint of a smile, as if savoring some memory awakened by the song.

A hush fell over the room as Isobel's husky voice lingered on each phrase of the song, with her accompanist supplying a gentle chord here and a delicate trill there. The respectful silence made the loud squeak coming from a chair near the edge of the room all the more startling. Heads swiveled in the direction of the squeak, eyes stared as a stern-looking elderly woman rose, seized her handbag and walking stick, and stalked from the room, but Isobel carried on. She seemed so caught up in the world evoked by the song as to be oblivious of her surroundings, unruly though an audience member might be.

"That *was* a sad one," she declared as the last few notes of the song faded away, but before the applause began. When the applause died down and it was possible to be heard again, she said, "Let's cheer things up with something fun. Shall we?" She glanced around the room as if inviting agreement. A few people nodded and she nodded back, smiling mischievously as her eyes continued to roam.

Then the roaming stopped and, as if addressing one particular person, a woman about Isobel's own age sitting at a table near the front, she went on. "You know, we Arborville girls weren't as goody-goody as some people thought. I could tell stories"—she looked into the distance and laughed—"but I won't, just now at least."

She nodded at her accompanist and offered him a mischievous smile. He played a few chords, but before she began to sing, she added, "This one isn't really Irish—but it's got clover. That's the same thing as shamrocks, right?"

Bettina, by this time, had returned to her seat next to Pamela. As Isobel belted out the opening lines of "Roll Me Over in the Clover," she grabbed Pamela's arm and gave a delighted giggle. Then she reached for another shamrock cookie.

A few people began to laugh, and the heads that had bobbed to "Whiskey in the Jar" commenced bobbing again. But apparently not everyone was delighted with the choice of material. The woman Isobel had seemed to address before launching into the song slipped out of her seat, edged toward the side wall, and tiptoed quickly to the entrance.

The remainder of the concert was something of an anticlimax, though the audience members smiled, tapped their feet, and swayed back and forth as "The Harp That Once Through Tara's Halls" gave way to "My Wild Irish Rose," followed by "Erin Go Bragh," "Mother Machree," "Foggy Dew," and "How Are Things in Glocca Morra?"

It was coming up on one thirty when Isobel leaned toward the microphone and said, in her husky voice, "You've been a great audience and we're going to wind things up now. But first"—she flung out an arm—"let me introduce this handsome guy at the piano. Nate Riddle!"

Then, with a saucy head-toss, she belted out the

opening lines of "The Wild Rover." Verse followed verse until, nearing the song's conclusion, Isobel spread her arms wide. The tempo slowed and she lingered over the last few words as if plumbing them for every bit of meaning. The piano punctuated the end with a resounding chord, Isobel dipped forward in a dramatic bow, and the room echoed with the sound of applause.

After another bow, and a generous round of kisses blown to the audience and her accompanist, Isobel darted back through the doorway from which she had emerged.

"She's really something," Bettina declared when normal conversation was possible again. "'Arborville's own,' the pianist said. It's amazing that I've lived here all this time and I never came across her before. But I got some good photos for the *Advocate*."

Many shamrock cookies remained on the platter in the middle of the table, and servers were circulating with fresh pots of coffee. Soon chatter and laughter had replaced the sounds of Isobel's voice and the accompanying piano. Bettina had been drawn into conversation by the woman sitting on the other side of her and Pamela was content to drink her coffee and nibble on a shamrock cookie—just a simple butter cookie, really, with buttercream icing tinted green, but the shamrock shape made it festive and fun.

"Will she come back out, I wonder," inquired the gray-haired woman with the bright green scarf from across the table. She and the others who had turned their chairs around when Isobel began to sing were now facing the table again. "She was sitting up there during the lunch"—the woman pointed at a table close to the piano—"next to the piano player."

"She certainly earned her coffee and cookies," said

the cheerful sixtyish woman sitting next to her. "And I'll bet a few people would even like her autograph."

"Yes," the gray-haired woman laughed, "her adoring public. And she's certainly not shy. So where is she?"

The same question seemed to have occurred to Meg Norton, the event organizer. Looking past the heads of the women facing her across the table, Pamela watched as Meg, a pleasant-looking woman in her sixties, with undemanding features and well-groomed hair tinted an inconspicuous shade of brown, made her way toward the door in the back wall.

She was gone no more than two or three minutes. When she emerged, she was still alone, but she no longer resembled herself.

Her expression evoked the cover graphics of a pulp paperback: a desperate woman with forehead creased, eyes wide, and mouth distended as if frozen in mid-scream. Meg did not scream, however. Instead, she clapped her hands, like a schoolmarm calling for order. Due more, perhaps, to the expression on her face than to the handclap, the room fell suddenly silent. It was as if a plug had been pulled on the laughter and chatter.

"Isobel is dead!" Meg announced. "She's just . . . dead!"

Instantly, Bettina was on her feet. She snatched up her phone and launched herself toward the doorway where Meg stood.

"Where are *you* going?" called a voice as she passed.

"I'm a reporter," she replied, slowing down only briefly. "Bettina Fraser from the *Arborville Advocate.*"

Suddenly the festive room was no longer festive. No

one spoke, not even in shocked whispers directed to tablemates. The fanciful decor—featuring giant shamrocks with leaves the size of dinner plates, tissue honeycomb rainbows, papier-mâché leprechauns, and pots of foil-wrapped chocolate "coins"—seemed a puzzling mockery of the mood that had descended over the gathering. Even the cheery ensembles, which included green sports jackets for some of the men, now appeared out of place.

Without quite thinking about what she was doing, Pamela leapt from her seat and followed Bettina as she wove between tables, nearly catching up with her as they approached Meg, who still stood in the same spot from which she had made her announcement. But instead of speaking to Meg, Bettina veered around her and swerved into the hallway that led to the back entrance of the rec center. Pamela reached her friend's side just as Bettina screeched to a halt in the doorway of the office that had been pressed into service as a green room.

Bettina lifted her phone, steadied it with both hands, and aimed it at the body of Isobel Lister, who was sprawled across the office's linoleum floor with her eyes staring sightlessly at the acoustic tile ceiling. The desk chair and a coat rack had been tipped over, and Isobel's long blonde hair was in disarray, suggesting that her current state was the result of a vigorous struggle.

Pamela was about to speak—saying what, she wasn't sure—but her attention was drawn to something visible beyond the windows in the heavy double doors further along the hallway. She stepped away from Bettina's side, leaving her focused on her task, and approached the double doors. They opened onto a small patio, beyond which was the parking lot that served the police station and the library.

Wanting to get a better look, she pushed one of the doors open and leaned outside. A van with the words "Beauteous Blooms of Timberley" lettered on the side in an elegant script was parked at the edge of the lot closest to where she stood. The driver's head swiveled toward her (the door had made a scraping sound as it opened), then swiveled back to face straight ahead. The van's engine awakened with a snarl and the van sped toward the parking lot's exit.

A voice from behind Pamela was calling Bettina's name. Pamela turned to see that Meg had gathered her wits and was putting her organizational talents to use, albeit in a situation she had probably never imagined.

"Bettina," she repeated, "I've called the police, and they should be here momentarily. I'm sure they would want the crime scene left just as it is." She directed her gaze toward Pamela, who had pulled the heavy door shut with a clang but was still standing near it. "Pamela! No one should be back here. Let's all return to our tables."

Two officers had already arrived by the time Pamela and Bettina slipped into their seats. Pamela recognized both officers, Officer Sanchez—Arborville's only female police officer—with her sweet heart-shaped face, and Officer Anders, trying to disguise his gentle boyishness by frowning.

Exempting herself from her suggestion that all three of them return to their tables, Meg met them at the room's entrance. A subdued hum of conversation had replaced the silence that followed her grim announcement, making it impossible to hear what she was telling the officers or how they were responding. But she gestured toward the doorway in the back wall and soon the small procession—Meg in a pea-green pantsuit and the officers in navy blue—was making its way across the polished floor.

"The next thing that will happen is that Clayborn will come," Bettina said, addressing her comment not to Pamela but to their tablemates. Pamela herself was quite aware that, after examining the crime scene to determine that it really was a crime scene, the uniformed officers who responded to the 911 call would summon Arborville's chief, and only, detective.

It was a curious fact that, idyllic a town as Arborville was, murders were not unknown to its small police department—murders carried out by *nice* people, people one would have thought were the very last people to ever do such horrible things. And more curious still, Pamela seemed often to be at hand when the murders were discovered—or sometimes to actually stumble upon the bodies herself. With a talent for noticing things overlooked by others, she sometimes realized the identity of a killer even before the police did.

Meg accompanied the two officers as far as the door leading to the back hallway and the crime scene beyond. Apparently being told by Officer Sanchez not to follow them any further, she lingered near the door, keeping a vigilant eye on the luncheon guests, perhaps having been tasked with making sure no one left.

Five minutes passed. Then Officer Sanchez appeared in the doorway and spoke briefly to Meg. Meg clapped her hands, the buzz of conversation ceased, and Officer Sanchez announced, in a firmer voice than one would have suspected from her sweet heart-shaped face, that everyone was to remain and the police would be taking statements.

At that moment, Detective Clayborn arrived, moving purposefully across the polished floor in his nondescript sports jacket. The expression on his homely face was nondescript as well, save for the slight tightening around the eyes that Pamela had come to recognize as signaling curiosity.

CHAPTER 2

As soon as Bettina turned into her driveway, the front door of the Frasers' house opened and a portly man wearing a plaid shirt and bib overalls stepped onto the porch, accompanied by a shaggy dog that was nearly half as tall as he was. The man hurried down the walk that led from the porch to the driveway, followed by the dog, reaching Bettina's faithful Toyota just as she emerged.

"Dear, dear wife!" exclaimed the man, who was Bettina's husband, Wilfred. "It's nearly five p.m. Woofus and I have been so worried—though I know St. Patrick's Day celebrations can be quite lively." He bent to study Bettina's face. As if responding to an unspoken signal, he held out his arms and Bettina sagged into an embrace.

"Pamela"—Wilfred gazed across the Toyota's roof to address her—"what on earth has happened?"

Though not included in the hug, Pamela felt nearly as comforted as if Wilfred's arms surrounded her as well. His genial presence, and even that of the timid but solicitous dog—who was at that moment sniffing her foot—soothed the chaos unleashed in her mind the moment Meg made her startling announcement.

"Isobel Lister is dead." Pamela sensed that her expression was bleak, and once the words sank in, Wilfred's face mirrored that bleakness.

"How tragic!" he exclaimed. "She was such a lively person, and not that old—though we're all getting up there." Wilfred himself was approaching seventy, and he referred to Bettina as his child bride.

Bettina stirred against his chest and a muffled voice, or more like a wail, emerged from the region of the overalls' bib: "She was murdered, Wilfred. She didn't just . . . *die*."

"We must all go inside," Wilfred declared, "and sit down."

As if he understood his master's words, Woofus led the way, and soon the three humans were sitting around the scrubbed pine table in the Frasers' spacious kitchen, while Woofus occupied his favorite spot against the wall. To make the little gathering complete, Punkin the ginger cat soon crept in to nestle against Woofus's shaggy flank.

The kitchen offered consolations beyond a cozy atmosphere and comfortable chairs. From the direction of the stove came the aroma of simmering corned beef, traceable to a large two-handled pot on a back burner. It blended with the aroma of something sweet and bread-like, with a hint of caraway seeds, emanating from the oven.

"I suspect," Wilfred said, noticing the new arrivals appreciating the significance of the aromas, "that the

corned beef dinner I've planned won't be the first
corned beef you've eaten today."

"That *was* the luncheon menu." Bettina leaned over
and squeezed her husband's hand. "But what else
could they serve for St. Patrick's Day, really? And not
everyone in the seniors' group has a spouse who's as
talented a cook as you! A lot of them probably even
live alone and were just as glad to have their main meal
at lunchtime." The catch in her throat as she spoke suggested that, despite her seeming focus on the mundane,
she was still tremulous from that afternoon's events.

Wilfred had been happy to take over cooking duties
when he retired—as well as setting aside his suits for
bib overalls—and Bettina had been happy to relinquish
kitchen duties. She had been a willing but uninspired
cook, serving the same seven meals, in the same order,
week in and week out for most of her married life.

"It smells delicious," Pamela said, "and I could eat
corned beef every day if given the chance."

"We'll be having beer with dinner"—Wilfred rose
to his feet—"and we'll be eating soon, but I think a
glass of beer would go just right at the moment."

He headed for the refrigerator and set out three
frosty bottles on the high counter that separated the
cooking area of the kitchen from the eating area. Then
one by one he tipped them over three of Bettina's tall
Swedish crystal glasses, tilting the glasses too as the
rich golden liquid lapped toward the rim and formed a
creamy layer of foam.

By the time the beer was delivered, Bettina had collected her thoughts. Without waiting to be prompted,
she filled Wilfred in on the details of the crime, starting
with Meg's announcement that Isobel was dead and

ending with the growing realization, once the police arrived, that her death had not been an accident.

"And whoever killed Isobel," she concluded, "did it between one thirty, when the concert ended, and one forty-five, when Meg went looking for her and found her dead."

Wilfred had listened, sipping his beer. Now he spoke. "The Listers are an old Arborville family, you know."

"Lister Street!" Pamela exclaimed. "Of course!"

Wilfred nodded. "Named after her grandfather. He was the mayor, for several terms. Quite the pillar of the community. And her great-grandfather built the commercial building on Arborville Avenue that houses the Union Bank, with the apartments up above." Wilfred was a member of Arborville's historical society and was thus a repository of obscure facts about the town.

He glanced toward the stove, closed his eyes, and sniffed. "I sense my soda bread is just ready to come out," he announced, "and that means it's time to start my potatoes and cabbage."

He stood up, and Bettina stood up too. "I'll set the table," she said, and took a few steps toward the doorway that led to the dining room. Pamela herself would have been happy to eat in the kitchen, but she knew that Bettina, delighted as she was that Wilfred now did the cooking, loved the ritual of setting the table with her favorite sage-green pottery and her other pretty things. Besides, that ritual would provide a welcome distraction from the topic uppermost in both their minds.

In the dining room, Bettina opened a drawer in her sideboard and took out napkins in a rich shade of brown, with stripes of gold, green, and red. "We'll use these," she declared. "They have the green stripes, for

St. Patrick's Day, and my dishes are green besides, and for the placemats, we'll . . ." She stooped to burrow further in the drawer, happily murmuring to herself until she bobbed up with a set of oval placemats in a honey-colored rattan.

"You know where the plates are." She nodded at Pamela with a smile as she began arranging placemats and napkins around the table. "And the flatware."

Pamela smiled back and headed obediently for the kitchen. There, she gathered plates and knives and forks and spoons, but paused to watch Wilfred in his ministrations at the stove. The large two-handled pot still occupied one back burner, but a saucepan had been put into action on the other. The slightly jiggling lid, with wisps of steam escaping at its edges, suggested that the contents were being subjected to vigorous boiling.

Wilfred, the very picture of a devoted cook in the apron that covered him from chest to knees, was tending more personally to the contents of the wide frying pan on the burner closest to him.

"Cabbage," he explained, noticing Pamela's interest. "I used to just cut it in quarters and boil it with the corned beef, but it's much better this way. I chop it up like I was making coleslaw and then sauté it in butter."

Indeed, the aroma coming from the pale green cabbage slivers that Wilfred was gently stirring with a long wooden spoon was recognizable as cabbage, but the butter had browned in a way that lent a caramelized dimension to the humble vegetable.

An oblong platter waited on the high counter, with a carving knife and large serving fork staged next to it. And the soda bread, a golden-brown dome with crisscross slashes in the top, had been removed from the oven and placed on a wooden cutting board.

Back in the dining room, Pamela arranged the plates and flatware on the placemats Bettina had set out, while Bettina transferred her candleholders—gleaming pewter with sleek Scandinavian lines—from the sideboard to the center of the table and lit the candles. Just as the second flame flickered to life, Wilfred appeared in the doorway.

"Please be seated, ladies," he said, his face ruddy from bending over the stove and his smile anticipating that his efforts would be appreciated.

He retreated to the kitchen, only to step forth again a few moments later bearing the oblong platter that had been waiting on the high counter. It now contained a goodly slab of corned beef, deep pink in color, and surrounded by small oval potatoes with their pale skins still intact. He set it near the head of the table and headed back the way he had come.

A few more trips to the kitchen brought the sautéed cabbage in a pottery bowl, the soda bread on its wooden cutting board, a large cube of butter on a little plate, and the knives and serving forks and spoons that would be needed to carve and slice and scoop the bounty before them. The final trip brought the tall crystal glasses, newly refilled with beer.

Wilfred's customary place was at the head of the table, the most convenient spot for access to the kitchen, and Bettina's was at the foot, with Pamela along the side facing the kitchen doorway. After sliding into his chair, he took up his impressive carving knife, steadied the corned beef with the serving fork, and delicately carved off several slices.

"Pass your plates, ladies," he requested, looking up with a pleased smile.

Pamela and Bettina complied, and soon their plates

were returned, amply supplied with broad strips of the glistening meat, clusters of the small potatoes, and mounds of the sautéed cabbage. While Wilfred served himself, Bettina set to work on the soda bread, first cutting the loaf in half by lining her knife up with one of the slashes that formed the crisscross on top and then cutting one half into crosswise slices. The butter made its way around the table, to be spread liberally on the bread and dabbed in pats on the potatoes once their steaming interiors had been exposed.

No meal at the Frasers' house was officially underway until Wilfred had taken up his utensils and uttered a jovial "Bon appétit!" Once that ritual had been accomplished, no further words were spoken for some time, since mouths were occupied savoring the results of Wilfred's industry.

The corned beef was juicy and tender, with a hint of salt and more than a hint of the bay leaf and spices that had gone into the corning process. The potatoes, plain but for melted butter, were the perfect counterpoint to the meat. And the slight bitterness of the cabbage, though soothed by the caramelizing effect of Wilfred's special cooking method, enlivened the simple meat-and-potatoes combo.

Bettina was the first to react, but even before she spoke, the admiring gaze that she directed at her husband offered a preview of the words to come.

"The luncheon was good," she said, "but *this* is the best St. Patrick's Day meal I have ever eaten."

"Dear wife"—Wilfred struggled to affect a serious expression—"I have cooked corned beef and cabbage for St. Patrick's Day every year since we've been married. Do you mean to say—"

Bettina interrupted with a laugh. "Last year's was

the best I had ever eaten—until this year's. And next year's . . ."

"I don't see how this year's could be improved upon," Pamela cut in. "You have truly outdone yourself, Wilfred. And I never want to eat cabbage cooked any other way again—except, of course, the special coleslaw that you make in the summer."

She speared a bite of corned beef with her fork, raised it to her mouth, and followed it with a slice of potato and then a bit of cabbage.

The pace of eating slowed as plates began to empty, and the conversation's focus widened. Wilfred noted that spring was just around the corner, and with it would come the pleasure of watching shrubs blossom and perennials awaken from their underground slumber. Bettina wondered aloud when pansies would be available at the garden center, and—with a complete change of topic—when Pamela's daughter Penny would be coming home from college for spring break. They chatted on along those lines for some time, pausing only to accept second helpings and remark once again on the deliciousness of the offerings.

At last plates were definitively empty and sighs of contentment had replaced speech. Wilfred, however, had one more treat in store. He quickly cleared the table, insisting that Pamela and Bettina remain in their seats.

From the kitchen came the sound of the refrigerator door opening and closing, and then the whirring clatter of an electric mixer, after which the refrigerator door opened and closed again. Delay increased anticipation until, humming a little tune with a faintly Irish flavor, Wilfred entered bearing one of Bettina's Swedish crystal bowls. He lowered it to the table with a flourish.

Visible through the clear crystal were layers of cake, pudding, and whipped cream, ending with more whipped cream—a billowy expanse sprinkled with shards of dark chocolate.

"Irish Coffee Trifle," he announced. "Bowls coming right up." He whirled around and darted back to the kitchen.

The bowls were Swedish crystal too, and he filled them with generous scoops of the trifle, whose alternating layers brought to Pamela's mind something she'd seen on the nature channel—an episode dealing with varicolored strata in cliff faces.

That image was dispelled by Pamela's first taste—though the taste was layered too. The cake was a rich pound cake drenched in strong coffee tinged with whiskey. Vanilla pudding mellowed the coffee's bitterness, and the whipped cream offered a sweet and airy counterpoint to both cake and pudding, with the surprise of bittersweet chocolate.

Bettina's reaction evoked a contented feline as, with her lips curved into a half-smile and eyes closed, she began to purr.

"We certainly didn't have *this* at the luncheon," Pamela said. "What an inspired creation!"

Wilfred tipped his head in acknowledgment of her praise and they all concentrated for a bit on their trifle, skillfully manipulating their spoons to make sure each mouthful contained a morsel of cake, a sampling of pudding, a bit of whipped cream, and a chocolate shard. Bettina finished first and gave a hopeful glance at the crystal serving bowl.

"There's plenty more." Wilfred scooped a generous second helping into Bettina's bowl and turned to Pamela, who was just capturing a last dab of whipped cream.

"No—really." Pamela set down her spoon. "I just can't eat another bite."

Bettina's spoon paused halfway to her mouth and she tilted her head in Pamela's direction. "That's why you're thin and I'm not," she said with a laugh. "I can always eat another bite."

Wilfred was in the process of serving himself a second helping, but the serving spoon halted in midair and he focused on his wife. "You could not be more beautiful!" he exclaimed.

Indeed, Bettina might have been plump, but she dressed with exceptional flair, in carefully coordinated ensembles that would have been at home in the closet of the most devoted fashionista. The fact that Pamela, whose tall and slim physique seemed made for stylish clothes, dressed day in and day out in jeans and casual tops was a continual mystery to her.

Bettina's bowl empty once again, she contemplated it with a satisfied sigh. "What a wonderful meal!" she said. "And what a comfort to be here at home with my husband, and my pets"—she glanced toward where Woofus and Punkin still lay—"and my best friend, after . . . after"—her face fell and her head sagged forward—"after . . . what happened."

The serving spoon clunked against Wilfred's bowl. With a tender expression that creased his forehead and made his eyes seem large and dark, he gazed down the length of the table and said, "Dear wife, put the luncheon out of your mind. There's no reason to dwell on it."

"There is though," Bettina wailed. "The *Advocate*

will want a story, and I'll have to talk to Clayborn, soon. Maybe even tomorrow."

Her shoulders drooped and she stared ahead bleakly. But suddenly her posture changed. Her spine stiffened and she lifted her chin, as a quick intake of breath parted her lips.

"I forgot!" she exclaimed, and she sprang from her chair, leaning on the table for a speedy liftoff.

She darted through the arch that divided the dining room from the living room and seized her handbag, green today to match her luncheon outfit, from the sofa. By the time she slid back into her chair, she had already pulled out her phone.

"I took pictures," she murmured, fingers busy on the phone's screen.

Bettina had suddenly undergone a remarkable transformation, apparently triggered by recalling that she was indeed "Bettina Fraser of the *Arborville Advocate*," as she had identified herself that afternoon to the assembled seniors.

"Here! Look!" She handed the phone to Pamela. "The crime scene."

Pamela took the phone and leaned to the side so Wilfred could see the screen too. Bettina had in fact captured the crime scene, which Pamela had glimpsed while peering over Bettina's shoulder: Isobel lay on the floor of the small office, sprawled between the doorway and a desk. Nearby were a chair and a coat rack, both tipped over.

Something was odd about the image though. During the concert Isobel had been wearing a sweater— Pamela was sure of this because she had particularly noted the bright chartreuse yarn from which it had been knitted. In the crime-scene photo, she was fully clothed, but instead of the sweater she was wearing a long-sleeved T-shirt, like something you'd wear under a sweater if you were concerned that the wool might be itchy. It was also green, but a more subdued shade.

"Where did the sweater go?" Pamela asked, handing the phone back to Bettina. The question was addressed more to herself, since Bettina couldn't possibly know the answer.

"What sweater?" Bettina stared at the screen.

"It's not there," Pamela said, "but during the concert she was wearing a sweater."

"Maybe she just got hot." Bettina continued staring at the screen. "I get hot sometimes. She was hopping all over the place while she was singing."

"It wasn't something a person could easily slip on and off, like a cardigan," Pamela said. "It was a pullover, and rather tight-fitting." She leaned over so she could glimpse the screen too. "Scroll back to the ones you took during the concert."

Bettina complied, stroking the screen with a carefully manicured index finger.

"See." Pamela pointed to the screen, where an image of Isobel, leaning toward the microphone with a dramatic expression suggesting insupportable yearning, had appeared.

Bettina continued to stroke the screen, and more images of Isobel flashed by: joyous, scornful, nostalgic, wistful.

"I do remember the sweater now." Bettina nodded. "I remember thinking that she was quite brave to wear that color, at her age. Those neon shades can be very unflattering to older skin."

"Someone who wanted that sweater was lying in

wait for her when the concert ended?" Wilfred had left his chair and was standing behind Bettina, bending over her shoulder to concentrate on the photos. "Did anybody jump up from the audience and follow her when she retreated?"

"I didn't really notice," Pamela said. "Of course I didn't imagine at the time that anything out of the ordinary was about to happen. People just went back to drinking coffee and eating cookies."

"Could someone have gotten into that room by another route?" Wilfred asked.

"It's along a hallway that leads to the rec center's back entrance"—Pamela tilted her head to look up at Wilfred—"and in fact . . . in fact . . ." Her words trailed off. She closed her eyes and covered her face with her hands. "*Think!*" she commanded herself.

Yes, those two things, separate things, went together, and she hadn't made the connection until now. She grabbed Bettina's arm.

"Bettina!" she exclaimed. Bettina responded with a startled squeak.

"Do you remember that woman at our table talking about flowers being delivered for the luncheon, white flowers like for a funeral, with a card that said, 'In deepest sympathy'?"

"I do." Bettina nodded.

"While you were taking those pictures of the crime scene, I happened to look out at the parking lot through the windows in those doors that lead outside."

"And?" Wilfred had gotten caught up in the story too, and he and Bettina spoke in unison.

"I saw a florist's van, Beauteous Blooms of Timberley, and when I pushed the door open the driver saw me and tore out of the parking lot."

"So he delivered the inappropriate flowers and then waited around until he thought Isobel had finished singing and was alone in that office . . . ?" Bettina's words came slowly, as if she was working out the details as she spoke.

Wilfred had returned to his seat at the head of the table. "Advertising that you're planning to kill someone—i.e., here are some flowers, in advance, for the funeral—and then doing it, and making your getaway in a van easily traceable to Beauteous Blooms of Timberley doesn't seem very smart," he observed.

"No, it doesn't." Bettina and Pamela agreed.

They all sat in silence for a bit. Wilfred offered to make coffee, but Pamela pointed out that she'd left her house that morning—it seemed ages ago—and hadn't been home since and there were cats to be fed.

Bettina was on her feet first, heading to the living room, where she peered through one of the windows that looked out onto the street.

"Your house is completely dark," she announced. Pamela's house faced the Frasers' house midway down Orchard Street. "Didn't you leave any lights on?"

"I didn't know I'd be coming directly here after the luncheon," Pamela explained.

"Wilfred and I and Woofus will walk you home," Bettina said. "After what happened today, I'm just not sure Arborville is all that safe."

"I'll be fine," Pamela insisted, joining her friend in the living room, where Bettina's comfy sofa and armchairs, and her colorful accent pillows, created an atmosphere as warm and welcoming as Bettina herself.

Wilfred had followed them. He opened the front door and stepped out onto the porch. "It smells like spring," he commented.

"I'll be fine," Pamela repeated. After picking up her jacket from the arm of the sofa, she wrapped an arm around Bettina's waist and together they made their way to the porch.

The night was chilly, and a layer of clouds, glowing faintly with the ambient light from the city just across the river, hid the stars. But it did smell like spring, as if the earth was thawing and coming awake.

After hugs all around, Pamela set off across the street, with the Frasers, illuminated by their porch light, waving her on her way. She waved back at them when she reached her own porch.

CHAPTER 3

Pamela's house *was* dark, though even with her daughter away at school, she was not its only inhabitant. But cats are unable to turn on lamps—and anyway, perhaps they don't care to, as it is rumored they can see in the dark.

She always felt welcome when she returned home, however—even stepping into darkness. That was why she had remained on Orchard Street, in a house too large for one person or even two, after a tragic construction-site accident fifteen years earlier took her architect husband and left her a widow while yet in her thirties. He and she had bought the hundred-year-old house as a fixer-upper shortly after they married, and they had fixed it up, and now, living in the house, she felt her husband's presence all around her.

As she unlocked her front door and crossed the threshold, other more tangible presences manifested themselves in the form of furry whispers brushing past her ankles and a chorus of gentle complaints. She switched on the light in the entry, tossed her jacket on the chair that was its main piece of furniture, and proceeded to the kitchen, stepping carefully so as not to tread on a cat.

There were three of them. First was inky-black Catrina, adopted as a pitiful stray long ago and now sleek and self-confident. Second was Ginger, Catrina's daughter, born as one of six kittens after Catrina's impetuous dalliance with a rakish tom whose bold coloration Ginger inherited. Third was Precious, a purebred Siamese adopted more recently and quite aware of her refined elegance.

"Yes, yes, yes," Pamela murmured as she opened a can of liver and gravy and scooped it into a large bowl for Catrina and Ginger to share.

Before setting the bowl in the corner where the cats were accustomed to expect their meals, she removed a half-full can of seafood medley from the refrigerator and emptied it into a smaller bowl for Precious, who sometimes preferred her own menu. Dinner delivered, she refreshed the communal water bowl and left the cats in peace to enjoy their meal.

The cats taken care of, Pamela climbed the stairs to her office, where she pushed the button that brought her computer to life and clicked on the icon that opened her email program. Along with offers of coupons from the hobby shop and the office-supplies store, a new message from Penny Paterson arrived in her inbox.

Pamela and her daughter exchanged frequent emails and talked on the phone often—in fact they had just chatted that morning. So Pamela was surprised to see Penny getting in touch again so soon. Could something be wrong? Penny would have called though, and there had been no voicemails, either on the landline or the smartphone.

The reason for the email became clear, however, as soon as Pamela read the first few words, which were, "Lorie Hopkins's grandmother is in the Arborville seniors' group." She barely needed to read further to know how the message would proceed.

Lorie Hopkins was one of Penny's old friends from high school. She was away at college now too, but not at Penny's college in Boston. She kept close tabs on Arborville news—both good and bad, made sure to keep Penny updated, and had apparently learned quite rapidly about the unfortunate event that had marred the seniors' St. Patrick Day luncheon. Now Penny knew about it too.

"Lorie's grandmother recognized Bettina but she doesn't know you and I hope you weren't there with Bettina," Penny went on to say. "If you were, I hope I don't have to worry that you (and Bettina) will find some reason to think that you can do a better job finding the killer than the police can."

"No reason to worry at all," Pamela wrote in response, "and I hope Lorie's grandmother isn't too upset."

Back downstairs, Pamela settled in her comfortable spot at one end of her sofa and pulled her knitting out of her knitting bag. The project, a crew-neck pullover in tawny brown with a large black cat on the front, had been in progress since Christmas. The back, one sleeve, and the front—black cat and all—had been completed. All that remained was the other sleeve, at present only a few inches long.

Soon, the crisscrossing of needles and the looping of yarn worked their soothing magic, aided by the British mystery unfolding on the screen before her and the rumbling purrs of three dozing cats, Catrina on the sofa arm and Ginger along her thigh, and Precious on the top platform of the cat climber.

The next morning, after a quick trip down the front walk in fleecy robe and furry slippers, Pamela returned to her kitchen bearing that day's edition of the *County Register*. The whistling kettle announced that the water she had set to boil before making her dash was now boiling, but she ignored the whistle to extract the newspaper from its plastic sleeve and unfold it on the kitchen table.

As she had suspected, the murder of Isobel Lister was the day's most significant story. A front-page headline declared, in outsize capital letters, "Arborville's Isobel Lister Killed at Festive Seniors Event."

Absorbing the story itself would require sustenance. Pamela left the newspaper on the table, silenced the whistling with a twist of the knob, and tilted the kettle over the freshly ground coffee waiting in the filter cone of her carafe. The small kitchen was soon suffused with the dark and spicy aroma of fresh-brewed coffee, an aroma rapidly joined by that of whole-grain toast.

Pamela filled a wedding-china cup with the steaming coffee and transferred the toast to a wedding-china plate. She'd never seen the point in saving her nice china for special occasions—better to break the occasional cup or plate than keep it all hidden away except for Thanksgiving and Christmas. Seated at the table, she took a bite of toast and a sip of coffee, and then she bent toward the newspaper.

According to the *Register*, citing Detective Lucas Clayborn of the Arborville police, Isobel Lister had died the previous afternoon, after an apparent struggle, at the Arborville Recreation Center. She had just performed a concert of Irish songs for a St. Patrick's Day luncheon organized by the Arborville seniors' group. The medical examiner had not yet performed an autopsy—at least by the time the *Register* went to press—but Isobel appeared to have suffered some kind of trauma to the head in the office that was serving as a green room. It was noted that she had landed on the floor near the corner of a metal desk. The article went on to point out that the Listers had a long history in Arborville and many family members still lived in the town.

Pamela was just setting Part 1 aside, hoping that Lifestyle would offer less disturbing subject matter, when the doorbell chimed. She hurried into the entry, where a glance through the lace that curtained the oval window in the front door revealed her early morning caller as Bettina. The figure waiting on the porch was dressed in a cheery yellow garment that glowed against the faded hues of lawn and shrubbery, with Bettina's vibrant hair providing a bright pop of scarlet.

Bettina's mood as she crossed the threshold, however, was anything but cheery.

"Clayborn!" she fumed. "He has plenty of time to speak to that pushy Marcy Brewer from the *Register*, but he can't talk to a reporter from Arborville's own newspaper until Monday?"

Pamela stepped aside and motioned for Bettina to

follow her to the kitchen. There, she took another wedding-china cup from the cupboard and filled it with still-hot coffee from the carafe.

"Is there toast?" Bettina inquired. "And cream and sugar?" Pamela drank her coffee black.

"You know there is," Pamela said with a smile.

She slipped two slices of whole-grain bread into the toaster while Bettina fetched the sugar bowl from the counter and opened the refrigerator.

"I see the cream," Bettina said. "And I see some strawberry jam besides."

"Help yourself." Pamela used only butter on her morning toast but she was well-acquainted with Bettina's taste for sweet things.

While she waited for the toast to pop up, she took another wedding-china plate from the cupboard and staged it next to the toaster.

A few minutes later she and Bettina were seated across from each other at the small table. The cheery yellow garment had turned out to be a chic all-weather coat with a wide collar and oversize buttons. Bettina had removed it to reveal more yellow beneath—a cashmere turtleneck and lightweight wool slacks. Antique amber and silver earrings dangled from her earlobes.

Still in her fleecy robe, Pamela resumed the breakfast that had been interrupted by the doorbell. Meanwhile, Bettina added sugar to her coffee and, once the sugar was dissolved, dribbled in cream until the contents of the cup reached the pale mocha hue that she preferred. After taking a sip of her coffee and approving it with a nod and smile, she applied butter and jam to her waiting toast.

These processes lightened her mood, but the memory of her early-morning conversation with Detective Clayborn apparently still rankled.

"And so," she said, after sampling the toast and taking another sip of coffee, "not only did he talk to Marcy Brewer in time for her to get an article into today's *Register*, but he had the nerve to point out that since the *Advocate* only comes out once a week and the next one isn't due till Friday, I'll have plenty of time to file my story after I talk to him Monday and there's really no rush at all."

Bettina took another large bite of toast, then she almost choked. She waved back Pamela's expression of alarm, cleared her throat, and said, "I'm okay, really. I just remembered though"—she gritted her teeth—"he actually told me he thinks the crime will be solved by the time the next *Advocate* comes out. And I suppose Marcy Brewer will get that story too, and people will read the *Advocate* and wonder why Bettina Fraser isn't up to date on Arborville news."

"I guess he has leads?" Pamela's skeptical expression implied that she'd be surprised if the answer was yes.

Bettina shrugged. "He didn't let on. He's doesn't seem the teasing type, but perhaps the idea of keeping me in suspense until Monday makes him feel powerful."

"Perhaps." Pamela sipped at her coffee. "Or perhaps he's been reading one of those self-help books about the power of positive thinking. Envision it happening and it will happen."

"He doesn't seem like the self-help type either."

The conversation shifted to more mundane topics then, like the crocus beginning to appear up and down

Orchard Street and the forsythia coming into blossom. At one point, Pamela warmed the coffee remaining in the carafe and divided it between the two wedding-china cups. Bettina finished hers off in a few quick slurps, after adding sugar and cream, of course, and rose to her feet.

"Wilfred and I are taking the Arborville grand-children to the science museum in Rochemont," she said, while bending over to smooth out the creases in her slacks. "So I've got to get going." She looked up. "I hope you've got plans for the day, something inter-esting to take your mind off yesterday."

"A walk?" Pamela suggested. "A trip to the Co-Op for groceries? And some work for the magazine?"

Pamela's job as associate editor of *Fiber Craft* mag-azine allowed her to work at home most days, and fit the work into her schedule any way she liked.

"Work?" Bettina's voice came out as an alarmed bleat. "Today is Saturday."

"I don't mind." Pamela smiled. "I like my work. You would have talked to Detective Clayborn this morning if he'd been willing to see you."

"I like my work too." Bettina smiled back. "But maybe tonight? Maybe tonight you have plans to do something that isn't work? Something involving that handsome Wendelstaff College professor that you've been spending time with?"

"As a matter of fact"—Pamela was still smiling, but now the smile was provoked by Bettina's entertaining lack of subtlety—"yes, I do have plans to do some-thing that isn't work tonight. And, yes, the something does involve Brian Delano."

"You've been happier since you met him." Bettina tilted her head to examine Pamela's face, as if to confirm the truth of her statement. "I know you loved your husband, but fifteen years is long enough to mourn. And, yes, there was that sad detour with Richard Larkin and—"

The sound that emerged from Pamela's throat was so feral that even she was startled. And Catrina, who had been passing through the kitchen en route to the sunny spot that appeared on the entry carpet every morning, sped up and bolted through the doorway.

"We're not going to talk about him," Pamela said firmly. "Remember?"

"I do." Bettina closed her eyes and tipped her head forward. "But sometimes I just can't help it." She turned and followed Catrina into the entry.

Richard Larkin was a handsome single man who had moved into the house next to Pamela's about four years earlier. Bettina had urged Pamela to welcome the obvious interest he showed in his new neighbor, and Pamela herself had been attracted to him. But she'd been so unused to thinking of herself as a potential romantic partner that she'd resisted his overtures and he'd finally looked elsewhere.

By the time Pamela joined Bettina in the entry, she had slipped back into her coat and was just buttoning the last button, with perhaps more deliberation than was strictly necessary. In a small voice she murmured, "I'll never mention his name again."

"You've said that before." Pamela reached for the doorknob. "Lots of times."

"This time I really mean it." Bettina mustered a smile. "Have fun tonight."

After Bettina had gone on her way, Pamela returned to the kitchen. She washed the cups and plates from breakfast and then sat down at the table with a notepad, one of the many that came unbidden in the mail. On a sheet of paper bordered with tulips—notepads celebrating spring had begun arriving in January—she wrote "cat food" and then added the items that she herself would be eating in the coming week.

The walk to the Co-Op was brief, only six blocks, past wood-frame houses the same vintage as her own, with wide yards in which tiny green shoots were erupting from the earth and forsythia bushes were bursting into startling displays of neon yellow. When Pamela and her husband had been searching for a house those many years ago, Arborville had reminded them of the college town where they met and fell in love. It was small enough that most errands could be done on foot, and Pamela was happy to brave weather of all sorts, enjoying the meditative state that walking induced.

The Co-Op Grocery was an Arborville institution, with its creaky wooden floor and narrow aisles. Pamela tossed her canvas shopping bags in one of the carts lined up on the sidewalk and wheeled the cart through the automatic door that was the Co-Op's main concession to modernity.

Browsing among bins filled with globular fruits and vegetables in tidy pyramids, carrots and celery in orderly stacks, and leafy greens in disordered profusion, Pamela consulted her list and collected apples, oranges, potatoes, and ingredients for salad. A trip up and down a crowded aisle added cat food to the cart, and she emerged at the meat counter.

Cooking for one could be a challenge, but Pamela

liked to cook. She added an organic chicken and a pot roast to her cart and moved along toward the cheese counter and then the bakery counter.

She left the Co-Op with bulging canvas bags, so heavy that she had to stop and rest on the bench at the bus kiosk halfway to Orchard Street. But once she reached home, it was satisfying to restock the refrigerator and pantry, and she rewarded herself with a lunchtime omelet featuring a goodly amount of newly purchased Vermont cheddar.

Brian wasn't coming until six p.m. and the plan for the evening was dinner at his place—he liked to cook too—and then a quiet evening watching a film from his collection of classic movies. In the meantime, Pamela really did have work to do for the magazine. Three articles had arrived earlier in the week with instructions to copyedit them and return them by Monday morning.

She'd finished two and had intended to devote Friday afternoon to the third, but Friday afternoon turned out to be taken up waiting in the rec center as the police interviewed everyone who had been at the luncheon. So, sitting at the computer in her office, she opened the Word file labeled "Shetlands" and immersed herself in the world of the prized Shetland sheep whose wool is destined to become yarn. Skimming the article earlier she had learned that they live in special roofed pens on farms where the underbrush is trimmed regularly lest it snag their fleece. Also, to protect their fleece, they sometimes even wear coats. Her task now was to make sure that the article conformed to the style that *Fiber Craft* preferred.

She was happy, a few hours later, to save her work and close the Word file with a satisfied click. She rolled her chair back a few feet from her desk, raised her arms over her head in a back-easing stretch, and turned off the computer.

Brian Delano *was* handsome, in a dark and wolfish kind of way—though the hint of wolfish danger was usually neutralized by a smile that could verge on goofy. Tonight, though, he wasn't smiling. Pamela had welcomed him into the entry and fetched her jacket from the closet, but as if unaware that she was expecting they would leave right away for the short drive to his condo near the college, he lingered uncertainly near the arch between the entry and the living room.

"Are you okay?" Pamela asked, stepping toward him. "Do you want to spend the evening here instead? I could cook something."

"No, no." He frowned and studied the floor for a minute, gesturing as if to push away her suggestion. Then he looked up, focusing on her face so intently that the sensation was almost physical. "Pamela, I—" He reached out as if to touch her arm, but pulled his hand back and waved toward the sofa. "Shall we sit down?"

What could be going on? Pamela felt more puzzled than alarmed, though she had become aware of her pulse ticking in her throat.

The living room was dark, illuminated only by light spilling in from the entry. Brian sat with that light at his back, his face in shadow. Only his tone of voice revealed his emotion.

"I haven't been fair to you," he said. "I should have told you long ago—there's always been someone else."

"There has?" Pamela was aware that she sounded more amazed than woeful.

"I'm sorry." His head tipped forward. "I was trying so hard. I really like you."

"I like you too." They had never spoken of love.

"But I can't forget her. She's always in my mind, getting in the way." He stroked his forehead, perhaps in a futile effort to erase the memory.

"You mean"—Pamela leaned closer and tried to make eye contact—"you're not actually with her now?"

"She's with *me* though, in here." He tapped the side of his head.

"You told me long ago that you'd broken up with someone and it had been painful."

"She was that person. And I've tried to forget but I've given up. So now I think, maybe I can backtrack, start over with her and make things turn out better. I have to try . . . *that*, instead of . . . *this*." His hands fluttered in his lap and he gazed around the room.

Somehow Pamela gathered that by "*this*" he meant his relationship with her and the pretense that he now admitted it had involved.

Brian did not stay long after that. He went on his way seeming relieved—perhaps doubly, in that Pamela hadn't reacted with tears and his difficult errand was behind him.

For her part, Pamela closed the front door and returned to the sofa, this time turning on a lamp. It had been fun to have a boyfriend. Bettina had been right about that. But in a sense, she and Brian had been kindred spirits, though she hadn't realized it at the time. She hadn't forgotten her husband. Unconsciously, she tapped the side of her head, as Brian had done when he said, "She's with me . . . in here."

Plans for the evening had changed, so she climbed to her feet and headed to the kitchen. She felt empty in a way—not devastated, but more a case of being at loose ends. Busy-ness was the cure for that, and in the refrigerator an organic chicken was waiting to be roasted.

CHAPTER 4

It was Sunday morning. Pamela had just begun her journey back to her porch, newspaper in hand, when Bettina's voice commanded her to wait. She turned to see her friend hopping off the curb and launching herself across the street.

"There's nothing new about Isobel's murder," Bettina panted when she got closer. She was still in her robe, cozy and fleecy, but a fetching shade of peach and trimmed with lace. Scanning Pamela up and down, she added, "How are you this morning?"

"I'm fine." Pamela nodded.

"Feeling well rested?" Bettina's smile and raised brow emphasized her curiosity.

"Quite," Pamela said. "Why do you ask?"

"No special reason." Bettina shrugged. She studied Pamela's face for a minute and frowned, then she shifted her gaze to the ground and took a deep breath. The next words came out in a rush. "It's just that . . .

well . . . I was outside with Woofus last evening, around dinner time, and I noticed Brian—"

"Leaving?" Pamela cut her off.

"Well, yes. I noticed him leaving"—Bettina was still looking at the ground—"and . . . and . . . I was worried about you. It was so early, and you were supposed to have a date with him." Now she was staring at Pamela's face again, her lips in a firm line and a slight crease between her carefully shaped brows. It was the expression of a person who has risen to a difficult challenge. "I know you don't like to talk about personal things like that, but I'm your best friend, and Wilfred and I really care about you—"

Pamela took her arm. "I'm freezing," she said. "Come in the house."

They were greeted by the hooting of the kettle. Pamela hurried to turn off the burner and tip the kettle over the filter cone atop her Pyrex carafe.

"Do you want a cup?" she asked as the boiling water began to seep through the fresh grounds and a seductive aroma filled the little kitchen.

"I can't stay," Bettina said. "Wilfred is making coffee at home, but"—she stepped close and angled her head to make eye contact with Pamela, who was staring at the carafe as the level of the fresh-brewed coffee rose—"are things still okay between you two?"

"They're not *not* okay," Pamela said, "though it depends on what you mean by okay. We didn't have a fight."

"I mean *okay*!" Bettina paused with eyes and mouth open wide, an expectant pose she seemed willing to hold until satisfied with Pamela's answer.

Pamela took a wedding-china cup from the cupboard. "I hope you don't mind if I pour a cup of coffee," she commented as she commenced to do just that. Then she gestured at the table.

"I have to sit?" Bettina edged toward the chair she usually occupied. "And then you'll tell me what happened?"

Pamela nodded and they both took seats.

"Brian and I aren't going to be seeing each other anymore," Pamela explained after Bettina had settled into her chair.

"What?" Bettina reached across the table and grabbed Pamela's free hand. Pamela's other hand was holding her coffee. "But things were going so well," she wailed, her expression as distraught as if the relationship had been between her and Brian. "You poor thing!" Her fingers tightened around Pamela's. "What happened?"

"He feels he hasn't been fair to me." Pamela shrugged.

"Whoa!" Bettina reared back in her chair. "That weasel! That is the *most* cowardly excuse for a breakup that I have ever heard!"

"Bettina!" Pamela leaned forward. She laughed—she couldn't help it. "You've been happily married to a wonderful man for over thirty years. How have you had so much experience with excuses for breakups as to be able rank their degree of cowardliness?"

"Well . . ." Bettina looked at the table. "The most cowardly I've *heard of* then." She looked up. "Anyway, *you're* okay . . . ?" Her troubled expression demanded an answer.

"I wasn't fair to him," Pamela said. "I still think about Michael, and Brian wasn't the one to make me forget, though maybe someone could come along who could . . ." Or that someone *has* come along, said a voice in her head, but you missed your chance with Richard Larkin.

"You have to come to brunch." Bettina rose to her feet. "I know you, and I know you keep things inside, and you can't mope around here by yourself all day even though you say you're not upset."

Pamela stood up too and together they moved toward the doorway.

"Wilfred is making eggs Benedict," Bettina said as Pamela reached for the doorknob. "Come about eleven. But go fix yourself some toast now. You can't survive the next few hours on just black coffee."

Wilfred's brunch menu had been a huge success. He'd chosen to add asparagus to his usual eggs Benedict recipe in a nod to the approach of spring—though in mid-March the asparagus showing up at the Co-Op was still sourced from warmer climes. The long, delicate spears had been steamed until they were just tender, bathed in melted butter, and then layered with Canadian bacon and poached eggs on toasted English muffins. Generous dollops of homemade Hollandaise sauce, piquant with lemon and Dijon mustard, had finished off the creation.

After he cleared away the plates, from which every last tidbit had been gobbled up, the three friends lingered around the pine table in the kitchen sipping coffee and chatting. The Frasers weren't expecting Sunday callers, and so when Woofus raised his shaggy head and gave an alarmed glance toward the doorway that led to the dining room and the living room beyond, no one paid any heed. A moment later, however, the angle of his ears shifted to alert and he climbed to his feet. His gruff bark overlapped the sound of the doorbell.

"Possibly the Bible people," Wilfred explained as he rose. "They sometimes come around after church."

But the caller was not the Bible people. Pamela heard Wilfred offer a cordial, if surprised, greeting and then he ushered Meg Norton through the kitchen doorway. She looked as if perhaps she too had come from church, in her tidy pink skirt suit, accessorized with a silk scarf in soothing pastel shades.

"Meg!" Bettina stood up and reached out to offer a hug as Meg advanced into the kitchen. "Has something happened? Are you okay?"

Meanwhile, Wilfred had detoured past the cupboard where Bettina kept her pottery set and fetched a coffee mug. As Bettina led Meg to the one unused chair around the table, Wilfred inquired, "Coffee, Meg?"

"Oh, yes, please." She looked grateful. Pamela wondered if she'd been unsure how her unannounced visit would be received.

"This is unexpected!" Bettina's smile was cordial but hinted at surprise. "What can we . . . uh . . ."

Wilfred delivered the coffee and backtracked for the sugar bowl and cream pitcher. Meg added sugar and cream to her mug and took a big sip, then another—then a deep breath.

"Bettina," she said at last, "I don't think those photos you took on Friday should be published in the *Advocate*. I've been thinking about it all weekend and—"

Bettina reached out a carefully manicured hand, laid it on Meg's arm, and gave a gentle squeeze. "No, no, no, no, no!" An energetic headshake that set her scarlet waves to vibrating accompanied the words. "Of course not! The *County Register* might go in for sensational coverage of crimes but the *Advocate* is a family newspaper."

Meg exhaled. "That . . . is . . . a . . . relief." She spoke slowly, emphasizing each word. Then she eased her arm out from under Bettina's grip and added another spoonful of sugar to her mug. "The seniors were upset enough about what happened, without having to relive it in graphic detail when the *Advocate* comes out this week."

"I work closely with Detective Clayborn of the Arborville police, you know." Bettina replaced her hand on Meg's arm. "I took the photos because I was first on the scene—aside from you, of course—after it . . . happened." She shook her head sadly. "Such a tragic event, a tragic conclusion to what should have been a happy occasion."

"It *was* a happy occasion"—Pamela thought Meg sounded a little defensive—"until . . ."

"Yes," Pamela jumped in. "And Isobel is . . . was . . . certainly an entertaining performer."

"Quite the character too. Free-spirited. A real bohemian." Meg seemed to welcome the new conversational thread.

"I understand the Listers are an old Arborville family." Pamela nodded toward Wilfred in acknowledgment of her source for that information.

"Isobel was something of a black sheep," Meg said. "But the Listers always welcomed her when she turned back up in Arborville after an adventure. And she always had a free place to stay."

"The Lister Building," Wilfred chimed in. "They kept an apartment empty for her."

Woofus had arisen from his favorite spot and meandered across the floor to nuzzle Wilfred's leg. For a few moments, Wilfred absentmindedly stroked the dog's head, then he pushed his chair back and climbed to his feet, leaning on the table to assist the process.

"Woofus is telling me it's time for a walk," Wilfred explained, as he reached back to untie his apron. He hung it on a hook near the door to the utility room and collected Woofus's leash.

As he and Woofus left the kitchen, Meg began to rise, but Bettina gestured for her to remain seated. "No need to leave just because Wilfred is going out," she said. "There's plenty more coffee and . . ."

"No more coffee, thanks." Meg settled back into place. "But I will stay and chat a bit."

Pamela bit her lips to suppress a smile. Bettina had a nose for news as well as an incorrigible curiosity. (Or were those both actually the same thing?) Meg had organized and presided over the luncheon and was now sitting right in front of her. It was clear Bettina was not about to waste the chance to extract any and all details about the circumstances surrounding Isobel's murder.

Bettina's mobile features arranged themselves into the expression that enabled her to draw out even the most resistant interview subject: avid interest tempered with concern.

"Someone at our table mentioned a flower delivery . . ." She let the sentence taper off in a suggestive way.

"Oh, that!" Meg threw her head back and contemplated the ceiling. "Funeral flowers! Like some kind of horrible foreshadowing, as it turned out later, and then it was downhill from there. The florist delivery man had already gone when I realized how inappropriate the arrangement was for a festive luncheon, and I'd no sooner hidden them than the Wiccan arrived."

"The Wiccan?" Bettina smiled slightly, a smile that seemed to invite clarification.

"This *woman*"—Meg sighed—"named Liadan Percy showed up demanding equal time to make a presentation about the Wiccan view of St. Patrick's Day. They don't like him—I figured that much out—because the Wiccans follow the old Celtic rituals that Christianity replaced."

"Oh, my goodness!" Bettina raised her fingers to her lips. "I had no idea there were any Wiccans in Arborville. I wonder if Wilfred knows they're here."

"She was incredibly insistent and it took me forever to get rid of her. She was *very* annoyed that I wouldn't let her speak to the group, and meanwhile the high school volunteers were asking me all kinds of questions about how I wanted them to do the meal service. And Isobel was late and I was wondering if we were going to have entertainment after all." As if reliving this stressful episode, Meg seized one hand with the other and began to twist her fingers violently, alternating hands to allow each to twist and be twisted.

Without glancing at her fingers—though Pamela was staring at them fixedly, concerned for their well-being—Meg went on.

"When Isobel finally arrived, she seemed very flustered, as if she'd been arguing with someone. But I didn't have a chance to ask her if the Wiccan woman had accosted her, and then later of course . . ."

"Of course." Bettina nodded sympathetically. "Such a shame that happened too, because you had put together a lovely event for the seniors' group—the decorations, the food . . . those shamrock cookies were divine.

And the program of Irish songs . . . a lot of heads were bobbing and feet were tapping."

"And a lot of people were walking out . . . including one of our newest members, Cheryl Hagan." Meg had seemed momentarily cheered by Bettina's praise, but now her smile turned into a grimace. "I'll admit 'Roll Me Over in the Clover' was a bit off-color—though Marilyn Gilroy was laughing her head off and she's the president of the St. Willibrod's Women's Auxiliary. But I don't know why that other woman left, the one who left first. Who could object to 'Danny Boy'?"

"Who was she?" Bettina inquired.

Meg shrugged. "I don't know. I'd never seen her at any of the other seniors' events."

"Well"—Bettina shook her head sadly—"it would be a shame to lose a new member over a risqué song, or a potential member over 'Danny Boy.' And they'll really be missing out. The Arborville seniors' group enriches so many people's lives. The *Advocate* has been covering their activities forever."

"I hope Cheryl Hagan comes back," Meg said. "She's actually an old-time Arborvillian who grew up here. She left for college and then raised her family in Rochemont, but her daughter ended up in Arborville. Cheryl's husband is gone now and she moved back to Arborville to be near her daughter."

The sound of the front door opening and the jingle of a leash announced that Wilfred and Woofus had returned from their walk. A few moments later he stepped into the kitchen, greeted the three women with a courtly bow, and proceeded on to the utility room with Woofus's leash. Woofus took up his spot along the wall near the sliding glass doors that opened to the patio—a spot he favored because it gave him a view of squir-rels.

Meg stood up. "I've got to get going." She sighed. "But thank you for the coffee, and for listening—and I'm so relieved those photos of yours aren't going to end up in the *Advocate*. I do hope they help the police. The sooner Detective Clayborn can figure out who did this and why, the better. I don't think the seniors are going to be interested in any activities until the case is resolved—and I hate to think of them sitting at home feeling depressed."

Bettina and Pamela saw Meg to the door, and Pamela was about to follow her onto the porch when Bettina whispered, "Stay a minute." After a detour to pick up her handbag from a side table, she led Pamela to the sofa.

CHAPTER 5

"I'm curious about this Wiccan," Bettina said, reaching into her handbag and coming up with her phone. "Do you remember what Meg said her name was?"

"I didn't exactly catch the first name." Pamela tightened her lips into a puzzled twist. "It wasn't a common name. But her last name was Percy—I remember that because it didn't seem like a name a witch would have."

"Wiccan, Percy, Wiccan, Percy, Wiccan, Percy," Bettina murmured as her fingers busied themselves on the screen of her device. "Wiccan, Percy, doesn't like St. Patrick's Day. Wiccan, Percy!"

Bettina held her phone out at arms' length. "She has a blog. And her first name is Liadan."

Pamela moved closer and both stared at the little screen. The website's graphics were striking. A green field sloping down from rugged cliffs as a gray sky glowered above formed the banner's background. Against it, the words "Liadan Speaks" were spelled out in letters shaped from sinuous lines that twisted and interlocked with no visible beginning or end.

"We Are Not Snakes" was the title of the most recent blog post. Both skimmed the post, which described St. Patrick ("though he's no saint to us") as a representative of an evil patriarchy who, by introducing Christianity to Ireland, destroyed the woman-centered Wiccan traditions. According to the blog post, the "snakes" that he drove out of Ireland—a story long associated with his myth—were actually Wiccans, whom he derided as pagans, when actually Wiccans are adherents of an ancient and noble religion.

"Well!" Bettina turned to Pamela. "She certainly has some strong views. I wonder if she's the reason Isobel showed up flustered and late for the luncheon. Once Meg turned Liadan away, she could have been lurking outside the rec center buttonholing whoever came along."

Bettina glanced at her phone. "Here's the post before the snake one," she said, shifting the angle of the phone so Pamela could see the screen too. "Wiccans Have Always Celebrated Easter" was the title.

Liadan explained that Christianity grafted the Christian holiday of Easter onto an ancient celebration of the spring equinox. Wiccan tradition called it Ostara, which sounds like "Easter," and with good reason, she said. Both words come from the name of an ancient goddess associated with dawn and new beginnings and thus with spring.

"And Ostara will be upon us before we know it," she concluded, "so start planning your Ostara altars now."

"Interesting," Bettina commented as she put her phone

to rest. "How about a little more coffee? Today's a lazy day for me."

"Not for me, I'm afraid. *Fiber Craft* calls." Pamela stood up.

"I'll stop by tomorrow though?" Bettina rose as well. "After my meeting with Clayborn?"

"Sure." Pamela nodded. "I'm curious to hear what he says."

Monday morning Pamela awoke eager for Bettina's promised visit. With the cats fed and her own breakfast and coffee out of the way, she was sitting at her computer checking over her copyedited versions of "Care and Feeding of Shetlands," "Piecework Masterpieces from the Wellfleet Collection," and "Depictions of Fixed-Beam Looms in Ancient Egyptian Tomb Frescoes" when the doorbell's chime summoned her downstairs earlier than she had anticipated.

"Well," Bettina declared as she stepped across the threshold, "Clayborn hustled me away as fast as he could, but at least there was fresh crumb cake at the Co-Op."

She thrust a white bakery box at Pamela and unbuttoned her cheery yellow all-weather coat. Beneath it was a form-fitting sheath dress in a lively shade of violet. On her feet were kitten heels in the same violet and she had accessorized the outfit with a necklace and earrings of Murano glass beads in which mingled colors created a kaleidoscopic effect.

Pamela led the way to the kitchen, where she set water boiling in the kettle, slipped a fresh filter into her carafe's filter cone, and poured in the extra coffee she had ground when she made her own coffee first thing that morning.

"I would think," Bettina said as she fetched wedding-china cups, saucers, and plates from the cupboard, "that if he had made any progress in the case he would have crowed about it, since it's to his advantage to let the residents of Arborville know what their tax dollars are paying for."

Pamela added forks, spoons, napkins, a knife, and a spatula to the table setting and asked, "Did you show him the photos on your phone?"

Turning from the refrigerator with a carton of cream in her hand, Bettina made a sound that resembled air escaping from a rapidly deflating balloon. "Oh"—she affected a pompous tone—"the county's CSI unit took much better ones. They're professionals, you know." She poured the cream into the cut-glass cream pitcher with such energy that some slopped over the rim. "*Hello*"—her gaze shifted to a spot in the middle of the kitchen and she spoke as if to an imaginary person— "I'm a professional too, a professional journalist. There is such a thing as investigative journalism, humble weekly though the *Advocate* might be."

Pamela offered a damp sponge to wipe up the spilled cream, and when that chore was done, she nestled the sugar bowl next to the cream pitcher. Once Bettina was seated, with a steaming cup of coffee in front of her, the process of adding just the right amount of sugar and cream provided enough distraction that she was silent while Pamela settled into her own chair with her own coffee. Further distraction was provided by cutting and serving generous portions of crumb cake.

A substantial bite of crumb cake followed by a long sip of coffee restored Bettina's good humor, and when she spoke again it was to praise the crumb cake as tasting even better than usual. Pamela wasn't sure it was even better than usual, but the Co-Op bakery counter's crumb cake never disappointed. The cake part was light, but rich and buttery, with a hint of lemon, and the crumb topping was even richer and more buttery, and it was infused with a hint of cinnamon.

Pamela, however, had more questions about Bettina's meeting with Detective Clayborn. "Did you show him the other photos you took?" she inquired. "The ones where Isobel is wearing a sweater that isn't in the crime scene photos?"

"I did not." Bettina's coffee cup paused halfway to her mouth, and the smile with which she had reported on the crumb cake vanished. "Because if Clayborn wasn't interested in my crime-scene photos I'm not going to do his work for him by providing him with what could be a very important clue."

"It could be a clue—to *something*." Pamela nodded. "But, as you said the other day, maybe she just felt hot and took it off."

"Possibly." Bettina nodded back. "However, in the photos it isn't on the desk or on the floor—or anywhere else that I could see. And I studied those photos really hard before I showed them to Clayborn."

"I wonder if Meg told him about the funeral flowers." Pamela had been maneuvering her fork to tease off a bit of crumb cake but she looked up from her task.

"She did—and I did too. But he said killers don't usually warn people of their plans ahead of time. So I didn't tell him about the florist's van you saw that had probably been parked by the rec center's back entrance during the whole luncheon, and I didn't tell him about Liadan Percy. Let him do his own detective work if he's going to be such a smarty-pants." Bettina followed this declaration with a snort that reminded Pamela of a cat sneezing.

Pamela pointed out that Meg had probably told Detective Clayborn about the Wiccan when he interviewed her.

"Well"—Bettina tossed her head and snorted again—"he can follow up then if he wants. It's none of my business."

Catrina wandered into the kitchen just then. She halted near Pamela's chair and gazed up at her mistress, her amber eyes glowing with uncharacteristic intensity against her inky black fur. Pamela suddenly felt herself shiver.

"What if *we* talked to the Wiccan." She blurted it out almost before she knew what she was saying.

"Why?" Bettina squinted across the table.

"Liadan could really be the person who did it," Pamela said. "It all fits together. Let's say the murder wasn't premeditated and the flower delivery was just a mistake. After Meg refused to give Liadan equal time, she could have visited Isobel in the green room after the concert to chastise her for supporting the patriarchy by celebrating St. Patrick. The conversation could have escalated—I'll bet Isobel could be quite feisty."

"They argue—yes!" Skepticism abandoned, Bettina had become quite caught up in the scenario. "And the argument becomes physical!"

"And all that laughter and chatter after the concert could easily have drowned out the sounds of an argument."

"Hmm." Bettina closed her eyes and raised a carefully manicured hand to her forehead. "Maybe the *Advocate* could use an article on alternative views of St. Patrick's Day—or this Ostara/Easter connection. And what's this Ostara altar she talks about in the blog?"

Pamela had been leaning forward, excited about this explanation for the unfortunate disruption of the St. Patrick's Day festivities. But suddenly she slumped back in her chair.

"What about the sweater?" she whispered. "And the florist's van lurking around long after the delivery? How do we explain those if Liadan is the killer?"

Bettina frowned. After a moment she seemed about to speak, but Pamela's phone, the landline, rang before any words emerged. Bettina lifted the handset from its cradle on the wall and handed it across the table to Pamela.

After saying hello, Pamela listened briefly and then responded by saying, "I'm sorry but you have the wrong number. This is the residence of Pamela Paterson, not Pete Paterson."

Passing the handset back to Bettina, she said, "I've always been in the directory as 'P Paterson.' I guess there's another one."

"What did they want? And shall I heat up the rest of the coffee?" Without waiting for an answer, Bettina headed for the stove.

"They wanted their screens fixed. I guess Pete Paterson is a handyman."

Bettina was carefully monitoring the progress of the coffee-heating project, watching for the tiny bubbles around the edges of the liquid that would indicate it was just shy of boiling. But she shifted her gaze to Pamela for a moment.

"You might have cost Pete Paterson a job," she observed. "That person might call somebody else instead of figuring out that there are two P Patersons."

"What could I have done?" Pamela saw the wisdom in Bettina's observation. Maybe Pete Paterson was seriously in need of work and a job fixing someone's screens could have made a significant difference in his cash flow.

"Look up the number for the other P Paterson—or here, I'll do it in a minute." Bettina switched off the flame under the carafe, thrust her hand into a protective oven mitt, and carried the carafe to the table, where she refilled both cups.

Even before adding sugar and cream to her coffee, she took her phone from her handbag and, after a minute of effort involving fluttering fingers, announced that she had found Pete Paterson, handyman, based in Arborville.

"Write down this number," she said. "Then if you get more calls looking for him you can give out the correct number."

Pamela fetched the notepad with the tulip-bordered pages and complied. The relevance of the missing sweater and the lurking florist's van to the scenario that had the Wiccan killing Isobel was forgotten as the two friends shared an additional piece of crumb cake and savored their second cup of coffee.

"I'll get in touch with Liadan Percy," Bettina told Pamela before they parted at Pamela's front door. "And then I'll call you. Maybe we can talk to her about St. Patrick and Ostara altars this very afternoon."

When Bettina had gone on her way, Pamela climbed the stairs to her office and resumed the process of checking over the copyedited articles before attaching them to an email and sending them off to her boss. She dawdled at the computer for a bit, rereading an email that had come the previous evening from Penny—about a job fair she had gone to on campus, a design project she had gotten an A on, and a new vintage clothing store that had opened near her campus.

She was about to depart, allowing her monitor to nap, when a new message popped up in her inbox. It was from her boss, Celine Bramley, and the stylized paperclip that accompanied the name of the sender and the subject line indicated that it brought with it attachments.

"Thank you for getting those back on time," the text of the email read. "Attached are three more—to be evaluated, not copyedited until I give the go-ahead. I need them back by Friday. And did the FedExed book I sent for you to review arrive yet?"

Across the top of the message, abbreviated titles gave hints of what Pamela would find when she opened the Word files: "Civil War Quilts," "Scottish Tartans," and "Virgin Mary Knits." She suspected she wouldn't be hungry for quite some time after indulging in the crumb cake with Bettina, so she opened "Civil War Quilts," whose full title was "To Make a Virtue of Necessity: Quilters and the War Effort, 1861–1865," and set to work.

The article included photographs of quilts in the author's possession, as well as ones preserved in museum collections. Before reading the article, Pamela skimmed over the pictures and was puzzled to see that most of the quilts were unremarkable and, moreover, many were in threadbare condition. But when she turned to the text, she understood: the article was more about the historical context of the quilts than their aesthetic value.

Cloth was in short supply as the war dragged on, especially in the South, where ports were blockaded. But the soldiers needed warm bedding, so the quilters welcomed any scrap of fabric, no matter how humble. Though they could have sewed the scraps together any old way, the impulse to create beauty triumphed even here, albeit with simple quilt block patterns and hasty assembly. Once completed, the quilts were put to use—often hard use, and washed and rewashed. Nonetheless, the quilts whose images accompanied the article were as personal and distinctive as any Pamela had seen.

As she read, she pictured the women who had made the quilts—mothers, sisters, and wives of both Union and Confederate soldiers—plying their needles while too aware of the fearsome battlefield scenes the quilts would come to witness. Technically the women might have been enemies, but they would have been united by their common devotion to the craft they shared.

"Definitely publishable," she murmured to herself even though she was barely halfway through.

At that moment, however, the ringing telephone interrupted her progress, and she answered to discover Bettina on the other end of the line.

"Liadan Percy is anxious to talk to me," Bettina said. "She's delighted that I want to present the residents of Arborville with another perspective on the holiday they just celebrated. So be ready to leave at one p.m. I'll pick you up."

Pamela made a note of where she had left off reading and closed the Word file. Downstairs, she ate a sandwich made from leftovers of Saturday night's solitary chicken dinner and was just rinsing her plate when the doorbell chimed.

"You have a FedEx parcel." Bettina handed over the bulky envelope as Pamela swung the door open.

"Something to review for the magazine," Pamela explained as she set the parcel on the table in the entry.

Liadan Percy lived in an old wood-frame house that had been carved up into apartments long ago. It was one of several houses, never grand, along the busy street that crossed Arborville Avenue and led to the George Washington Bridge. It had almost no front yard, as if the street it faced had grown in importance, and thus width, over the decades and gradually encroached upon the house's original land.

Pamela and Bettina climbed wooden steps to a small, rickety porch, rang one of several bells along the doorframe, and then climbed a wooden staircase to the second floor. There, Liadan was waiting in her doorway. She greeted them and ushered them into a dim and shadowy room that was nonetheless strangely welcoming. Heavy curtains hid the windows and the only light came from flickering candles.

"Please sit," she said, gesturing toward a sofa upholstered in a dark, velvety fabric. A long wooden bench with a carved back faced the sofa, and between bench and sofa was an ornate table. On the table was a tray bearing three pottery mugs filled with some fragrant potion.

"Don't worry," she said with a merry laugh. "I'm not

going to cast a spell on you. Sit down and have some cider."

She perched on the bench facing them, picked up one of the mugs, and took a sip after murmuring a few unintelligible words.

"A thank-you," she explained, "to our great mother, the earth, who provided us with the fruit that made this cider possible."

Bettina and Pamela joined her in sipping the cider. It was a rich brew, slightly warm, that distilled the very essence of apples, with a hint of spice as well. Bettina set her mug back on the table and took out her phone.

"I'll record, if you don't mind—so I'm sure to get all the details correct."

Liadan nodded. "You can start with my name, my Wiccan name, which I chose in the ceremony that welcomed me into the coven to which I still belong. Liadan means "gray lady" in Celtic, and I guess that's true now—though I wasn't gray then. I just liked the sound of it."

Liadan was, in fact, gray—with an unapologetic mass of springy salt-and-pepper curls cascading to her shoulders, which were draped in a rustic wool shawl fastened with a large brooch shaped like a complicated rope twist.

Sitting next to Bettina, Pamela couldn't see her friend's face—and the room was very dim besides—but from the tone of Bettina's voice she could picture the earnest expression, touched with concern, that Bettina assumed when touching on difficult matters in her interviews.

"I never knew, until now," she said, "that St. Patrick's Day wasn't a holiday that everyone liked—at least everyone who has a fondness for corned beef and cabbage. But then Meg Norton mentioned that you'd requested equal time to speak on the Wiccan view of St. Patrick's Day at the luncheon."

Liadan's reaction was another merry laugh—a laugh that left her wiping her eyes with a corner of the shawl. When she had composed herself, she leaned forward to peer at Bettina. Her eyes seemed to enlarge as she stared with a catlike fixedness.

"I'm very intuitive," she whispered. "It's one of my gifts."

Pamela felt the sofa quiver as a tremor passed through Bettina. But Bettina's voice didn't betray her unease. "That must be useful," she murmured.

"It is," Liadan went on. "You're here from the *Advocate*. And so, yes. Detective Clayborn *did* speak to me about the murder of Isobel Lister. And I realize that in the view of some people—maybe you—I could have wanted Isobel dead for fostering the celebration of the person who destroyed the Wiccan culture in Ireland. But the Wiccan creed is 'Harm none. Do what you will.'"

A gentle meow coming from somewhere behind them drew Pamela's and Bettina's attention to a shadowy doorway in the apartment's back wall. A cat emerged, a pale cat with darker markings on its tail and ears. It was hugely, gigantically pregnant, and it meandered in a lumbering fashion past the end of the sofa toward the bench where Liadan was sitting.

She watched its slow progress, smiling in a maternal way. When it reached her feet, she carefully scooped it up and nestled it on the bench beside her. Then she turned her attention back to Pamela and Bettina and said, "Witches' cats don't have to be black, you know.

This is my sweet girl, Luna, and she's right in tune with the seasons. We Wiccans celebrate the spring equinox—which as it happens is today—as Ostara, which heralds the coming of new life."

"Is that like Easter?" Bettina asked.

"Easter took the name from the pre-Christian holiday," Liadan said, "and a lot of the symbolism too, like eggs. But Easter moves around and Ostara always marks the equinox. I'll be putting the finishing touches on my Ostara altar this evening."

She pointed to an attractive piece of furniture along the wall that had probably served as a dining room sideboard in an earlier life. A long linen cloth covered its top, and a five-pointed star shaped from twisted vines hung on the wall above it, set off by two symmetrically arranged vases containing pussy willow branches.

"But back to the matter at hand—" Liadan leaned forward once again and focused her catlike gaze on Bettina. The cat did likewise, and Pamela was startled to see that one of its eyes was blue and the other amber. "*Someone* killed Isobel. Was it because of the St. Patrick's Day connection? That remains to be discovered. And by the way, she wasn't really Irish. She had a wide repertoire, or so I've heard, and could be Edith Piaf if that's what the gig called for—or even Janis Joplin."

"Versatile." Bettina nodded. "But she certainly threw herself into those Irish tunes."

Liadan laughed, but not as merrily as before. "Now that I think of it, if anybody would object to the luncheon and the concert—more than I did, and for different reasons—it would be Siobhan O'Doul. Have you heard of her?"

"Not really?" Bettina sounded hesitant, as if she

feared that not having heard of Siobhan O'Doul would mark her as hopelessly out of touch with Arborville society.

"She's a local genealogist," Liadan explained, "focused on tracing and reclaiming her Irish heritage—and she's quite the crusader against what she calls 'Irish minstrel shows.'"

"I can see how Isobel's performance could offend someone like that," Bettina said. "But would she *kill* a person for putting on a fake Irish accent?"

Liadan shrugged. "Her grandfather was in the IRA."

CHAPTER 6

Bettina's first words once they were settled back in her car were, "She likes cats."

"Um-hm." Pamela reached for her seatbelt.

"And I liked her." Bettina watched as Pamela buckled herself in, and then she twisted her key in the Toyota's ignition. "I can't think of any reason she would have taken the sweater, and the person who killed Isobel is undoubtedly the same person who took the sweater."

"Most probably." Pamela nodded.

"Besides"—Bettina pulled away from the curb and executed an alarming U-turn—"Clayborn interviewed her and hasn't arrested her, so I think we should talk to this Siobhan O'Doul. The sweater was green—even though it wasn't a very Irish shade of green—and Isobel wasn't really Irish and Siobhan could have thought her wearing it on St. Patrick's Day especially while she sang those songs was a complete travesty."

They drove a few blocks in silence, with Bettina

frowning slightly. As they neared the corner of Orchard Street, she spoke again. "Then there's the 'Harm none' thing."

"And the florist's van," Pamela added. "We never linked Liadan with the florist's van."

"Let's say—" Bettina braked suddenly and Pamela lurched forward, glad for her seatbelt. A skateboarder had appeared out of nowhere and swerved off the sidewalk just as Bettina swung the steering wheel to turn onto Orchard.

Once the skateboarder was safely across the street and the Toyota was moving, Bettina took up her thought again. "Let's say the killer ordered the flowers to be delivered as a threat—cease and desist with this insulting fake-Irish performance or it will be your funeral."

"That does make sense," Pamela said, "except that the florist's van hung around long after the flowers had been delivered."

"Puzzling," Bettina agreed. "But it will be easy enough to drive up to Beauteous Blooms in Timberley and find out who ordered those flowers."

They had reached the Frasers' house. Bettina pulled into the driveway and parked the Toyota beside Wilfred's ancient but lovingly cared-for Mercedes.

"And I'm curious to meet this Siobhan O'Doul. She sounds like someone I *should* have heard of, as a reporter for Arborville's weekly newspaper. I can work her into my St. Patrick's Day article—two views of St. Patrick's Day celebrations, both negative. But putting Ostara and the altar and the eggs and all in there too will make for a crowded article, so I'll wait and cover that angle when Easter gets closer."

Back at home, Pamela finished reading the article on Civil War quilts and wrote an enthusiastic recommendation that it be published. She was midway through the article on Scottish tartans, quite dizzy with references to specific clan patterns tossed about as if, in the absence of any accompanying drawings or photographs, the reader could bring to mind the image of an Arbuthnot tartan as opposed to a MacAlister tartan, or a Cameron tartan as opposed to a Muir tartan.

"No, no, no," she murmured to herself. An article like this one fairly screamed for lavish illustrations, and she skimmed the rest of it and wrote a quick note suggesting that the author supply pictures and resubmit.

It had gotten to be nearly five p.m., though the sky behind the curtains at her office windows was still bright, thanks to daylight savings. Pamela saved her file, closed Word, and raised her arms in a stretch that seemed to compel her lungs to expand and draw in a long, refreshing breath. Then she rolled her chair back, rose, and stepped out into the hall.

She was greeted by Catrina, who bounded ahead and beat her mistress to the kitchen by a full minute. The sound of cupboards opening and, particularly, the aromas of tuna and shrimp-liver medley that were released once the can opener did its work attracted Precious and Ginger. Soon Precious was feasting on tuna from her own bowl, and Catrina and Ginger were sharing large scoops of shrimp-liver medley.

Pamela stored the remaining half a can of tuna in the refrigerator, leaving the door open while she pondered the contents with her own dinner in mind. There was plenty of chicken left, though she'd eaten chicken for lunch. When Penny was still at home, Pamela had always cooked real dinners for the two of them, trying to keep life as much as possible the same as it had been when Michael Paterson was still alive. And she'd kept up the habit even with Penny in college, though now one dinner could serve for many nights.

So chicken it would be, but not merely sliced and eaten cold. She removed the half-eaten carcass from the refrigerator and set it on the counter. In search of inspiration, she took her Fannie Farmer cookbook from her cookbook shelf and scanned the index. After a few minutes of browsing, her mind was made up. What could be cozier and more comforting on a chilly spring evening than creamed chicken on toast?

But no sooner had she launched her white sauce than she was interrupted by the telephone's ring.

"Good news!" Bettina announced without preamble. "Siobhan O'Doul will be more than happy to talk to me—first thing tomorrow morning, and I know you'll want to come along."

"Wouldn't it make more sense to go to Beauteous Blooms first?" Pamela crossed the floor carrying the phone's handset and continued whisking her butter and flour mixture. The metal whisk scraped against the aluminum pot with a pleasing rhythmic jingle. "Once we talk to the florist we might realize Siobhan is completely out of the picture."

"We might," Bettina agreed, "but as Wilfred says, 'A bird in the hand is worth two in the bush.' Siobhan volunteers at Ellis Island, the Immigrant Museum, and she has to be there by eleven, so if we want to meet her it's tomorrow morning, or who knows when we'll get another chance. She sounded kind of prickly."

With that, Bettina announced she would pick Pamela up at nine a.m. and Pamela was left to focus on her white sauce.

* * *

The first impression was of books—books filling shelves that reached from floor to ceiling, books stacked haphazardly on tables, open books balanced face down on the arms of overstuffed chairs and on the dusty-looking sofa. The house that contained the books was a small, old house on a curiously shaped lot formed by a curving street that disrupted the strict grid governing most of Arborville's real estate.

Siobhan O'Doul's greeting lacked a smile, but she stood aside and ushered them into the book-filled room. Pamela and Bettina looked at each other. Their hostess was the same woman who had stalked out of the luncheon, making no effort to be inconspicuous, as Isobel launched into "Danny Boy."

"Just take your coats off, move those books out of the way, and have a seat." Siobhan gestured toward the sofa and then lowered herself with some difficulty into a nearby chair. Leaning against the chair was a gnarled walking stick that resembled a croquet mallet.

"So," she said, glancing from Pamela to Bettina, "which one of you is Bettina Fraser?"

"I am." Bettina pointed to herself. She had dressed with her usual flair and was wearing a lavender cashmere turtleneck and matching wool slacks. Lest the lavender seem too sedate, she had accessorized the outfit with a bold necklace that combined oversize silver beads with freeform nuggets of turquoise.

Siobhan raised an arm to check her watch. "You said you wanted to interview me for the *Advocate*. Okay, but be quick about it. I've got to be on my way soon."

Bettina glanced at Pamela, a slight smile twisting

her brightly painted lips. Perhaps the glance was a
warning, Pamela realized when Bettina spoke—because
her approach was far from her usual deferential interview manner.

"I guess you didn't care for the entertainment at the
luncheon the other day," she said.

"No, I did not." Siobhan resembled a slightly younger
version of Nell Bascomb, with her white hair floating
around her lined face and her pale blue eyes. But whereas Nell's resting expression was kindly amusement,
Siobhan's was anything but, as if she made no effort to
contradict the gravity that tugged down the corners of
her thin-lipped mouth.

"Have you toured the Immigrant Museum at Ellis
Island? Have you visited the Hunger Monument in
lower Manhattan? Can you imagine what it would have
been like to have nothing to eat but a potato and then
cut into it to discover it was moldy?"

She paused for breath. "My great-grandmother came
here from Ireland as an indentured servant, happy to
sleep on a cot in a corner of the kitchen when she wasn't
scrubbing pots, and grateful to have a full stomach in
exchange for twelve hours a day of work."

In a small voice, Bettina ventured, "But that was a
long time ago. Things are different now."

"Yes!" Siobhan reached for the walking stick to
steady herself as she half-rose from her chair. "Now
it's all shamrocks and leprechauns and cheap tee-shirts
that say, 'Kiss me, I'm Irish.' And half the time the
people wearing them aren't even really Irish. And the
ones who *are* Irish should be ashamed of themselves."

"What's wrong with celebrating?" Bettina said.
"And a little bit of fun?"

"Irish heritage is so much more than that, and it deserves study . . . and respect." Siobhan continued leaning on the walking stick and pulled herself to her feet. "And now," she added, "I must be on my way."

"She could at least have offered us coffee!" Bettina exclaimed as Siobhan's front door closed behind them. "What a sour person!"

"She had a point though." Pamela had recently copyedited an article that dealt with the Irish linen industry in the mid-1800s. The author had pointed out that Northern Ireland, where the industry was centered, had escaped the worst effects of the potato famine because the income from linen enabled people to buy food. Those in the south hadn't been so lucky. "Earlier generations of Irish came here came because they were desperate."

"Well, she didn't have to be so sour. That's no way to convert people to your point of view."

They had reached Bettina's faithful Toyota. "And I still think she could have offered us coffee," she observed as she unlocked the passenger-side door. "But no matter." She lifted her wrist to consult her pretty watch. "We're in time for waffles at Hyler's."

Ten minutes later, Pamela and Bettina were settled opposite each other in one of Hyler's comfortable booths. The booths, featuring worn wooden tables and benches upholstered in burgundy Naugahyde, lined the luncheonette's side walls. At the back was a lunch counter with seating furnished by a row of stools, also upholstered in burgundy Naugahyde. The rest of the floor was taken up with wooden tables surrounded by straight-backed wooden chairs. A large plate-glass window looked out on the sidewalk, Arborville Avenue, and the bank and shops across the way.

They had arrived in the lull between the breakfast crowd and the coffee-break crowd, and in place of the usual laughter and chatter only a few quiet conversations could be heard. But the aroma of breakfast still hung in the air—coffee, of course, with an admixture of toast, bacon, ham, and sausage.

No sooner had they sat down than a server delivered the oversized menus that were a Hyler's institution. Now she returned with a pot of coffee, which she tilted over the heavy cream-colored mugs that waited on the paper placemats.

Bettina was already studying her menu, and all that was visible of her was a pouf of scarlet hair above the menu's top edge.

"I thought your mind was made up for waffles," Pamela commented as she picked up her own menu.

"It is." Bettina's voice came from behind the menu. "But I have to decide what to have with them. Smoked salmon is even a possibility."

The waffle breakfast was a Hyler's specialty, but available only until eleven a.m., so being at Hyler's in time for waffles was an unaccustomed treat.

"I think I'll have mine with ham," Pamela said, barely needing to glance at the menu. "And a glass of orange juice."

"Sausage for me." Bettina lowered her menu, which the server took as a signal to approach with her order pad. The order was placed for waffles with ham, waffles with sausage, and two glasses of orange juice, and she went on her way.

Bettina busied herself for a few moments adding

sugar and cream to her coffee. Pamela, who eschewed sugar and cream, took several sips of her coffee, black, willing the caffeine to tame the disordered ideas swirling in her mind.

"Siobhan's walking stick would make a good weapon," she said after Bettina had sampled her coffee and pronounced it perfect. "In fact, I think those sticks are weapons, or once were." Taking Bettina's alert stare as a sign of interest, she went on. "It doesn't look like the medical examiner has released details from the autopsy yet. Detective Clayborn didn't have any news for you yesterday and if Marcy Brewer had gotten any kind of scoop there'd have been an article in the *Register* this morning."

Bettina continued to stare. Then her brightly painted lips parted in a wide smile. "I get it," she exclaimed. "The medical examiner would know if she died from a blow to the head from something made of wood rather than cracking her head on the corner of that metal desk when she fell."

Pamela nodded and pulled her phone from her purse, commenting, "I think that walking stick is a shillelagh. The nature channel had a feature about Ireland the other night—leading up to St. Patrick's Day, I suppose—and there was an interview with a man living out in the middle of nowhere who makes them by hand from wood he scavenges."

She keyed "shillelagh" into the search panel on her phone and in a moment was reading aloud: "Shillelagh, blackthorn walking stick, or old Celtic fighting cudgel." She studied the images that came up on the screen. Shillelaghs varied in form. Some—the most primitive ones—looked like they had been created by taking a stout branch with a sturdy limb extending from it and sawing the branch above and below the limb. The limb became the walking stick and the remains of the branch it had sprung from became a useful grip for the walker's hand—or a lethal knob capable of doing quite a bit of damage if the stick was wielded as a weapon.

She extended the phone across the table.

"Yes, yes!" Bettina bent toward the little screen. "That walking stick of Siobhan's did look like this. And one of these could certainly do a lot of damage."

But the discussion of the shillelagh's murderous potential was interrupted by the arrival of the waffles.

"I'll be right back with your juice," the server said as she lowered two large platters to the table and turned away. Butter and syrup, standard features of Hyler's breakfast table setting, were already at hand, and the juice arrived a moment later.

The platters were oval and the waffles were round. Each waffle occupied one end of its platter, with its irregular edges overlapping the platter's rim and the accompanying ham or sausages tucked in at the platter's other end.

Pats of butter melted satisfyingly into the crisp golden-brown grid that formed the waffles' surface, and the thick syrup spread and pooled even more satisfyingly. To make the generous round of waffle more manageable, Pamela sliced it into the quarters scored by the waffle iron and piled the quarters in stacks of two each.

Bettina, meanwhile, had already taken her first bite and a dribble of syrup was making its way down her chin. She seemed oblivious to it, however, as her lips curved into a close-mouthed smile and her eyes crinkled with pleasure. Her "umm" was as musical as a snatch of song.

Pamela was not as vocal, but as she sampled her own waffle she had to agree with Bettina's estimation. Waffles in general were uniquely designed to serve as vehicles for melted butter and syrup, and this waffle managed to deliver the maximum sweet, buttery pleasure while still retaining its own crisp integrity.

The sausages that accompanied Bettina's waffle were plump, and browned to glistening perfection from their time on the grill. She steadied one with her fork, releasing a few beads of fat as the tines went in, and carved off a bite. Meanwhile, Pamela turned her attention to the thick slice of ham that shared the platter with her waffle. An exploratory taste revealed that its smoky, salty flavor offered a savory complement to the sweetness of the syrup-bathed waffle, and one taste led to many. Occasional sips of orange juice provided a refreshingly tart contrast.

Neither Pamela nor Bettina spoke for some time, except in monosyllables that confirmed the reputation of Hyler's storied waffles. When the platters were empty, except for a sliver of ham fat, a bit of sausage casing, and a few streaks of syrup, the server approached to refill the coffee mugs.

A goodly swallow of coffee shifted Pamela's attention from the pleasures of the table back to the puzzle that had brought her and Bettina out for their early-morning errand.

"It occurs to me," she said, after Bettina had finished sugaring and creaming her fresh mug of coffee, "that after Siobhan walked out in the middle of 'Danny Boy,' she could have reentered the rec center through the back door, and she could have been waiting in the green room to pounce on Isobel as soon as the concert was over."

"Pounce on her with the shillelagh." Bettina nodded, and her earrings, which were large nuggets of turquoise that matched her silver and turquoise necklace, swayed.

"But there's still the Beauteous Blooms connection." Pamela lifted her mug in a gesture like a toast. "Drink up and we'll be off to Timberley."

CHAPTER 7

The route to Timberley lay north along County Road, with Arborville to the east and the county's nature preserve to the west. In an earlier era, County Road had been a major thoroughfare connecting the small towns of northern New Jersey with the farms and orchards that supplied them with sustenance. Now, in place of travelers on foot and horseback, horse-drawn carts, and carriages, cars and trucks traversed the smooth asphalt that had replaced the rutted dirt.

Pamela was enjoying the ride, and the distraction provided by the trees speeding by, with their spindly branches brushed with the barest hint of green. Overhead, the sky was pale blue but for massed clouds like a woolly flock of sheep.

Soon Bettina was negotiating the twists and turns that would bring them into Timberley's commercial district. After a few minutes their speed slowed as they joined the parade of cars cruising past the charming shops that drew shoppers looking for something a little more special than Arborville or other towns to the south had to offer: shops where one could find cheese imported from France, or velveteen party dresses for little girls, or handmade gold jewelry. Even the shops themselves—with their awnings and hand-painted signs and fanciful window displays—contributed to Timberley's distinction.

Beauteous Blooms was next to a candy shop whose window featured all manner and size of chocolate eggs, chocolate chicks, and chocolate bunnies, inhabiting a landscape made springlike with liberal amounts of raffia Easter grass. In the window of Beauteous Blooms next door, rustic baskets held clusters of daffodils and tulips forced from bulbs.

A silvery bell tinkled as Bettina pushed the door open, and from behind a long counter a slender man in a pale blue sweater that flattered his blond good looks greeted them. Behind him, tall glass doors protected the flowery contents of a refrigerated case.

"What can I do for you ladies?" the man inquired.

Pamela was happy to let Bettina remain in the lead. They hadn't exactly discussed why Beauteous Blooms would feel it was a stranger's business to know who had placed a particular order.

"You delivered the most beautiful funeral arrangement to an address in Arborville last Friday." Bettina augmented her smile with a flirtatious head tilt.

"St. Willibrod's Church on Arborville Avenue." The man returned the smile, but it faded quickly and was replaced by a concerned forehead pucker. "I hope I'm not speaking to a bereaved family member . . . Losing a loved one can be so difficult."

Pamela often had to stifle a laugh at the theatrics to which Bettina resorted in her investigative exploits, but this time Bettina's surprise was genuine.

"They were meant for the church?" She took a step backwards and seemed to struggle for balance. "Really?"

"Of course." The concerned forehead pucker remained. "Where else would they go?"

"To the Arborville rec center, which was hosting a St. Patrick's Day luncheon for the seniors' group," Bettina said, adding, "I'm involved with the group—though I'm not a senior, of course"—she winked—"and we were concerned that maybe there'd been some kind of mix-up."

"Argh!" The man closed his eyes and flung his head back. "No complaints from the woman who ordered them yet, thank goodness—but maybe there were so many floral tributes that she didn't notice hers was missing." He stepped over to a computer monitor at the end of the counter, tapped in a few quick keystrokes, and spoke.

"The Lasting Remembrance All-White Tribute, to be delivered by noon March 17 to St. Willibrod's Church at 182 Arborville Avenue."

Bettina, meanwhile, was busy with her own device. "The rec center is at 128 Arborville Avenue," she said. "It looks like your delivery man transposed the numbers."

"He's my nephew"—the man shook his head wearily—"taking a gap year before college, though in my mind I call it a 'nap year.' If he's not mixing up a delivery, he's asleep. How I wish he was at school, somewhere far, far away. Apparently it didn't occur to him that a St. Patrick's Day luncheon was an unlikely destination for the Lasting Remembrance All-White Tribute."

A gentle tinkle announced the arrival of another visitor, this one bent on placing a rush order for red roses to acknowledge a forgotten birthday. Pamela and Bettina withdrew to let the proprietor of Beauteous Blooms focus on his customer.

Soon they were settled back in Bettina's faithful Toyota, but before inserting her key in the ignition, she pulled her phone from her handbag again.

"I'm just curious," she explained as her fingers, with their bright orange manicure, fluttered over the screen of her device. In a moment she was speaking into it.

"Bettina Fraser from the *Advocate* here," she announced crisply. "Just checking on a detail. Was there a funeral at the church last Friday?"

She listened, hummed in acknowledgment to whatever the response had been, and murmured thanks.

"That florist was on the level," she reported as she tucked her phone away. "There really was a funeral at St. Willibrod's on St. Patrick's Day."

"I suppose the delivery man wasn't lurking in the parking lot behind the rec center for any sinister purpose, but just grabbing one of his naps." Pamela laughed. "And he sped away when he saw me because he didn't want to be caught goofing off."

Bettina was silent as she twisted her key in the Toyota's ignition. The car's engine came alive with a grumble and she pulled away from the curb. Pamela waited until they were once more on County Road, but heading south, to speak again.

"We were thinking the funeral flowers suggested premeditation," she reminded Bettina. "The killer sends the flowers as a spooky threat that something bad is to come and then makes good on the threat by attacking Isobel in the green room after the concert."

Bettina nodded and said, "But we were also thinking that if Liadan or Siobhan was the killer, the murder likely grew out of a discussion that escalated into an argument and turned physical. So if one of them did it, it wasn't premeditated."

Pamela replied with a nod of her own. "Now we know the flowers had nothing to do with it."

"I really don't think the killer was Liadan." Bettina slowed as they approached a stoplight that had just turned yellow.

"Because she likes cats." Pamela laughed. "And the Wiccan creed is 'Harm none. Do what you will.'"

"Not just that." Bettina braked and swiveled to face Pamela. "Liadan showed up in advance to ask Meg for equal time to speak about reasons *not* to celebrate St. Patrick's Day. It would have been stupid to kill Isobel after being so obvious that she disapproved of the event."

"But"—Pamela raised an admonitory finger—"she could have lost her temper. People often do things they hadn't planned when they've been carried away by their emotions."

"She didn't seem like the excitable type." Oblivious to the fact that the light had turned green, Bettina continued to face Pamela. "Siobhan, on the other hand—"

The thought was interrupted by a chorus of honking horns. Bettina stomped on the gas pedal and the Toyota lurched forward.

". . . is quite old and seems arthritic." Pamela finished Bettina's thought for her after the Toyota had slowed to a more sedate speed.

"That wasn't what I was going to say." Bettina frowned but kept her eyes on the road.

They were passing the nature preserve now. Come summer, wildflowers would decorate the spaces where the woods gave way to the road's shoulder, but for now wan tufts of grass were the only greenery.

"I was going to say," Bettina went on, "that Siobhan seemed grumpy."

"She *was* grumpy," Pamela said, "and like someone convinced that her views were the correct views. And the shillelagh definitely looked like something that could be used as a lethal weapon—and they definitely were in times past."

Bettina slowed to make the turn onto Orchard Street and said, "I wonder how we can figure out if Siobhan has an alibi for St. Patrick's Day between one thirty and a quarter to two."

Back at home, Pamela collected her mail from her mailbox, deposited most of it into the recycling basket that sat at the ready in the entry, and hung up her coat. The afternoon was nearly half over and Knit and Nibble met that evening. Ginger and Precious were nowhere in sight, but Catrina was relaxing on the sofa.

After a day that had already included a visit to Siobhan O'Doul, brunch at Hyler's, and a trip to Timberley, with a meeting still to come, relaxing on the sofa seemed like a good idea, but Pamela found it hard to do absolutely nothing. Fortunately, she could combine relaxing with work for *Fiber Craft*.

The FedEx parcel that had arrived the previous day still waited on the mail table. Soon Pamela had joined Catrina on the sofa and was immersed in *Shaker Communities and the Feminist Sensibility: The Paradox of Women's Work.*

CHAPTER 8

When Pamela and Bettina stepped into Holly Perkins's stylish living room that evening, Nell Bascomb was already settled on the loveseat, with its orange and chartreuse print upholstery, and Karen Dowling and Roland DeCamp occupied the streamlined ochre sofa. But two chairs with angular chrome frames and dark green leather seats and backs sat empty. They faced the sofa across the coffee table, which was a freeform slab of granite on spindly legs.

Holly's dramatic appearance reflected the same bold style choices as her living room's décor, which also involved walls the color of graphite, enlivened by a bold sunburst wall clock. Holly's luxuriant raven hair was accented tonight by a streak of bright green. Enormous silver hoops hung from her earlobes and her ensemble, all black, consisted of leggings, chunky boots, and an oversize sweater that seemed knitted from yarn as thick as rope.

"Make yourselves comfortable!" Holly gestured toward the chairs after she had taken their coats.

"It looks like we're all here," Bettina commented as she lowered herself into one of the chairs.

"Not quite." Holly still hovered near the door, though a pair of knitting needles and a skein of yarn in an empty spot on the long sofa indicated that she had already claimed a seat. "Imogene is coming back—she still can't decide whether she wants to join or not."

"We didn't invite her to join," Bettina commented.

Roland looked up—he was already hard at work on a few inches of ribbing. "No," he agreed, "we didn't."

Holly raised her hands as if to fend off their observations. "I know, I know," she said. "We all have to agree on new members, so I didn't promise her anything. But she just lost her aunt—in a very shocking way."

"Oh, that's right!" Bettina looked chastened. "She's Imogene Lister! Of course! I absolutely did not make that connection."

"Yes!" Holly's dark eyes grew large. "Isobel Lister is—*was*, I guess I should say—her aunt. And what a finale for the St. Patrick's Day concert! The Arborville seniors will be talking about it for the rest of their lives!" She focused on Bettina. "You must have been there—I remember you saying you were going to cover the luncheon for the *Advocate*."

"I *was* there." Bettina had opened her knitting bag but held off reaching inside. "And I have to tell you that—"

She was interrupted by Nell, speaking in tones uncharacteristically severe. "We do not need to discuss this tragic event," she said, her faded eyes in their nests of wrinkles glancing first at Bettina and then shifting to Holly. "Not now, not ever. Our gossip will not help the police solve the crime." Nell, in her eighties, was by far the oldest member of the knitting group.

Bettina would have been silenced anyway, because the doorbell's ring overlapped with Nell's words and Holly exclaimed, "That must be Imogene!"

Aside from Holly's gracious, "Please come in," Imogene was greeted by silence. Would saying, "I'm so sorry about your aunt," violate Nell's commandment? Pamela wondered. And apparently the other Knit and Nibblers were faced with the same quandary.

Holly led their guest to the sofa and Imogene took a seat. The full complement of knitters accounted for, Holly picked up the skein of yarn and the needles that had marked her place and sat down between Karen and Roland, with Imogene on Karen's right at the sofa's end.

Though both blonde and young, the two women could hardly have been more different. Karen was slender and delicately pretty, with a sweet and shy manner. Imogene, on the other hand, was not slender or fine-featured, and her platinum hair was not natural. Once she had acknowledged Holly's greeting, and the welcoming—but silent—nods of the others, her face settled into an expression that suggested a self-pitying belligerence.

The silence stretched on to the point that even Roland, normally happy to forgo conversation in favor of concentrating on his knitting, began to stir uncomfortably. Holly, sitting next to him, noticed. She glanced across the coffee table at Bettina, who was busy at what Pamela knew to be the sleeve of a royal-blue sweater destined for her oldest son. Holly's eyes strayed to Pamela's face. Pamela offered an unhappy smile and a shrug.

With a sigh, Holly sat up straighter and said, "I guess we can now say spring has officially started, as of March 20th."

As a conversational gambit, it may have been trite, but it served the purpose.

"We certainly can." Nell jumped in enthusiastically, as if to atone for condemning her fellow knitters to silence. "And the nature channel had the most interesting program the other night, about how people have been celebrating the spring equinox forever, since back when religions were based on the cycle of the seasons. Now it overlaps with Easter but it's much older."

"It's called Ostara, by Wiccans anyway!" Bettina lowered her knitting to her lap. "I was just interviewing a Wiccan for the *Advocate*. Wiccans aren't really witches, you know. They believe people should live in harmony with nature, and they observe all kinds of holidays based on what the sun is doing. The spring equinox is just one of them."

"There are Wiccans in Arborville?" Roland's lean face, above his immaculate shirt collar anchored by a perfectly knotted tie of expensive silk, was serious.

Bettina laughed. "I just said they're not really witches, Roland. No need to be alarmed."

"I know they're not really witches, but I wouldn't think people living in Arborville would have to . . . worship *nature*. There are certainly enough churches in this town."

After her initial comment, Nell had returned to her project, which Pamela now realized involved not knitting needles but a crochet hook. But her busy fingers stilled for a moment and she leaned forward from her perch on the loveseat.

"Being respectful of nature is a noble impulse," she said. "And the cycle of the seasons provides so many opportunities for celebration—new life in the spring, and midsummer with the longest day, and then the harvest, and after that everything gets dark so people light candles . . . And celebrating is such a human impulse, a break in the routine."

"Speak for yourself. I like routine." As if to emphasize the point, Roland's next needle thrust was particularly vigorous. Roland indeed took his work as a corporate lawyer seriously—so seriously that his doctor had recommended he take up knitting as a means to de-stress. "I have never thought the town Easter egg hunt was a sensible expenditure of tax dollars—not to mention all the Christmas carryings-on," he concluded. "I can't believe the size of my tax bill and it goes up every year."

"Oh, for heaven's sake!" Bettina made the sound that reminded Pamela of a cat sneezing. "You can afford it, Roland, and the children love the Easter egg hunt. You're always such a spoilsport."

"I'm *not* always a spoilsport." Roland's muttered words seemed addressed to his knitting project rather than the group, as he focused on his looping yarn and crisscrossing needles. He turned to Holly, who was sitting next to him on the sofa. "You don't think I'm a spoilsport, do you?" he inquired in uncharacteristically plaintive tones.

Holly swiveled to face him and offered a smile that displayed her perfect teeth and brought her dimple into play. "I like the Easter egg hunt," she said, "even though Desmond and I don't have children yet. That's just one of the things that makes this amazing town so amazing."

"This is the first year Lily will be old enough for the Easter egg hunt," Karen added in her meek voice.

Before Roland could object that the question of whether or not he was always a spoilsport remained unresolved, Holly found a new focus for her smile and her dimple.

"And what new and interesting project is our dear Nell working on?" she inquired, leaning toward the loveseat. "And I see a crochet hook instead of knitting needles. How talented you are!"

Nell ceased plying her crochet hook and held up a small circular object about the size of a coaster one would put under a drippy glass. It had been worked from delicate yarn in a pale green, around and around in a spiral.

"It's a nest," Nell said, "or it's going to be a nest. I'm just getting to the part where the sides start to curve up in a bowl shape."

"A nest!" Holly's knitting slipped into her lap as she released it to free her hands for an energetic clap. "A nest!" she repeated. "That is awesome. And we were just talking about Easter eggs."

Roland joined in, perhaps seeking to make up for his earlier ill temper. He even smiled. "What will you do with the nest?" he asked, lowering his knitting and tilting his head attentively.

"It's for rescued baby birds," Nell explained, "or even baby squirrels. They fall out of their own nests and people find them. I just learned last week that the

Wildlife Center in Timberley needs them, nice soft crocheted nests, or even knitted ones, especially in the spring and summer."

"I would love to make a nest!" Holly's enthusiasm lent an extra glow to her radiant good looks. "Will you teach me?"

"Absolutely!" The gaze Nell directed at Holly was fond. Holly's love of all things midcentury modern encompassed home furnishings and food—as well as, apparently, humans who had experienced the 1950s first-hand, and when she joined the knitting group some years earlier she had immediately bonded with its oldest member.

Holly gestured toward the swath of knitting in her lap. Its magenta color and the shaggy yarn from which it was worked made it resemble the pelt of some fantastical creature. "I'm just finishing the second sleeve of my jacket," she said. "And then all I have to do is sew the pieces together. So next week I'll be ready to start making nests. I always wanted to know how to crochet."

"They don't take much yarn, as you can see." Nell held the small project aloft. "So you can use up leftover odds and ends—but the yarn can't be too fuzzy because the little toenails of the birds and squirrels get caught."

"I'd like to crochet some nests too." Karen spoke up in a small voice. She and Holly were best friends— though with her lively personality, Holly was definitely the leader. Karen displayed her knitting project and added, "I'm almost finished with what I'm making too."

It was a dress, Pamela knew, but a doll-sized dress. At a previous meeting of the group, Karen had passed around a pattern book for knitted doll clothes and had declared her plan to knit an entire wardrobe for her daughter's favorite doll.

"I'll give the crocheting a try too," Pamela said. She had only one sleeve to finish and the tawny brown pullover with the black cat on the front would be done.

No one else indicated a wish to make nests, perhaps because their current projects were nowhere near completion and they feared losing momentum if they set them aside. Bettina, who was never speedy, had been at work on the royal-blue sweater sleeve since January, but Pamela knew that her aim was simply to finish the garment in time for the following Christmas. Roland, too, was working on a gift—a pale yellow sweater in a fancy, lacy stitch for his mother's birthday. In Imogene's case, a long column of knitting, pale in color and with an interesting texture, hung from her needles, but since it was hard to know what it was, it was hard to know how much longer she intended it to be.

The knitters knit in near-silence for a bit, a silence broken only by clicking needles and an occasional murmur as someone counted stitches or checked a pattern to verify a detail. Pamela finished a row and closed her eyes for a few moments to rest. When she opened them, she was staring at the striking sunburst clock that dominated the wall behind the sofa.

The minute hand was the tiniest fraction to the left of the bold "12" at the top center. At the very moment that it lurched to close the gap, a deep voice from the sofa proclaimed, "It's eight o'clock." Roland raised his eyes from the expensive watch that adorned his wrist and added, "Break time." He lowered his knitting onto the elegant briefcase he used in place of a knitting bag.

The spot that Holly had occupied on the sofa was

empty—she had slipped from the room while Pamela's eyes were closed. Now she appeared in the arch that separated her living room from her dining room to announce that coffee and tea would be ready very soon and people should join her in the dining room. She added that she hoped they all liked grasshopper pie.

Suddenly, unexpectedly, Imogene burst into laughter. "I haven't heard anybody talk about grasshopper pie for ages," she said. The laughter had softened her expression into an appealing vulnerability. "My grandmother used to make it. At first I thought it really had grasshoppers in it."

Karen and Imogene rose from the sofa and headed toward the arch. Roland rose too, but he stood aside in a gentlemanly way to let them take the lead, and he bowed slightly to indicate that Nell and Pamela and Bettina should go ahead as well.

Holly's dining room was furnished with vintage furniture from the 1950s, a table-and-chair set and a sideboard all made of pale wood and sleek in design. The table held plates and cups and saucers in an eye-catching shade of pink, not china but from Holly's collection of Melmac. Napkins and silverware sat at the ready too, as well as sugar in an elegant chrome sugar bowl and cream in a matching cream pitcher.

As the aroma of coffee began to drift in from the kitchen, Holly entered the dining room bearing a large wooden tray. She set it on the table with a flourish and stepped back looking pleased. "Grasshopper pie!" she announced

The pie's filling, rimmed by a crust composed of chocolate cookie crumbs, was a vivid shade of green. Shavings of dark chocolate decorated its surface.

Shivering with anticipation, Bettina leaned forward to examine the pie more closely. "I smell mint," she observed.

"Crème de menthe," Holly explained. "That's a key ingredient of grasshopper pie." She picked up the pie server and a knife tucked alongside the pie on the tray. "Would someone like to serve the pie while I fetch the coffee and tea?"

Bettina was happy to oblige and, with one long stroke sliced the pie in half. "I'll do eight," she said, "and there will be one left for Desmond."

She continued slicing, and by the time Holly returned carrying her vintage chrome coffee pot in one hand and her squat pottery teapot in the other, she had transferred four of the slices to Melmac plates. The vivid green contrasted strikingly with the pink color of the plastic dinnerware.

Holly made sure Nell and Karen were provided with tea, and then commenced pouring coffee for the others. Bettina continued serving the pie, and soon the group was clustered around the granite coffee table. Its surface was just large enough to accommodate seven plates and seven cups and saucers. Holly had given up her seat to Nell—the loveseat was too far from the coffee table for easy access—and pulled a dining room chair up to the coffee table's end.

Bettina was the first to taste the pie, raising a fork on which was balanced a freeform morsel of fluffy green with a dark brown cookie-crumb edge. Once the morsel had entered her mouth, she closed her eyes, and motions of lips and jaw indicated that the bit of pie was being quickly dispatched.

"Divine!" she declared, opening her eyes.

As if they had been waiting for her to speak—not that the verdict had been in doubt—the six remaining people took up their forks in unison and began to carve off tidbits of the pie's creamy interior and toothsome crust. Soon hums of pleasure echoed around the table, followed by enthusiastic praise.

"Not really too sweet," Nell commented, "and anyway, the slices are just the right size."

That was Pamela's view as well. The slight bitterness that still lurked in the dense chocolate flavor of the cookie crumbs provided a nice balance to the filling, which owed its sweetness to marshmallows and its extra richness to whipped cream. And the minty effect of the crème de menthe offset the sweetness too. A sip of black coffee added another contrasting flavor.

Even Roland spoke up, in a voice as formal as if he was offering an evaluation of a colleague's professional performance. "Excellent job with the refreshments tonight," he observed. "And quite appropriate to the season."

"You noticed!" Holly's fork clunked against her plate as she set it down and swiveled to face Roland. "I kept thinking *green, green, green*. What can I make that's green?"

The tiniest frown marred Karen's smooth forehead. "Well, the pie *is* green," she said, "but why?"

"St. Patrick's Day! *Duh!* But the crème de menthe didn't make it green enough so I put in some food coloring too." Holly laughed, but the laugh cut off abruptly as she gulped and raised a hand to her mouth. Her nails, painted with metallic silver polish, glittered. "I wanted to make something for St. Patrick's Day," she murmured, glancing at Nell. "Is it okay if I say that?"

Imogene frowned too, less delicately than Karen

had. She leaned over to get a look at Holly's face, shifted her gaze to where Nell was sitting on the other side of Karen. Then for good measure, she studied Pamela's face for a second and then Bettina's.

"Is there some reason you all don't . . ." Her voice trailed off. She closed her eyes. Her features relaxed as they had earlier when she laughed. "You're worried about me?" she asked in tones so amazed that Pamela felt sorry for her, and all the more sorry when Imogene added, "People don't usually care enough to worry about me."

When no one said anything, she went on. "You don't need to be afraid that mentioning St. Patrick's Day will remind me of what happened to my aunt."

"We're all so sorry for your loss." Sitting in the chair next to Bettina, Pamela could only see her friend's scarlet hair and one of the bold copper earrings with which she had accented her deep indigo ensemble. But from Bettina's sympathetic tone she could picture the puckered brow and the gentle smile that accompanied the words.

"Yes," Nell chimed in, as Holly and Karen nodded, and Roland's features froze into an expression that suggested a cross between concern and physical discomfort.

"Thank you." Imogene half-rose and turned this way and that in order to make eye contact with everyone. "Thank you," she repeated. "You're all so kind, and thoughtful. It means a lot to me."

She sat back down. "Isobel was my favorite aunt, and I'm really going to miss her." Karen reached over and grabbed her hand.

"Will the funeral be held here in town?" Bettina inquired.

"Oh, of course." Imogene responded quickly, and in a matter-of-fact voice, as if the answer was obvious. "Isobel was a Lister, after all, and they always have to do things up in a big way. It's to be at St. Willibrod's, with a reception afterwards at Caleb's Table, on County Road. I heard my mother on the phone discussing the menu first thing this morning. There are to be oysters, among other things." Her lips stretched wide in a sarcastic smile. "All the best people serve oysters when they bury their loved ones. The thing is"—she laughed, more like a snort—"I'm the only one who really loved her."

She half-rose and surveyed the group again. "You're all invited. Ten a.m. at St. Willibrod's. And come down to Caleb's Table afterwards—for the oysters."

There was still pie to be eaten, which was fortunate—because, with Imogene's sad revelations, once again silence had descended on the Knit and Nibblers. Pamela carved off a good-sized morsel from her slice, enjoyed once again the interplay of chocolate and mint, and the contrasting textures of cookie-crumb crust and creamy filling.

She followed up the bite of pie with a sip of coffee and was surprised to find that the coffee was still agreeably hot. Imogene's revelations had been so moving that Pamela felt as if she had watched a drama unfold—yet not much time had elapsed at all.

When people did speak again, it was to repeat their praise of Holly's grasshopper pie as they lowered their forks onto plates now empty but for streaks of green and chocolate brown against the lively Melmac pink.

Even Imogene joined in the praise, the sweet treat seeming to have restored her equilibrium. She was the first to join Holly in ferrying plates and cups and saucers back to the kitchen, and Karen jumped up to help too. Soon the granite surface of the coffee table was bare once again and Nell had moved from the sofa back to her perch on the brightly upholstered loveseat.

Knitting resumed—as well as Nell's steady crochet work that was gradually shaping yarn into an object resembling a delicate handle-less teacup. Needles clicked steadily as quiet conversations arose here and there. Karen and Holly conferred in soft murmurs while keeping their eyes focused on their busy needles, and Bettina leaned across the coffee table to chat with Imogene.

From what Pamela could hear, Bettina was doing her kindly best to make Imogene feel comfortable and welcome, inquiring how long she'd been knitting, what types of yarn she preferred, and whether she'd ever succumbed to the temptations of the fancy yarn shop in Timberley.

The time passed agreeably in this way, with Pamela happy to think her own thoughts and enjoy how satisfyingly her sweater sleeve was nearing completion. The rhythm of her needles and busy fingers had induced such a meditative state that she might well have knit on for hours had she not been brought back to reality when Roland began to stir.

She looked up from her work to see him hefting his briefcase onto his lap. With a solid clunk, the tongue of his briefcase latch snapped back. He lifted the cover and began to carefully arrange his yarn and the pale yellow beginnings of the gift sweater within.

The other occupants of the sofa took their cue from Roland, hoisting knitting bags from the floor and tucking away needles, yarn, and projects.

Imogene carried her work in an interesting bag that could stand on its own, open, at the knitter's side or on the floor. It could also be closed and carried. A frame constructed of wooden dowels supported a fabric sack that hung like a sling, supported by two wooden dowels threaded through casings at the sack's top. Those wooden dowels formed the bag's handle when the bag was closed.

As she lifted the bag, grasping one of the dowels that formed the handle, the dowel came loose from the frame, slipping out of the hole that anchored it. The bag tipped onto its side and remnants of yarn, stray needles, rumpled clippings with photos of knitted objects, and a few small knitted squares in various colors spilled onto Holly's carpet.

Karen was sitting next to Imogene, and she leaned over to help pick up the odds and ends that had spilled. Bobbing back up, she displayed knitted squares in black, bright chartreuse, and pale pink.

"Are you doing a color-block project?" she inquired.

"Color block? What?" Imogene had lifted the deconstructed knitting bag onto her lap and was trying to re-anchor the errant dowel.

"Like that." Karen pointed toward the loveseat, where an earlier knitting project of Holly's was draped over one of the loveseat's arms. It was a color-block afghan, and Holly had created it by knitting squares and rectangles in shades of orange, turquoise, vibrant green, and gold and sewing them together in a random pattern.

"No," Imogene said. "They're just swatches. If I'm making something that has to fit just right, I knit a swatch first, to make sure that I'm not knitting so tight or so loose that the sweater or whatever ends up too small or too big."

"That sounds very advanced," Karen said. "I've never made a swatch."

"I have." The voice was Roland's. "Knitters who take their knitting seriously always make swatches."

Bettina was busy tucking away her swath of royal-blue knitting, careful that no stitches slipped off the needle from which it hung. But she stifled a snicker. Pamela glanced over to see that her friend had turned quite pink with amusement. Then she glanced at Roland.

He was on his feet, briefcase in hand, and ready to depart—with the satisfied expression of someone who has put in a productive few hours and dispensed a bit of wisdom as well. Holly scurried to the closet to fetch his coat.

CHAPTER 9

"Honestly!" Bettina and Pamela were barely halfway down Holly's front walk when Bettina exploded. "What a pompous character Roland is!" Her voice modulated into an unconvincing baritone. "Knitters who take their knitting seriously always make swatches." Speaking in her normal tone, she added, "I guess I'm not a serious knitter then, because I've never made a swatch."

They were silent as they walked the rest of the way to the curb, where Pamela's serviceable compact waited. And they were silent as they settled themselves into their seats. It was not until they were coasting down the hill toward Arborville Avenue, with Pamela's headlights carving bright tunnels through the darkness, that either of them spoke again.

"I think we should invite Imogene to join Knit and Nibble," Bettina announced suddenly, as if giving immediate voice to an idea that had just popped into her brain.

Pamela slowed as she reached the intersection with Arborville Avenue. "You won't get any argument from me," she said.

As if, in fact, Pamela had offered an argument, Bettina went on. "The poor thing just seems so forlorn. I have a favorite aunt, and though I certainly always felt loved by everyone in my family—not just her—I would be very sad to lose her even now. Holly would vote yes, I'm sure, and Karen always does whatever Holly does, and Nell is a warm-hearted soul . . ."

A few cars passed, and when the way was clear to turn Pamela pressed down on the gas pedal and swung the steering wheel to the left. "We never exactly spelled out that the vote has to be unanimous," she pointed out.

"But we always said everyone has to agree. That's the same thing, isn't it?"

"I suppose." They were cruising along Arborville Avenue now, approaching Orchard Street, where a street-lamp illuminated the lawn and shrubbery of the stately brick apartment building at the corner. "We don't know that Roland would be opposed," Pamela added. "It's just that he likes procedure to be followed, and Holly seemed to be suggesting that if Imogene wanted to join Knit and Nibble she would automatically be in."

"Well!" The half-laugh that accompanied the syllable suggested that the discussion was about to take a less serious turn. "If she became a member she and Roland could bond over their mutual love of swatches."

Soon Pamela was edging toward the curb in front of Bettina's house, where a porch light and a soft glow behind the living room curtains signaled a cozy atmosphere within. After murmured thanks for the ride and a half-hug, Bettina reached for the door handle. But before she clicked the door open she said, "I'm going to the funeral. What about you?"

"The oysters do sound tempting." Pamela's teasing smile wasn't visible in the darkness and Bettina's reaction was swift.

"That isn't why!" she exclaimed, not sounding amused at all. "People don't take the *Advocate* seriously, but *I* do, and Isobel Lister's murder is a big story, and Clayborn never goes to the victims' funerals when he's working on a case, and so he has no idea how much a person can learn from watching and listening, and at the receptions too, oysters or not."

Bettina had become quite breathless, and she left off speaking to pant for a moment. But she wasn't through, and soon resumed again.

"Besides that, he was very cocky the last time I met with him and . . . and *scornful*, like he was laughing at me. But I *am* a journalist—a *serious* journalist, though the people who leave the *Advocate* out on their driveway to get rained on and be squashed by their cars don't appreciate that—and I know how to get to the bottom of things."

"What time do you want to leave tomorrow morning?" Pamela asked as she leaned toward Bettina for another hug, a more complete one.

First came the police-car escort, with lights on the roof flashing spasmodically and the siren hiccupping in short blasts. Then came the hearse, monumental but sleek, bearing an impressive load of exotic flowers piled atop the chamber that housed the casket. Cars, many cars, followed, their slow progress and illuminated headlights indicating that they were part of the procession en route to Isobel Lister's final resting place.

That resting place was a cemetery up a steep hill from St. Willibrod's Church, atop the cliffs overlooking the Hudson River. It was a very old cemetery, predating St. Willibrod's and all of Arborville's other churches, from an era when Arborville was not yet Arborville, but merely a collection of orchards and farms.

The St. Willibrod's parking lot, which during the funeral had been filled nearly to capacity, emptied gradually as cars maneuvered toward the exit and joined the procession. Pamela's serviceable compact was nearly the last car to exit and commence the slow journey up the hill. But eventually she and Bettina reached the crest of the hill, drove through the cemetery's ancient iron gates, and parked. The parking area was a wide expanse of gravel that gave way to acres of grass, the colorless grass of mid-March, dotted with tombstones. Overhead, the sky hung low with clouds shading from pale to dark as if by a spreading stain.

Paths crisscrossed the grass, and in the distance they could see a cluster of people in dark clothing, presumably gathered at the gravesite. Other people in dark clothing were converging on the cluster and still other people were just picking their way across the gravel lot.

Bettina opened the passenger-side door and lowered a foot gingerly to the ground. "I should have remembered the gravel," she muttered, "and not worn my good pumps. I've been up here for funerals before and come home with my shoes totally destroyed. The gravel just chews them up. Especially suede."

With a sigh, she turned sideways, lowered her other foot to the ground, and stood up. The shoes in question today *were* suede, black suede, with a narrow heel and pointed toe. They complemented a double-breasted black wool coat with a nipped-in waist. A triple strand of large pearls was visible at the neck, matching pearls dangled from Bettina's earlobes, and she carried a black-suede clutch. Pamela wore her cozy down coat, with black pants visible beneath.

Bettina took a few tiptoeing steps across the gravel, then sped up until she reached the edge of the grass, though Pamela, with her longer stride, was there first. Proceeding toward the gravesite with its cluster of people, they passed tombstones of all sorts.

Off to the left was a group so worn by wind and weather that they seemed natural outcroppings rather than anything shaped by human hands, some still upright, others tilted or tipped. Several steps further on, however, were some carved from gleaming marble, ornate and angular, with elaborate script spelling out names, and birth and death dates that suggested the people whose graves they marked had only recently taken up residence in the cemetery.

The crowd around the gravesite was so large that Pamela and Bettina, lingering at the outer fringes, could only get glimpses of the deep rectangle that had been carved into the earth. Presumably it already contained the casket, because a serious man dressed in sober black had just scooped a shovelful of dirt from a pile at the grave's head and tipped it into the grave. Elsewhere in the crowd a solemn voice spoke words whose rhythms identified them as biblical, though the words themselves were hard to make out.

Pamela was straining to identify the speaker, but Bettina's attention had been drawn elsewhere. She stepped away and began to roam among the tombstones and larger grave monuments clustered nearby. Meanwhile, the people standing around the gravesite became less interested in the official proceedings and more interested in their immediate neighbors. Conversations sprang up here and there, hands were shaken, and hugs were exchanged. The crowd broke into smaller units as people began to stroll back across the grass to the parking area.

Bettina was still inspecting tombstones and had roved quite far afield. Pamela, on the other hand, edged closer to the grave and peeked inside. She recognized the casket from the funeral service, constructed from wood as smooth and glowing as would suit a piece of fine furniture. It rested at the bottom of the deep excavation, with the few symbolic scoops of dirt that had accompanied the final prayer scattered over its polished surface.

The last group to leave had just turned away. The serious man in sober black—perhaps a representative from the funeral home—was escorting a well-dressed couple who looked to be in their sixties and an attractive young woman, equally well dressed, across the lawn. Two men in tidy work clothes, cemetery employees Pamela imagined, waited discreetly off to the side.

Bettina approached, shaking her head and smiling an amazed smile. She gestured back toward the cluster of graves she had been examining.

"The cemetery is full of Listers," she announced. "All those"—her gesture became more vigorous—"are Listers. Everywhere."

"They're an old Arborville family," Pamela said. "Remember?"

"*Very* old." Bettina nodded. "Some of those tombstones go back to the early eighteen-hundreds."

"Deep roots in town." Pamela nodded back. "I guess that's why there was such a huge turnout for the funeral. And I expect the reception will be quite something."

She turned toward the parking area and took a few steps. Bettina followed her lead and soon Pamela's serviceable compact came into view, in a parking area now considerably emptier than it had been when they arrived.

"I *did* see the mayor." Bettina was panting a bit, after exerting herself to keep up with Pamela's long strides. "And a couple of people from the town council. And one of Wilfred's friends from the historical society. And of course Meg Norton was here, and I think I recognized that cute man—Nate Riddle was his name?—who played the piano for Isobel's concert."

They had reached the car. Pamela took her keys from her purse.

Caleb's Table had not always been Caleb's Table, and like the cemetery, it dated from an era before Arborville was Arborville. Situated on County Road, it had started life as an inn, offering food, drink, beds, and fresh horses to weary travelers.

The original building was unchanged, sturdily constructed from the pink sandstone readily available in that part of New Jersey. Symmetrical windows with dark-green shutters flanked the doorway, and little dormers looked out up above from beneath a peaked roof. Inside, the white-plastered walls, wide-plank floors, and a fireplace with a hearth that nearly spanned an entire wall had remained unchanged for more than two centuries.

It was tempting to imagine that the inn had offered solace to generations of mourners over the centuries, as the bereaved repaired to its cozy confines for a meal and a drink after laying a loved one to rest in the cemetery up the hill. Now it was offering solace to the Listers and the large crowd of Arborvillians who had turned out to help them mourn.

And now the inn's pink sandstone walls housed an upscale restaurant. It drew diners from far and wide to sample its vaunted farm-to-table menu—never mind that for most of its existence the inn's food offerings would have been farm to table by necessity. The inn had been expanded too, with a large addition on the back, invisible from County Road and thus detracting not at all from the building's eighteenth-century charm.

As soon as Pamela and Bettina stepped through the front door of Caleb's Table, on the heels of an older couple who had preceded them up the walk and followed closely by a cluster of younger people, it was obvious that a party was underway. The room they had entered was unoccupied, but from a doorway at the side of the broad hearth came waves of chatter and even laughter.

The small group of which they were now a part made its way toward that doorway and the larger room beyond. Just within the larger room was a coat-check booth, where a cordial young woman helped them off with their coats and issued claim checks. Large as the room was, it was crowded, crowded with people surging around a long buffet table at its far end and crowded with people standing in line at the bar near the buffet table, though servers were circulating with champagne flutes on trays as well.

But nearer at hand a shorter line of people waited to pay their respects to the well-dressed couple and the attractive young woman Pamela had noticed being escorted across the lawn at the cemetery.

"Her next of kin I suppose," Bettina whispered as she leaned close and touched Pamela on the arm. "We should say something to them."

They had been lingering near the end of the line and, though discreet, Bettina's whisper had been overheard. A small woman in a chic navy-blue suit turned toward Bettina and said, "That's Isobel's brother, Isidore, and his wife, Barb. He's Isidore the Fifth—the Lister men have been named Isidore for ages. The girl is their daughter Iris. The other daughter should be here too, but she's—"

A familiar voice interrupted and Imogene Lister edged between Pamela and Bettina. "She's here," Imogene announced in tones that were anything but discreet. "She wouldn't miss it for the world." She turned toward Bettina and added, "If my mom knows how to do anything, it's put on a good party."

Barb Lister broke off speaking to a white-haired

woman who had seized both her hands. She lifted her head and frowned as she focused on her daughter. "Get over here," she mouthed. Freeing a hand from the white-haired woman's clutch, she fluttered her fingers in an urgent beckoning gesture.

"Gotta go!" Imogene strode to the head of the line and slipped into place between her father and her mother.

Pamela and Bettina looked at each other. "Poor thing!" Bettina whispered.

Pamela nodded agreement. Imogene's careless attitude had struck her as an affectation, an attempt to hide what Pamela knew was a more genuine grief than that expressed by her family. Imogene's eyes had shown signs of recent tears, with pink rims and moist lashes.

Soon it was their turn to greet the Listers and add their condolences to the many that had already been offered. First in the lineup was Isidore Lister, fittingly, since he was Isobel's closest kin. He was a tall man, fit for his age, with a thick head of silvery-gray hair. His air of self-confidence was enhanced by well-shaped lips, deep-set eyes under a strong brow, and a large but shapely nose.

Glancing back and forth between him and Imogene, Pamela was struck by the family resemblance. Isobel had resembled her brother too, and the bold features had suited her outgoing manner. Imogene, on the other hand, seemed mastered by her looks—with puzzled eyes reflecting a sensitive soul unable to summon the boldness demanded by her appearance.

Bettina took the lead, tilting her head to meet Isidore Lister's gaze, reaching for the hand he offered, and murmuring, "I'm so sorry for your loss. Isobel was an amazing and talented woman."

Pamela took the hand as Bettina released it and added, "Yes, such a very sad loss."

They moved on and Bettina, unexpectedly, offered Imogene a hug, which she seemed grateful to accept. At that point the slow parade of mourners paying their respects to the bereaved family came to a halt, not because of the hug, but because a server, a slender young man in a white shirt and black bowtie, had appeared at Barb Lister's shoulder.

"Excuse me, ma'am." He leaned close to her ear and she tipped her head in his direction, a frown disturbing her well-tended skin. "The champagne is going faster than we anticipated. Do you want us to keep serving champagne or just offer wine when the champagne runs out?"

"Add another case of champagne to the bill, of course." The sharp tone in which she uttered the last two words implied that there had been no need to even inquire. She turned toward Bettina and seemed to will her forehead back to smoothness.

"Thank you for coming," she murmured before Bettina even had a chance to speak. "So kind."

Barb Lister was a lovely woman, with fine features in an oval face and dark hair that fell in graceful waves past her shoulders. Given that she must have been in her sixties, the color doubtless owed more to her hairdresser's art than to nature, but the effect was flattering in the extreme. And her elegant suit, tailored from black crepe, suited her delicate frame.

Her other daughter, Iris, stood next to her, nearly her mother's double but thirty or more years younger. She had the same fine features, and dark hair like the natural shade Barb's must have been in her youth, and a petite body clothed, like her mother's was, in black.

Bettina moved on, taking Iris's hand and repeating the words she had offered to Isidore.

"Thank you," Iris responded, with a sad smile that enhanced her beauty. She squeezed Bettina's hand and then reached for Pamela's. "Thank you both so much." She nodded toward the people milling about in the large room. "Please have some refreshments." The smile became a bit mischievous. "I believe there's plenty of champagne."

"And oysters!" From behind them came Imogene's mocking voice as they turned away.

The noise level had risen just since they arrived, probably due to the free-flowing champagne. In fact, were it not for the somber garb, the party room at Caleb's Table could have been hosting a genuine party. Many faces wore smiles as champagne flutes were raised and people stepped away from the buffet table bearing plates laden with exotic hors d'oeuvres.

"I think I'd like to start with food," Bettina commented. "It's a bit early for champagne, but it's definitely lunchtime."

They began to thread their way through the crowd, edging past clusters of chattering guests and veering around people suddenly breaking away from one conversational grouping to join another or visit the buffet or the bar.

As they reached the midpoint of the room, a woman's voice called out, "Bettina! Bettina Fraser!" Bettina had been leading the way, and when she stopped Pamela nearly collided with her. They steadied themselves and began to swivel their heads this way and that looking for the source of the voice.

A woman detached herself from a particularly large conversational cluster, all older women, and Pamela recognized Meg Norton. Meg carried a champagne flute and looked quite a bit more cheerful than she had been the last time Pamela and Bettina spoke to her. As if aware that her apparent mood was unsuitable to the occasion, she blinked few times and tightened her lips, and her face assumed the undemanding expression that Pamela recalled.

"I'm so glad you came!" She advanced and used her free hand to grab one of Bettina's. "Moral support, you know. And these ladies"—she pointed toward the group she had detached herself from—"have been so understanding and kind. They were at the luncheon and they all—*we* all—agree that what happened to Isobel there could have happened anywhere."

"Of course!" Bettina offered a partial hug, being careful not to jostle Meg's champagne. And as if to change the subject, she added, "Quite a nice reception the Listers have arranged. Don't you think?"

"Very! Very!" Meg took a large sip of champagne. She glanced here and there. "In fact, this room would be a wonderful venue for the senior group's Christmas party. It's never too soon to start planning."

"Never too soon." Bettina nodded sagely. "Well begun is half done," as my Wilfred would say. "The longest journey begins with the first step."

"I'll have to remember to pick up the manager's business card before I leave." Meg raised her champagne flute and tilted it for another sip. "I don't think the seniors are going to want to go back to the rec center for quite some time."

As Meg began to elaborate on that theme Bettina nodded sympathetically, though after a bit Pamela noticed her friend casting longing glances at the buffet table. Normally, Bettina deployed her social skills to great advantage, coaxing people to talk whether they wanted to or not and extricating herself when conversations became awkward or stretched on longer than she wished.

But Pamela, who was feeling hunger pangs, decided to take action. Touching Meg on the arm as a graceful way of interrupting, she said, "Have you tried any of the food yet? We just got here and haven't had a chance."

For a moment Meg looked as startled as if Pamela's question had touched on some secret vice. She rallied though, perhaps realizing that she was being gently chided for her monolog. "Oh! Oh!" She herself glanced toward the buffet. "No, I haven't. But you must. You should. People are raving about it."

Bettina took over then, offering Meg another quick hug and saying, "I think we will then, and you take care, dear." She stepped away quickly before Meg could answer, and Pamela hurried along after her.

The crowd at the buffet table had thinned somewhat since they entered the room, but the quantity of food had not diminished. Just at that moment, a server in what seemed the uniform—black pants, white dress shirt, black bowtie—was replenishing platters that held toast triangles garnished with various toppings.

"Oysters!" Bettina announced even before she picked up a plate from the pile at the end of the table nearest them. "I think I see the oysters!"

Indeed, there were oysters, broiled on the half-shell, with bits of spinach and hollandaise sauce. But the oysters were halfway down the table. First came per-

fect open-faced tartlets, holding generous scoops of
caviar decorated with dabs of sour cream, and then
mini-sausages accompanied by a bowl of mustardy
sauce, and tiny lobster rolls, and water chestnuts wrapped
in crispy bacon, and stuffed mushroom caps, and a
sumptuous array of cheeses that ranged in color from
white with blue veins to a ruddy gold.

By the time they reached the oysters, their plates
were nearly full, but there was much more to come,
starting with the platters of toast triangles. Some were
topped with shrimp spread, others with a rustic pâté,
still others with a creamy white cheese and what, on
closer inspection, proved to be shredded brussels sprouts.
A tray of raw vegetables was arranged so artfully that
it resembled a seventeenth-century still life, and the
amazingly tiny deviled eggs were identified by the
server refilling the platter that held them as quail eggs.

"Very cute when they're still in their shells," he
said. "Speckled."

Pamela and Bettina stepped away from the buffet
table with heavy-laden plates and edged toward the
nearest wall, where a pair of French doors gave a view
of a vegetable garden currently in a dormant mid-
March state.

"Umm, umm, umm," Bettina hummed between bites
of a caviar tartlet, before nibbling a mustardy mini-
sausage from the toothpick that speared it.

The assortment of food really was amazing. The
broiled oysters were surprisingly manageable, with the
shell serving as a utensil from which they slid easily
into the mouth. The spinach and hollandaise sauce
added contrast and richness to the mild oyster flesh.
And it was hard to decide whether the shrimp spread,
which blended a hint of cayenne with its mayonnaise

base, or the rustic pâté, which was enhanced with a slice of gherkin, made most impressive use of its toast triangle vehicle—though the less-traditional cheese and brussels sprout garnish was definitely in the running as well.

Pamela and Bettina were happy to concentrate on their food in silence, while enjoying the ebb and flow of the crowd, as people—some strangers, some familiar faces from Hyler's and other Arborville venues—refilled their plates or exchanged empty champagne flutes for full ones.

Pamela was quite willing to relinquish her plate, empty but for two oyster shells, when a server strolled by bearing a large tray on which several other empty plates were already stacked. But Bettina set off in quest of more . . . "Of everything," she said, when Pamela asked.

By the time she returned, with deviled quail eggs prominent in her selection, Pamela had been provided with a glass of champagne and had been joined by Marlene Pepper, who she greeted with her social smile.

Marlene resembled Bettina in shape and age, though her smooth hair was its natural gray-blonde color and her wardrobe ran to the unremarkable, like the navy pantsuit she had chosen for the funeral and reception.

Marlene had engaged Pamela in the usual sorts of pleasantries, asking after Penny and the cats, but acknowledging Pamela's responses with only distracted nods. It was clear that her real conversational target had been Bettina, because the moment Bettina reappeared, Marlene's engagement level rose.

"Quite the event, isn't it?" she commented, surveying the room with a sweeping glance that started at the Listers, still lined up near the door and now accepting thanks from departing guests, and ended at the buffet table. "I guess they had to do it, given that they're *the Listers* and all, and blood is thicker than water—though she must have been a constant source of embarrassment to them with all her carryings-on."

"She *did* lead an adventurous life, from what I've heard," Bettina responded before popping a deviled quail egg into her mouth.

Marlene seized Bettina's arm, causing the plate she was holding to tilt alarmingly. She leaned close to Bettina's ear, where her nose grazed the large pearl dangling from Bettina's earlobe.

"So who do you think did it?" she whispered so audibly that a few people standing nearby turned and stared. "One of her lovers?" Marlene went on. "I heard there were quite a few. I'm not sure I could keep that up at seventy but I guess Isobel had"—she paused and a wrinkled forehead suggested deep thought—"*energy.*"

Pamela discovered that—excluded as she was from the conversation—she had been drinking her champagne at a much faster pace than she realized. The delicate flute was completely empty, and before she knew what was happening, a server had darted forward, claimed the empty flute, and thrust a full one into Pamela's hand.

As Marlene talked on, Bettina responded with polite monosyllables while consuming a caviar tartlet, a toast triangle with shrimp spread, a cracker piled with blue cheese, another deviled quail egg, and a mini lobster roll.

Pamela sipped the fresh glass of champagne which, if nothing else, was refreshingly chilled. Despite the fact that people were beginning to leave, the room seemed no less crowded and Pamela felt her cheeks growing hot. . . and the noise becoming oppressive. The French doors leading out to the vegetable garden were only a few yards away, and Marlene and Bettina were totally focused on each other.

With a few quick steps, Pamela reached the doors, grasped a knob, and pulled. The door opened and she slipped through, closing it gently behind her.

CHAPTER 10

The draft of cold air that greeted her was welcome, and she took a few deep breaths. She was still holding the champagne flute, but she planned to be outside for only a few minutes, just enough to regain her composure. Meanwhile, the garden offered a pleasant diversion.

The kitchen garden contributed mightily to the restaurant's high standing among connoisseurs of fine food, since it provided the chef with ultra-fresh ingredients during the long growing season that had given New Jersey its reputation as the Garden State. Now, however, most of the carefully laid out beds still reflected the ravages of the winter just passed, with nothing visible but tangles of withered vines, stubby remnants of dried cornstalks, and rumpled furrows from which root vegetables had been extracted.

But the section devoted to herbs showed more signs of life. The sage, a sturdy shrub with narrow gray-green leaves, had survived the cold, as had the rose-mary, its spikey branches bristling with needles almost like a Christmas tree.

Pamela strolled a bit farther, wondering what plantings were destined for beds that were now merely expanses of untilled earth and examining the clever chicken wire and stake construction waiting, perhaps, to host climbing beans.

The wing of the building that housed the party room had provided some shelter from the wind, but as she neared the far edge of the garden, a chilly gust reminded her that her coat had been left behind in the coat-check booth. And with no pockets to tuck them into, her fingers were becoming stiff and bloodless.

She retraced her steps past the herbs and the withered vines until she reached the French doors. The sounds of laughter and chatter reached her faintly through the glass. She could see Bettina's back and, facing Bettina and the French doors, Marlene Pepper gesticulating energetically despite the nearly full champagne flute in her hand.

She reached for a doorknob, already imagining the soothing warmth just beyond the doors' glass panes. But the knob wouldn't turn. Her fingers merely slid on the cold metal. She tried the knob on the other door, with the same effect.

Of course! It made sense. To avoid party crashers, the party room could only be entered through the restaurant's front door. She tried waving at Marlene Pepper, but Marlene was so engrossed in whatever she was telling Bettina that her eyes were focused only on her conversation partner.

Pamela sighed, and shivered. Then she made her way through the garden again, heading for the side street that led down to County Road. Walking fast, and feeling a bit self-conscious about the champagne flute she still carried, she turned onto that street and proceeded toward the intersection.

But halfway to her destination, she was distracted by an angry voice, a male voice. "Just where do you think you're going?" it demanded.

"I—I—" She spun around to face the sound, which was coming from the far side of a car parked across the street.

"I was just . . ." she continued, until she realized the question hadn't been directed at her.

Visible over the roof of the car, which was a bright red Fiat, were the head and shoulders of a man well into his seventies. His pointed beard and meticulously shaped moustache gave him a distinguished air, and the dark tie and crisp shirt collar visible between the lapels of his overcoat suggested he'd dressed for a serious occasion, like a funeral. In fact—Pamela blinked and stared—he was one of the people who had been clustered around Isobel's grave at the cemetery.

"What's it to you?" inquired another male voice as the car door opened. The speaker emerged from the car and the older man glared at him.

Pamela could only see the second man from the rear, but something about him seemed familiar as well. She studied him for a moment, and then realized that the familiar thing was his hair. Artistically long, and dark but with graying streaks at the temples, it curved over his collar in a careless swoop. The second man was Nate Riddle, the piano player who had accompanied Isobel for her final concert, and Pamela's main view of him had been from the back.

When the older man didn't answer, the second man

went on. "If you must know," he said, "I'm here to pay my respects to Isobel's family. I guess you didn't see me at the funeral."

"Oh, I saw you all right," the older man said. "Faking like you actually cared about her. You can quit that now. She's dead."

"I *did* care about her."

"Yeah, yeah. Isobel was too smart to take you seriously. No woman in her right mind believes that a man twenty years her junior has anything other than his own interests at heart when he comes on to her with a lover-boy act."

"It wasn't an act." Nate Riddle's voice tightened. "I loved Isobel."

"Well, she didn't love you, bud." The older man raised a leather-gloved hand with his index finger extended. "I was number one in that department."

"I doubt it"—Nate Riddle laughed—"for a lot of reasons."

"Meaning?"

Nate Riddle laughed again.

The older man ignored the laughter and went on. "Isobel played the game as well as you did, bud, but I was number one. And by the way—speaking of playing—if you were so devoted to Isobel, who was that woman hanging around in the cemetery parking lot waiting for you to finish pretending to be sad?"

Without answering, Nate started to cross the street. The older man's gaze followed him, and Pamela, who had slowed to a snail-like crawl while eavesdropping on the conversation, quickly sped up.

As she reached the corner, she could hear footsteps

behind her, and as she made the turn onto County Road, Nate, with his longer strides, caught up with her.

"Bringing your own glass?" he inquired pleasantly as he caught sight of the champagne flute in her hand.

"No." She laughed. "I was looking at the garden and I got locked out. Don't go through the French doors unless you're prepared to make a big detour."

"Thanks for the tip." He added a genial smile, seemingly recovered from his recent encounter. They reached the restaurant's front door and he opened it and ushered Pamela through, bowing.

Bettina scarcely seemed to realize that Pamela had been gone. With a gesture that mimed holding something large and round, Marlene Pepper was emphasizing a point she'd just made, and Bettina turned to Pamela and asked, "Can you imagine such a thing?" as if Pamela had been there the whole time.

"Uh . . . no! No, I can't," Pamela replied, wondering what she was being tasked with imagining. But the answer became clear as Marlene continued.

"So anyway," she said, "we'll be offering the unclaimed community garden plots on a first come, first served basis starting next week. And of course we'll do the pumpkin competition again in the fall, though I doubt if anyone will beat last year's champion."

"I don't see how they could." Bettina added a companionable nod, though she sighed with relief when Marlene was summoned away a few minutes later.

"My goodness, that woman can talk," she commented as Marlene was led off by one of her other friends. She turned to Pamela and a concerned furrow appeared between her carefully shaped brows. "You're shivering!" she exclaimed, grabbing one of Pamela's hands. "And your hands are frozen. What on earth is happening to you?"

Pamela managed a laugh despite her chilled state. "I've been outside," she said.

"What? Outside? Why?"

"Let's get our coats." Pamela took a step toward the entrance. "I have lots to tell you. And I want my coat."

On the way to the coat-check booth, they paid their respects once again to the Listers, and soon they were heading toward the small lot at the side of the restaurant where Pamela's serviceable compact waited. As they walked, Pamela described to Bettina the circumstances that had led to her excursion out of doors and—more importantly—the interesting confrontation she had witnessed.

"A love triangle?" Bettina's breathy tone and wide eyes implied wonderment. "Who would have thought? But she was a captivating woman, and who's to say that a fifty-year-old couldn't be just as captivated as a seventy-year-old—though he could have loved her but not *loved* her. I love Woofus, but not the same way I love Wilfred."

"Do you think one of them could have killed her?" They had reached the car and Pamela unlocked the passenger-side door for Bettina. Bettina settled herself and waited until Pamela had taken her own seat behind the steering wheel to answer.

"The older one maybe? She invites him to the luncheon and the concert—"

Pamela interrupted. "He looked familiar—and there weren't that many men there, so the ones that *were* there kind of stood out."

"Then," Bettina went on, "he thinks he detects a

deeper connection between Isobel and the piano player than just singer and accompanist. She was definitely flirting with him—and he with her."

"So the older man pays a visit to the green room afterward—"

"—And we know Isobel had a lot of spirit." Bettina took up the thought. She swiveled toward Pamela and, though hampered by the fact that she was sitting in the seat of a car with her seatbelt fastened, reenacted Isobel's reaction as she imagined it, arching her back and placing her hands on her hips.

"How dare you?" she exclaimed, her voice reverberating in the enclosed vehicle. "You don't own me and I'll do whatever I like!"

"And maybe he says he thought they were committed to each other and he doesn't like to see her being so . . . welcoming . . . to other men's admiration," Pamela suggested.

"I've known a lot of men!" Bettina gave a careless toss of her head, setting the scarlet tendrils of her hair in motion. "You're just one of them. So take it or leave it!"

"Oh, Bettina!" Pamela raised her fingers to her mouth. "That's awful. Do you think she would really have said a thing like that?"

Bettina shrugged and grinned a mischievous grin. "Anyway, whatever she said, things escalated from there and . . ."

Pamela inserted her key into the ignition and a few moments later they were underway, both mulling over the possibility that a lover's jealousy had been the cause of Isobel's death. On the right, the nature preserve sped by, and the intersection with Arborville's main east-west street loomed ahead. Orchard Street was several blocks beyond that, but as they neared the intersection, Bettina clutched Pamela's arm and commanded, "Turn here."

"What? Why?" The car lurched and Pamela steadied the steering wheel. Bettina's grip on her arm and urgent command had startled her.

"Just turn," Bettina repeated, "and I'll explain."

The light had begun to change and Pamela slowed to a stop.

"The library," Bettina said. "The coloring book club meets in the library on Wednesday afternoons."

"And?" The syllable came out sounding more skeptical than Pamela intended, but Bettina was not put off.

"I did an article on the club for the *Advocate* last month," she explained. "Most of the women are in the seniors' group too. If the older man was sitting in his seat from the time the concert ended till Meg came out to announce that Isobel was dead, he couldn't possibly be the killer. At least a few of the coloring book women are bound to have noticed, because like you said, there weren't very many men at the luncheon."

When the light turned green, Pamela made the turn.

The coloring book club used a small meeting room tucked into a back corner on the library's main floor. Bettina led the way past the circulation counter and down a long aisle created by tall shelves filled with books. The upper half of the meeting room's front and one side wall were glass, making it soundproof but not claustrophobic. Through the glass they could see ten women, most of them older, gathered around a long table. Each had an open coloring book in front of her and a collection of crayons or markers or colored pencils nearby.

"It's really kind of like needlework," Bettina commented as they drew closer, "filling in little spaces with pretty colors. Probably very relaxing. And they chat while they're working, like Knit and Nibble."

"I don't see a Roland though," Pamela said with a laugh.

By the time they reached the meeting room, a few women had noticed their approach, and as Bettina turned the knob and pushed the door open, she was greeted by a chorus of hellos.

"That was such a nice article," a woman at the far end of the table exclaimed. She was dressed for the occasion in a sweatshirt with the words "Don't bother me. I'm coloring" lettered across the front. She added, "It brought us two new members, Sue and Kirsten."

The women sitting on either side of her smiled and tipped their heads.

Bettina introduced the first woman as Dorothy Evers and continued talking with the group, settling into a chair that she pulled up to the table from a few spares against the wall. Pamela helped herself to a chair as well. Many of the women continued coloring, looking up every once in a while to add something to the conversation. Others seemed happy to take a break from their work.

From what Pamela could see, the artistic tastes of the club members varied widely. Some of the coloring books offered abstract designs that brought to mind the view through a kaleidoscope. Others were representational—a nature scene, or a still life with fruit and flowers, or dolls, or animals. Still others were fantastical, depicting dragons or otherworldly visions. A pleasant-looking white-haired woman in a pink sweater was working intently on an undersea scene, a diver rescuing a mermaid from the clutches of a giant squid.

As she watched, she became quite absorbed in the woman's progress. The diver was a silvery gray and the mermaid had blonde hair and a flesh-colored body, with tail color pending. At the moment, the woman was creating a variegated effect for the seaweed by juxtaposing several shades of green in parallel strokes.

Bettina's voice, however, cut into her reverie. "Eye candy! Yes, that probably is who I mean. Pamela!"

Pamela turned, startled at Bettina's seeming urgency.

"Would you describe the man at Isobel's concert as eye candy?"

"I—I suppose so." Pamela shrugged. "He was quite distinguished looking."

A woman—not the undersea woman—looked up. "Nice beard?" she said, stroking her chin. "Tall, very fit."

"He's mine!" exclaimed a woman with thick gray hair tamed into a braid.

"Really?" several voices asked in chorus.

"No. I wish."

As the women talked, it became clear that those who had been at the luncheon had been very aware of the handsome older gentleman in their midst.

"The seniors' group could use some new blood," one commented.

"Male blood, you mean," added another. "I hope he becomes a regular."

"I thought maybe he was a friend of Isobel's." Bettina made the comment in an offhand way. "But when she ducked away after she finished singing and so much time passed, he didn't seem very curious. Or did he?"

"I was sitting right next to him," said the woman with the braid. "In fact, we were talking about Italy. He goes there often and he speaks Italian. So romantic. And then Meg came out and said Isobel was dead, and of course nobody said much of anything after that."

"How did he seem?" Bettina asked. "Like I said, I thought maybe he knew her well."

"Shocked," the woman with the braid replied. "But then, everybody was shocked."

"Well," Bettina said as they walked across the library parking lot toward Pamela's car, "I guess that answers that question."

They didn't speak again until Pamela pulled up to the curb in front of the Frasers' house. But she'd been thinking, and as Bettina started to climb out of the car, she suddenly said, "We should have asked those women whether they noticed if the piano player left the room after the concert ended."

Bettina sank back into her seat. "Do you think the piano player could have killed her?" she asked, turning toward Pamela.

Pamela shifted position to face her. "As you said, Isobel was a captivating woman. Maybe he didn't just love her, but *loved* her, and they were doing more than just practicing her repertoire when they got together. And he didn't have a clue that he had a rival for her affections until the older man showed up at the concert."

Bettina nodded and her bright lips tightened into a grim line. "He follows her back to the green room to ask what's up with this other guy. And she gets angry . . ."

"And things escalate from there."

"Clayborn must have talked to him though, and he hasn't arrested him."

"He wouldn't seem an obvious suspect," Pamela pointed out, "unless Clayborn suspected a love triangle."

Bettina reached for her handbag and pulled out her phone. "We can find out right now whether Nate Riddle has an alibi." She continued speaking as she searched her phone's contacts list for an entry. "I'll call Dorothy. She was the person I first approached when I did the article for the *Advocate*."

Pamela was silent while Bettina spoke into her phone. The voice at the other end was audible, though too faint for Pamela to make out what it was saying, so she let her attention wander.

Despite the chilly day, a few people were out on Orchard Street. A woman strolled by, leading a dog as large as Woofus, but elegant and fine-boned, with long silky fur. Pamela watched them pass, then her glance strayed to the yard of Bettina's neighbor. In summer months the blooms of a climbing rose decorated the side of her neat brick house, but at the moment only a tangle of lifeless-seeming canes crisscrossed that wall.

After a few minutes, Bettina ended the call and lowered the phone to her lap. "He was there the whole time," she said. "Sitting on the piano bench."

"One less suspect," Pamela commented.

"We still haven't figured out whether Siobhan O'Doul has an alibi," Bettina remarked, as if the thought had just occurred to her.

"I'm working on it," Pamela said.

Bettina reached for the door handle, but before she opened the door, she turned to Pamela once again. "What are you going to do now?" she inquired.

Pamela shrugged. "Work for the magazine, I suppose. I've got a book to review."

"I'd invite you to dinner," Bettina said, "but Wilfred's going to be out all afternoon—in fact I have to remember to walk Woofus—and I'm cooking. It's just meatloaf and it's not as good as yours."

"I'm sure it is"—Pamela squeezed her friend's hand—"but I bought a pot roast on Saturday and I should do something with it."

"Plan on coming over Sunday night though." Bettina pressed down on the door handle. "Wilfred's been studying a new cookbook."

After parking in her own driveway, Pamela climbed the steps to her porch. There was mail in her mailbox, as she had expected, but there was also a glossy advertising flyer hanging from her doorknob. She collected mail and flyer, unlocked her door, and stepped inside. The cats were nowhere in evidence, not even Catrina— the sunny spot on the entry carpet that she favored for her morning naps being long gone at this time of day.

The flyer showed a verdant suburban yard and proclaimed, "Spring is coming. Call us now for your lawn care needs." Spring was coming—that was true. In fact, technically speaking, spring had already arrived, and it had already been greeted by Liadan Percy with her Ostara altar. The climbing rose across the street might still appear lifeless, but as she and Bettina left the library, Pamela had noticed crocus and snowdrops in a sunny spot near the library steps.

She took off her coat and sorted through the mail, consigning most of it to the recycling basket, along with the flyer. The nudge about spring had reminded her of something though. The lawn would look after itself, but when the screens had been taken down and put away the previous fall, she had noticed that they looked quite shabby, *very* shabby in fact. The metal screening was rusted in spots and some panels even had jagged tears.

She had made a note in her calendar to have them repaired, but she hadn't turned to that calendar page yet. Why not do something about them now though, while she was thinking of it? But who to call?

She wandered out to the kitchen and took the pot roast out of the refrigerator. As she closed the refrigerator, her gaze landed on a note fastened to its door with a magnet in the shape of a mitten.

"Pete Paterson," it read, and below the name was a phone number. Pete Paterson was the handyman who repaired screens—at least that's what the mistaken caller had wanted him for.

Now maybe she wanted him. She stepped over to the phone and picked up the handset.

CHAPTER 11

Pete Paterson followed Pamela down her driveway to her garage. She had opened the garage door, and checked that nothing was blocking access to the screens, as soon as she hung up the phone.

"Ah, yes," he said as they stepped into the dim interior, which smelled of earth and dampness. They walked toward the back of the garage, where the stack of screens was leaning against the wall. Each was nearly as tall as a person, and there were eight of them. "Old screens, and I guess you have old storm windows too. When was your house built, anyway?"

Pamela told him and he smiled. "Most people with these old houses put in modern windows long ago. Trading storm windows for screens every spring, and screens for storm windows every fall, is a hassle."

"It is," Pamela agreed, though Wilfred had always volunteered to do the chore after Michael Paterson died.

"I like old things too though. The frames of these are real wood, not that fake stuff they make the replacement windows out of." Pete stepped forward and gripped the top screen, one hand on each side. "Let's take a look at this guy out in the light," he said.

Pamela stood aside and let him pass. Pete Paterson was a trim man, not too tall, with a face that was attractive in an unremarkable way, like a model in a catalog for outdoor wear. His jeans looked new and his woolly buffalo-check jacket had been left unbuttoned, revealing a well-pressed denim shirt. His movements were quick and efficient, and there was something about him that reminded her of Roland—a kind of suppressed intensity.

He leaned the screen up against the outside of the garage and studied it, turning it over to examine the back as well. This particular screen was one of the worst. The metal screening was nearly black with rust and accumulated dirt. In a few spots it had pulled loose from the wooden frame, and the frayed edges resembled metallic fringes.

After a few minutes, he said, "It looked like there were about eight of them back there. Do you want to redo them all?"

Pamela nodded. "I might as well, though they're not all as bad as this."

"It's the same amount of work though. Take the old screening out and put new screening in. I'd have to charge . . ." He quoted a price.

"Fine," Pamela said. "Fine."

She accompanied him down the driveway and watched him lay the screen down in the back of his pickup truck. Like the jeans, the pickup truck looked new—sleek and a gleaming shade of metallic silver. Once that screen was stowed, he leaned into the truck's cab to fetch a small order pad and asked her for her phone number. Then he made a few notations on the top sheet, tore off the yellow copy beneath, and handed it to her.

"Pete Paterson," the heading read, "Jack of All Trades. No job too big or too small."

"I'll get the rest," he said. "Should take a couple days to fix them. I'll call you."

Back inside, Pamela got her pot roast started. She coated the roast with flour seasoned with salt and pepper, melted vegetable shortening in her Dutch oven, added the roast, and browned it. The final touch before slipping it into the oven was to mix catsup with a cup of water and pour the mixture around the roast. Some recipes called for tomato juice, but her mother had always done it that way and so she did too.

It would take a few hours for the roast to reach the tender falling-apart state that devotees of pot roast seek. In the meantime, *Shaker Communities and the Feminist Sensibility: The Paradox of Women's Work* awaited.

Noticing that Pamela had occupied her spot on the sofa unexpectedly early, Catrina joined her there, stretched against her thigh. The cat's reverberating purrs seemed quite the proper accompaniment to the author's descriptions of the domestic paradise the Shakers had created in their communities.

The tantalizing aroma of pot roast nearing a state of tender perfection had begun to seep from the kitchen into the rest of the house. In response to that, perhaps, or some internal clock, Ginger and Precious strolled into the living room. They came from opposite directions but each planted herself on the carpet at Pamela's feet and fixed her with a penetrating stare.

Pamela glanced at the clock on the bookcase nearby and realized that it was past six p.m. She'd been so caught up in the Shakers' philosophy of work, with men's and women's work defined by gender roles yet both considered of equal value, that she'd scarcely been aware of time passing. She marked her place and set the book aside. Sensing the motion, Catrina stirred too.

The small parade made its way to the kitchen, with Pamela in the lead. She refreshed the water in the cats' communal water bowl, took two clean cat food bowls from the cupboard, and bent down to study the labels on the cans in the cupboard where the cat food was stored. She had always found cat food labels misleading, even disturbing if one thought about them too hard. With images of fish or fowl, they often indicated what was contained within to be eaten. But by that logic, what was to be made of the ones that depicted cats?

Setting that thought aside, she murmured, "Liver tonight?" Without waiting for an answer, she seized the can, whose label did not show a liver but rather a shallow dish piled with a substance that resembled a rather tasty pâté. Once Catrina and Ginger had been served, she bent down once again and selected a smaller can whose label depicted a dancing shrimp.

She had just picked up the can opener, however, when the doorbell's chime distracted her from her task.

Can opener in hand, she stepped through the kitchen doorway and into the entry. Sunset was nearing, but the sky still had a twilight glow. Through the lace that curtained the oval window in the front door, she could see the silhouette of a tall figure dressed in dark clothes. She leaned closer to the stiff lace, angling for a better look, and realized that the visitor was her neighbor Richard Larkin.

At that moment, an irritated yowl erupted from somewhere very near and her body tensed. She spun around and saw Precious staring at her, opalescent eyes ablaze with blue fire.

"Yes, yes," she assured the cat. "You will have your dinner."

She reached for the doorknob and pulled the door open.

"I can't talk," she told Richard Larkin. "I have to feed a cat." But she left the door ajar when she returned to the kitchen.

He appeared in the kitchen doorway as she was setting a bowl containing something chopped and pinkish in front of Precious. The cats preferred to eat in a corner of the kitchen where one set of cupboards made a right angle with another, perhaps feeling protected, at least on two sides.

"I don't mean to intrude." He was dipping his head, as if a lifetime of being taller than the average person had made him wary of doorframes.

Pamela was happy her hands were empty now. She could clasp them behind her back to hide the slight tremor that had afflicted them. Richard Larkin himself seemed afflicted, though unless he was smiling, his long, bony face and strong nose had always made him appear serious, even stern.

She hadn't seen him for ages, except to wave in a neighborly way if she happened to see him in his yard. And she'd thought that the curious pull he'd exerted over her almost from the beginning had loosened—especially when Jocelyn Bidwell came into his life, which seemed a sign that any reciprocal attraction had waned. But her chest felt tight and she suspected her cheeks—though she was olive skinned and tended not to blush—had nevertheless grown rosy.

"I was wondering," he said, though the question was directed at the black-and-white tiles that covered the kitchen floor, "whether you might have . . . might know about . . ." His gaze drifted toward where the cats were finishing up their dinner and his stern features softened, then he raised his head and focused on Pamela. ". . . a cat."

Pamela laughed, gratefully, because the laugh relaxed her.

"A cat?" she asked, glancing toward the cats. "I have cats."

"I mean, a *new* cat."

Richard Larkin had been one of the people who claimed a kitten from the litter that Catrina unexpectedly presented Pamela with not long after being adopted as a woebegone stray. But Jocelyn Bidwell had considered the cat, one of three black males that Catrina produced, unlucky, and Richard had found the cat a new home.

"I'll . . . I . . . of course." *Of course, what?* she asked herself. *Of course you want a new cat?*

He was looking at her intensely, so intensely that now it was her turn to develop a profound curiosity about the floor tiles.

"I didn't mean to be presumptuous," came his voice.

"I don't know why I assumed you'd . . . know about how to find a cat . . ."

"Well," Pamela said, raising her eyes to meet his, "people often adopt cats from the shelter in Haversack, grown cats sometimes, whose owners can't keep them. That's one source." He was still looking at her, but not answering, so she went on. "I could ask around though. It's more fun to start fresh with a kitten."

"I would like that." He smiled again. "A kitten."

"Not black though, I suppose."

"It doesn't matter," Richard Larkin said. "It doesn't matter at all."

He backed up, dipping his head again.

Pamela saw him to the door. Before he stepped across the threshold he remarked, almost wistfully, that whatever was in the oven smelled delicious.

Leftover pot roast would make sandwiches, but sandwiches would need bread. And Pamela had toasted the last slice of whole-grain bread for breakfast. So the next morning, as soon as she had rinsed the cup and saucer and plate she had used and folded up the *Register*, she fetched the notepad with the tulip-bordered pages and sat back down at the kitchen table to make a grocery list.

Ten minutes later she was on her way up Orchard Street, squinting against the brisk wind, and carrying a few of the canvas tote bags that she used for shopping. It was a relief to turn onto Arborville Avenue and get out of the wind's direct path, and the five blocks to the south edge of Arborville's shopping district passed quickly.

As she approached the Co-Op, she could see a small crowd gathered near the automatic door, all facing the building's façade. This sight was not unusual, however. Long before the internet enabled Arborvillians to communicate with one another via the town's listserv, AccessArborville, there had been the Co-Op's bulletin board. And the bulletin board had remained, allowing people to sell (or give away) unwanted furniture, offer or solicit babysitting or housecleaning services, advertise yard sales, or alert the residents of the town to anything they were willing to commit to paper and tack to its long-suffering surface.

People often tacked up notices about free kittens. When Pamela herself had had kittens to give away, she had been alarmed at the surfeit of kittens on offer, almost despairing of finding homes for her own brood. Before collecting a cart and stepping up to the automatic door, she edged as close to the bulletin board as the small crowd would permit.

The high school was advertising a talent show, one of the churches was collecting food to prepare Easter food baskets for the less fortunate, and a bicycle in good condition was available for $35 on Catalpa Street. Many, many other notices competed for attention, so many that the effect resembled a haphazard collage. A few people backed away, apparently having seen their fill, and Pamela moved closer. But search as she might, she could not find any notices offering kittens, either free or for sale.

She circled around to where a rank of shopping carts stretched along the building's wall, claimed one, and glided through the automatic door toward the produce section. There, she collected a long cucumber sealed in a clear plastic sheath and studied the tomato selection. The large ones were promising, with their gleaming scarlet skins, and some even bore a hint of the hauntingly acidic tomato fragrance. But she knew from experience that they could deceive.

Where would they have come from in March? And how could *real* tomatoes, real *garden* tomatoes have withstood such a journey? It was better, she decided, to buy cherry tomatoes, which promised nothing that they couldn't deliver. She reached for a carton.

As she did so, however, she glanced up. The tomato offerings were displayed at the end of a long row of bins containing vegetables related to salad-making. That row of bins backed up against a parallel row of bins accessible to shoppers browsing in the next aisle over. Directly opposite her, a woman was scrutinizing a baking potato.

The woman was short and plump, with curly hair dyed black. She looked familiar, but not familiar like someone who'd been shopping at the Co-Op as long as Pamela had, or eating lunch at Hyler's as frequently as Pamela did. The woman put the potato down and picked up another. She was older, quite a bit older than Pamela and most of her friends, except Nell. She was about as old as . . . Isobel Lister. With a sharp intake of breath, Pamela dropped the carton of tomatoes and it landed back in its bin.

The woman examining the potatoes so carefully had been at the St. Patrick's Day concert, but she hadn't stayed for the whole program. She had slipped out after Isobel, looking right at her, had commented that she could tell stories proving that the Arborville girls weren't as goody-goody as some people thought.

It appeared that Pamela wasn't the only person who had recognized the woman.

"Why, Cheryl! Cheryl Radcliff!" A woman, also older, wearing a woolly beret at a jaunty angle, edged over from a bin containing the yams. "That's you, isn't it?—though I suppose it's not Cheryl *Radcliff* anymore, with the way the boys were already chasing you in high school."

The first woman made no response, and the woman in the beret went on talking. "Back in town? Are you living here now? I thought I recognized you at the luncheon the other day, but I wasn't sure."

There was still no response, though the first woman seemed to have lost interest in the potatoes.

The beret woman's eyes suddenly grew large and she raised a hand to her mouth to suppress an explosive gasp. "Oh, I'm so sorry!" she exclaimed. "Here I am chattering on and forgetting you and Isobel were such great friends." She shook her head. "A shame, just a terrible shame what happened!"

"I really do not know what you're talking about." The first woman's tone was cold, and a freeze had descended on her features.

"I hope you'll still want to be part of our seniors' group though." The beret woman was undeterred, though the first woman was now glaring at her. "Our events are usually very . . . I mean, what happened at the luncheon wasn't . . . though I know it must have made a bad impression . . ." Her voice trailed off.

"I was not at the luncheon," the first woman said. "And now, if you'll excuse me, I have grocery shopping to do." Abandoning the potatoes without making a selection, she propelled her cart to the end of the aisle and vanished around the corner.

The beret woman didn't watch her go. Rather, seemingly aware that Pamela had witnessed the whole exchange, she offered a shrug and a half-smile and returned to examining yams.

Pamela picked up the carton of tomatoes, added it to her cart, and proceeded on toward the leafy greens, where she slipped a bunch of kale into a plastic bag and settled it next to the tomatoes. After a stop at the fish counter for tilapia and a stop at the meat counter for fresh Italian sausage, she proceeded to the cheese counter. Usually she bought the Vermont cheddar, but there was still a bit of that left at home. The variety of cheese on offer at Caleb's Table the previous day had made her realize how limited her cheese horizons had become.

So after contemplating ovals and rounds and wedges, some coated with red wax, some riddled with holes, some so veined with blue that they resembled marble, some powdery white but oozing golden from cut edges, she came away with half a pound of stilton and a small log of goat cheese.

The last item on her list was bread. In that realm too, Pamela realized that she had long ago slipped into a comfortable rut. With all the possibilities lined up atop the glass display case, she inevitably chose a loaf of whole-grain bread, sliced and bagged. What would be an interesting change?

Before she could decide—and anyway, several patrons were in line ahead of her—she was distracted by a tap on her shoulder. She glanced back to see the woman wearing the jaunty beret. Without preamble, the woman began to speak.

"I know who she is. She's Cheryl Radcliff—or at least Cheryl Radcliff *as was*, like they say. She's probably married now. I don't know why she wouldn't admit who she was. Why would she move back to Arborville if she wanted to be incognito?"

The beret woman was considerably shorter than Pamela and was gazing up at her in a curiously imploring way. Perhaps she was embarrassed, Pamela decided, given that Pamela had been a witness to the encounter, and in fact had been staring unashamedly. It would be embarrassing to have an observer think one made a habit of accosting strange people and claiming to know them. And Cheryl Radcliff *as was*—if that was really she—had reacted so curtly. The woman in the beret must have felt like she was being scolded.

Pamela smiled, willing herself to inject a bit of warmth into her social smile. "I don't know if she's the Cheryl Radcliff you knew in high school—"

The woman interrupted. "She is. No doubt about it, though like I said, she probably has a different last name now."

"But that woman was definitely at the luncheon," Pamela went on. "I saw her there too. And her name *is* Cheryl, but it's Cheryl Hagan now."

"Oh!" The woman seemed relieved that this attempt at conversation was going more successfully than her previous one. "But you're not a senior . . ."

"Not yet!" Pamela laughed and the woman relaxed even more. "I was there with Bettina Fraser. She was covering it for the *Advocate*."

"The *Advocate*! I love the *Advocate* and I love Bettina's writing."

The small cluster of people between Pamela and the bakery counter had dissipated, as loaves, sliced and unsliced, were bagged, handed over, and lowered into carts. The counter attendant was just filling a bag with brioche buns for a man who was hesitating between wanting six or eight. He settled on eight, the bag was passed across the counter, and the counter attendant turned his attention to Pamela.

"Help you?" he inquired pleasantly.

"Uh . . ." Pamela realized her chance to adequately ponder the many alternatives to a whole-grain loaf, sliced and bagged, had passed, and she spoke up and made her usual request.

"Nice talking to you," the beret woman murmured as Pamela turned to go and she herself stepped up to the counter.

Her purchases paid for and stowed in her canvas totes, Pamela pushed her cart through the automatic door and out into the chilly sunshine.

"I'll take that if you're through with it." The speaker, who had just climbed out of a BMW parked at the curb, was Barb Lister. Her outfit was far cry from her somber funeral garb—a bright blue down jacket with a flash of chartreuse at the neck—but the dark hair flowing to her shoulders and the lovely features enhanced with carefully applied cosmetics were unmistakable.

"Sure." Pamela steered the cart across the sidewalk and rotated it so it was easy to grab hold of.

Barb Lister responded with a gracious thank you but seemed not to recognize Pamela. That was understandable, Pamela thought, given the many, many people the woman must have spoken with at the funeral and reception, but Pamela mustered her social smile.

"I'm Pamela Paterson," she said. "I'm so sorry

about the death of your sister-in-law. Imogene has been coming to our knitting group . . . I hope she, and you, and the rest of your family are doing okay."

"Thank you, thank you. You're very kind." Barb offered her own social smile. "Imogene loves the group," she added before wheeling the cart toward the automatic door.

CHAPTER 12

Pamela did not go directly home. Halfway down Orchard Street she veered right instead of left and rang Bettina's doorbell. Bettina answered still dressed in her robe and slippers, as Woofus lurked in the background glancing apprehensively toward the open door.

"Are you okay?" Bettina's glance was apprehensive too. "Has something happened?"

Pamela wondered if her expression portended bad news—it was true she had been thinking hard about the curious incident she had witnessed in the Co-Op produce department. Perhaps she was frowning. She made a conscious effort to relax her brow and smiled.

"I'm fine," she said. "I've just been to the Co-Op."

"Obviously." Bettina nodded toward the canvas totes. "And your bags look heavy. Come on in—there's still coffee. Some Co-Op doughnuts too."

"Just coffee would be great." Pamela followed her to the kitchen and set the bags on one of the chairs surrounding the scrubbed pine table. She settled herself into another.

"You have a fan," she said as Bettina set a steaming mug of coffee in front of her. "Somebody who loves the *Advocate* and especially loves your writing."

"Well, thank you!" Bettina reclaimed her spot, marked by a half-finished mug of coffee and a few sections of the *Register*. "Nothing new about the case," she remarked as she folded them and pushed them aside. She turned her attention back to Pamela. "And you detoured over here to tell me that? So sweet—especially after the mean thing that woman at the luncheon said."

"That's not the only thing I wanted to tell you though." Pamela took a sip of coffee.

"Oh?"

They were interrupted by the arrival of Woofus, who headed directly for the chair that held the canvas totes and began sniffing at the one that contained the fish and sausage. Pamela sprang up and moved the bags to the high counter.

"Tilapia and Italian sausage," she explained as she returned to her chair. "Anyway . . ." She took another sip of coffee and then described the encounter between the woman who slipped out of the luncheon after Isobel seemed to speak directly to her and the woman in the beret who claimed to recognize her as a long-ago friend of Isobel's.

"The woman in the beret identified her as 'Cheryl Radcliff,'" Pamela concluded, "and then accosted me at the bakery counter to insist that the other woman really was Cheryl Radcliff (or at least that had been her birth name), though she denied it vigorously."

"Hmm." Bettina's lips tightened into a meditative knot.

"She obviously doesn't want the connection with Isobel to come out. From what the woman in the beret said, it sounded like all three of them grew up in Arborville. Cheryl has been away for a long while and just came back, like Meg told us. But she didn't realize Isobel had come back too."

"That makes sense. And at the concert, Isobel recognizes her and then says she could tell stories about the Arborville girls not being as goody-goody as everyone thought. So she—Cheryl—thinks, 'Oh no. Those things I got up to in high school aren't going to be a secret anymore . . .'"

"And so she kills Isobel?"

Bettina was on her feet. "I think we have a new suspect," she exclaimed. "And Bettina Fraser, of the *Arborville Advocate*, is going to get to the bottom of Isobel Lister's murder before Lucas Clayborn does. And she's going to have another doughnut." She bent toward Pamela. "You're sure you don't want one?"

"No," Pamela smiled. "I'm not sure."

Soon a sage-green pottery plate containing many doughnuts appeared on the scrubbed pine table, along with napkins and refills of coffee, and the next few minutes were devoted to eating and sipping.

The doughnuts were glistening and plump, with a generous glaze of chocolate icing. The icing was almost too sweet, but the doughnuts themselves were yeasty, with a texture more like good French bread than cake, and so the overall effect was just right.

"So," Bettina said after a bit, pausing to lick a bit of chocolate from her fingers, "the next step is to figure out whether Cheryl and Isobel really knew each other here in Arborville when they were young. And I think the way to do that will be to look at the Arborville High School yearbooks in the library. I happen to know the library has them all, going way back, because I did an article on that very topic for the *Advocate*."

"Sounds good." Pamela had been about to take a sip of coffee but she lowered her coffee mug to respond. "When shall we do it?"

"I'm leaving in a while to babysit the Arborville grandchildren," Bettina said, "but how about tomorrow at about eleven? I know you'll want to walk but I don't—so I'll pick you up. Then we'll come back here for lunch. Wilfred is making a batch of his five-alarm chili."

Not wanting to overstay her welcome, Pamela finished up the last few bites of her doughnut and tipped her mug to drain the last few swallows of coffee.

"I should get going," she murmured, starting to rise. "I've got groceries to put away."

"Wait! Wait!" Bettina said suddenly and she gestured for Pamela to sit back down.

"What?" Pamela studied Bettina's face for a hint of what was to come.

"There's something I think you should know." The tone was serious. Bettina's eyes focused on Pamela's as if she, in turn, was searching for a clue to the workings of Pamela's mind. "But I'm not sure how to tell you . . . because it's about, you know . . ." She tipped her head toward the doorway leading to the dining room.

"What?" Pamela felt her heart lurch. "Something in the dining room? What's going on?"

"No, not the dining room. You know . . ." Bettina continued to tip her head toward the doorway and added a pointed finger, angling it so that, if walls hadn't been in the way, it would have been pointed at the street.

"Your neighbor, whose name I'm not supposed to mention. Wilfred was walking Woofus this morning, first thing, and"—she tipped her head again—"your neighbor was bringing in his copy of the *Register* and they chatted for a minute like they often do, and—"

Pamela interrupted. "Get on with it, please. Wilfred talked to Richard Larkin—there, you don't have to say it—and . . ."

"He and Jocelyn . . ."

Pamela raised both hands, fingers extended and palms facing outward, and Bettina stopped abruptly.

"They're getting married," Pamela said. "It's okay. It's their own business. I'm actually very happy for them. She's a lovely person." She took a deep breath.

"They're not." Bettina shook her head. A few scarlet tendrils, still disordered from sleep, flopped over her brows. "They're not getting married. They're not even together anymore."

"They're not?"

"They're not. Richard told Wilfred that Jocelyn went back to an old boyfriend."

Pamela crossed the street to her own house, barely aware of her surroundings. As she climbed the steps to the front porch she noticed that the mail had arrived, but later, standing in the kitchen, she realized she had forgotten to bring it in. She retraced her steps to fetch it, sorted most of it into the recycling basket, and climbed the stairs to her office, absentmindedly carrying her water bill.

Someone with kittens in need of homes might have posted on AccessArborville, she said to herself, and launched a search for that website. But no sooner had the list of new messages come up than she remembered that her groceries were still sitting on the floor in the entry.

Back downstairs, she put the groceries away. Then she sat at the kitchen table, buried her face in her hands, and commanded herself to breathe slowly and focus her mind, which had begun skittering this way and that the moment Bettina's startling announcement sank in. Richard Larkin was once more unattached. Was she glad? Well, yes, she had to admit she was glad. And was that why he wanted a cat—and why it was okay if the cat was black?

She climbed the stairs again. Seated once more in front of her computer, she noticed the bill from the water company lying next to the keyboard and was momentarily puzzled as to how it had gotten there. But now, with her mind less skittery, she scanned the headings on the listserv posts that had come in over the last few days.

No one was talking about kittens in need of homes. Many people, however, were talking about Isobel Lister. After a "speak no ill of the dead" disclaimer, one post empathized with the long-suffering relatives who tolerated her bohemian adventuring and always made sure an apartment in the family-owned building was waiting for her when she ran out of other options.

Others recalled her presence in Arborville before she left home: strutting around in crazy clothes that left nothing to the imagination, getting suspended from Arborville High every other week, organizing wild parties involving marijuana and who knows what else, sneaking into the rec department pool for nude midnight swims, forming a rock band whose name involved a vulgarity.

A lively debate had arisen, in fact, with those on one side—younger people—saying that Arborville could be awfully staid and they wished they'd been around in Isobel's heyday, and those on the other side saying that she had been a true black sheep and it was a blessing when she left, and they felt sorry for her brother and his family and all the ancestral Listers. Those Listers, who by the way were buried in the Arborville cemetery, had undoubtedly been rolling in their graves for decades and now they would finally get some peace.

And moreover, no matter what people thought of Isobel, nobody could have found it funny when she habitually referred to Arborville as "Arbor-vile."

It was a refreshing, then, to scroll down and discover a message headed "Has anyone else seen this knitter?" posted by a woman whose address Pamela recognized as being in the neighborhood people called The Farm—because it had been a farm for a few centuries before being sold to developers. Pamela knew the Knit and Nibblers were not the only knitters in Arborville. Many, many, many of her fellow residents knew the simple joys that a pair of knitting needles and a skein of yarn could bring.

But the knitter the woman from The Farm was inquiring about turned out to be . . . *a ghost*. At least that was her interpretation.

"I can see the cemetery from my kitchen window," the woman wrote, "and I don't really believe in ghosts but I can't think what else this could be. She waits until after dark and then she glides among the tombstones carrying something white. When she sits down with the thing in her lap, it looks like she is knitting."

"When did you start seeing her?" another woman inquired.

"St. Patrick's Day night," the first woman responded, "and every night thereafter."

"I thought I was imagining things," came another message. "I have not seen the knitting ghost, but I too live near the cemetery and ever since Isobel Lister was killed I've been hearing the most ghastly wailing every night. Like a banshee."

"It could not be a banshee," a man posted helpfully. "Or if it is a banshee it has nothing to do with Isobel Lister's murder. Banshees only wail before a death, not after."

Smiling to herself about men and their fondness for authoritative pronouncements, Pamela closed the AccessArborville site and opened the Word file labeled "Virgin Mary Knits." The article's full title was "Why Does the Virgin Mary Knit?" and the author was a medievalist at an Ivy League university.

Pamela knew that people had been knitting for a long time, even doing something like knitting as early as the third century. So it stood to reason that people would have been knitting in the Middle Ages. Naturally the real Mary, having lived before the third century, would not have been a knitter—nor would she have dressed like a medieval noblewoman.

Yet here she was in a splendid Italian painting dated between 1400 and 1410, wearing an elegant late-medieval dress and busily at work with four double-pointed needles and a supply of yarn in a lovely shade of pink. Her project resembled a simple tunic, created from the bottom edge up, and she seemed about ready to cast off, leaving an opening for the head. Somehow, working in the round, she had managed to give it sleeves that appeared to be of a piece with the body. Pamela was not sure it was possible to accomplish such a feat in real life. She suspected that perhaps the artist was not a knitter and thus his depiction of knitting lacked a certain verisimilitude.

The article's author was less interested in the mechanics of knitting than in the implications of a knitting Virgin Mary. In addition to its very real utility as a household craft, she pointed out, knitting had also become a hobby for upper-class women. Paintings like this one were intended to decorate churches and were commissioned by wealthy patrons. How delighted a patron must have been with a painting that showed the mother of Jesus in a pose that evoked the women in his—or perhaps *her*—own circle!

Pamela's evaluation suggested that the author add some discussion of the technique (if there was one) that could produce a garment like the one hanging from Mary's needles, noting that readers of *Fiber Craft* were likely to be as puzzled as she was by the sleeves. She read over her evaluations for the other two articles, saved her file, and closed it. She would skim them again in the morning and then send them off to her boss.

Back downstairs, Pamela made a quick pot roast sandwich. Lunchtime had come and gone, but the doughnut she'd eaten at Bettina's had kept hunger at bay. Once lunch was done, she decided the rest of the day would be devoted to household chores. She started a load of wash, vacuumed the downstairs carpets—which sent the cats scurrying for the stairs—and dusted the cupboards, cabinets, and shelves that held her collections of thrift-store treasures, as well as the treasures themselves. Finally, she fluffed up the needlepoint pillows that decorated the sofa, making sure the needlepoint cat was not standing on its head.

Such work was tiring, but there was still the kitchen floor to scrub, wash to be folded and put away, and the paper-recycling basket to be emptied into the bin at the side of the house.

It was past six p.m. by the time she headed out the front door with the paper-recycling basket. The sky was clear overhead, but to the west rich shades of amber and crimson marked the progress of the setting sun. She veered toward her driveway and made her way along the tall hedge that separated her property from Richard Larkin's. Through gaps at the top of the hedge where the bushy shrubs tapered, she could see that the light was on in his kitchen.

Cooking for himself now, she imagined. Sometimes, looking from her kitchen window, she had watched him and Jocelyn moving about that space together. She tilted back the lid of the recycling bin and dumped a week's worth of newspapers and junk mail and the odd magazine from the basket into the larger container.

She was on her way back to her porch when she heard a voice from the sidewalk call her name. She turned to see Richard Larkin standing at the end of the hedge.

"Hello!" she called, waving the hand that wasn't holding the basket. "How are you?"

He was several feet away and twilight had descended, making things seem not quite real. But as he stepped closer, she felt her breathing cease, and in a moment he was looming over her with that curious stern expression. She had to tilt her head to meet his eyes.

"There are no kittens," she heard herself say. "I checked the Co-Op bulletin board and AccessArborville." When he didn't respond, she went on. "But you could try the shelter in Haversack. That's where the Frasers got Woofus." He nodded. "I'll keep looking though," she added. "I'll keep my eyes and ears open."

The brief exchange about cats had been neighborly, not really that different from casual greetings called from driveway to driveway. She found she could breathe again, though he was an imposing presence in his navy-blue pea coat and boots. But suddenly he bent forward as if to scrutinize her through the gloom.

"How have you been?" he asked suddenly, as if the answer was important.

"Oh, I . . . uh. Fine, really," she said.

"And Penny?"

"She's fine." Pamela nodded. "And your daughters? I hope they're fine."

"They are." He nodded back. His dark-blond hair was shaggy, the way it had been when he first moved in next door, when she'd been sure the glamorous shaggy-haired stranger in the faded jeans couldn't be seriously interested in his quiet, widowed neighbor.

"Penny will be home for spring break," Pamela said. "I know she'd like to see your daughters if they'll be around. And maybe"—she took a deep breath—"we could all . . . do . . . something."

Her voice trailed off as he seemed to frown. "I don't know when they'll be here." It was hard to know if the hint of anger in his tone was directed at her suggestion, or a sense that as his daughters grew up they were slipping away from him.

He bid her goodnight and turned away. After he'd taken a few steps, he turned back and said, "I'm glad you're doing well."

Pamela headed for her porch, her mind awhirl as she recalled the breathlessness she'd felt in his presence and then his seeming dismissal of her hint—granted, it had been rather subtle—that she might welcome a renewal of his interest. But why approach her about a kitten, she wondered, if that hadn't been his own—subtle—hint that he wanted to reestablish contact?

Stepping over her threshold, she was met by a happy distraction in the form of three cats lined up on the entry's thrift-store carpet.

"I suppose you're hungry," she commented as she returned the recycling basket to its accustomed corner.

And, she realized, she was hungry too, and a piece of tilapia was waiting in the refrigerator to be sautéed and served with kale and brown rice.

An hour later, she had settled into her spot at the end of the sofa and was once again immersed in *Shaker Communities and the Feminist Sensibility: The Paradox of Women's Work* as Catrina purred at her side.

Extra coffee was needed the next morning. Pamela's night had been restless, and she had opened her eyes at six a.m., not sure if she had actually slept at all. With the sky still dark behind the eyelet curtains and the cats who shared her bed still deep in slumber, she had rolled over and managed to drift off.

When she woke again, the room was bright, but scattered fragments of a dream remained in her consciousness. Richard Larkin had been in it, minus the navy-blue pea coat, and in fact minus most of his clothes. Something, related or unrelated to Richard Larkin—she wasn't sure, since the fragments were rapidly slipping away—had involved Bettina and the Haversack animal shelter and even Woofus. And maybe cats.

In any event, real-life cats were stirring at her feet. Soon Catrina and Ginger emerged from beneath the bedclothes and stared at her until she pushed the covers aside and sat up. The hint of a headache that she had awakened with was more intense now that she was upright.

Downstairs in the kitchen, Pamela trusted her morning ritual to vanquish the effects of her troubled sleep and the sense of unease that still lingered from the dream. She set water to boil, fetched the *Register* and the *Advocate*, fed the cats, and ground more coffee than usual. Soon the little kitchen was filled with the comforting aromas of coffee and toast and she was sitting at the table with the *Advocate* spread out in front of her.

A quick glance through the *Register* had revealed no news about the Isobel Lister case, so she had set it aside in favor of reading Bettina's interview with Liadan Percy. She wondered what the readers of the *Advocate* would think of such a sympathetic portrayal of a witch, though Bettina's interview made it clear that the women who had come to be known as witches weren't really what people thought witches were.

Traces of her headache remained, but the coffee had helped. An additional cup would help even more, she was sure, so she rose and crossed over to where the carafe waited on the stove. Mission accomplished, she was just returning to the table when the phone rang. The sound startled her and her arm twitched, setting the dark surface of the coffee aquiver within the confines of the wedding-china cup. She set the cup down and reached for the handset.

CHAPTER 13

"Pete Paterson here," the caller announced, "and I've got your screens done. Shall I bring them by? Would ten a.m. be good?"

"Sure," she responded. "See you then."

Pamela resumed sipping at her coffee while continuing to browse through the *Advocate*, even lingering over the last few pages where the exploits of the high school sports teams were covered. Coffee finished, she put the newspapers in the recycling basket, rinsed the breakfast dishes, and climbed the stairs to her bedroom, pausing in the entry to smile at the sight of Catrina napping in her favorite sunny spot. How fortunate cats were to be able to sleep anywhere at any time!

Standing in front of her closet, she stepped into the jeans she had been wearing for the past few days, but she exchanged the previous day's blue turtleneck for another of her own creations, a V-neck pullover knit from an ombre yarn in shades of cream, yellow, and gold. In the bathroom, she combed the dark hair that hung straight to her shoulders and declared herself ready to face the day.

In her study, she skimmed over her evaluations of the articles on Civil War quilts, Scottish tartans, and the knitting Virgin Mary and sent them on their way. No sooner had they been dispatched than a new message popped into her inbox, from Penny, with news that she probably had a ride home lined up for spring break but she wasn't sure yet and in any event she could take the bus.

Pamela closed her eyes and leaned back in her comfortable chair. Something about Penny's message had tickled the spot where her brain still stored fragments of the previous night's dream. Richard Larkin's daughters must have been in it too, visiting their father while Penny was home for spring break. She was too sensible to believe that dreams could foretell the future, but clearly her unconscious mind had liked her idea of easing into a renewed connection with her neighbor by suggesting Penny get together with her old friends.

"Keep me posted," she responded to Penny. "I can drive up and get you if you don't want to take the bus."

The doorbell chimed then and she glanced at the clock—ten a.m. Pete Paterson was exactly on time.

"Good morning," he greeted her from the porch as she swung the door back. He was dressed as he had been when he came to pick up the screens, in the new-looking jeans and the well-pressed denim shirt topped with the rugged buffalo-check jacket. His gleaming silver pickup truck was parked at the curb.

She echoed his greeting and he smiled a quick smile that somehow left his eyes melancholy.

"You don't have to come out." His glance traveled from her face to her feet and, apparently judging that the sweater and jeans made her suitably dressed for the chilly day, he added, "Unless you want to, of course." He held out a hand. "Otherwise you can just give me your garage key."

"I'll give you the key," Pamela said. "Just a minute—it's in the kitchen."

Provided with the garage key, and instructed to ring the bell again to collect his payment, he went on his way. Not wanting to start a task that would just be interrupted, Pamela watched him through the window in her back door as, moving with a graceful energy, he carried the screens, one at a time, into the dark recesses of the garage. Half an hour later, he was back on the front porch, handing over the garage key.

"Come on in." Pamela stepped back and pulled the door open wider. "I'll get my checkbook."

He followed her to the kitchen, stood near the table while she made out a check, and handed over a receipt marked "Paid." As he pocketed the check, he said, "It looked like somebody worked on those screens sometime within the last hundred years—nice mitering jobs, pretty recent, on some of the frames. Was that your husband's work?"

"Oh." Pamela closed her eyes. Even after all this time, she still felt awkward telling the story. "It was his work," she said after a bit. "We bought the house as a fixer upper and . . . and . . . we fixed just about everything." A gesture and a glance around the room implied that the kitchen had been included in the refurbishing.

Pete laughed. "So he put in his time and now he likes to hire out the repairs?"

Pamela sighed. "It's not that. He's . . . dead."

It was Pete's turn to say, "Oh." The melancholy cast to his eyes suited his expression now, as his brow tightened. His lips remained parted as if he wanted to add more but wasn't sure what.

"It's all right." Pamela added a shrug to her half-smile. "It happened a long time ago."

"You stayed in the house?"

"I have a daughter," Pamela said, "so for a long time there were two of us here. She's away at college now."

"Where?" he inquired.

"Massachusetts."

He laughed. "They all go there from New Jersey. Far enough to be away but not so far that it's hard to come home for the holidays. I've got a son at college in Boston."

Pamela joined in the laughter. "That's where my daughter is. Is he your only child?"

"There's a daughter too. She's still in high school but she lives with my wife." He paused. "So it's just me at home now, in a big house. But I did a lot of work on it myself, when we first moved in, and I don't want to leave it."

"That's how I feel. I stripped wood and painted and even figured out how to wallpaper. So I see my own handiwork everywhere."

He smiled. "I love these old places, and Arborville is full of them." He glanced around the kitchen and added, "By the way, how did you find out about me?"

"Oh!" Pamela laughed again. "It's kind of a story. You're not the only P Paterson in Arborville."

"You're a P Paterson too," he said. "I noticed that on the check."

"So what happened was, a call came for you here . . ." She described Bettina's insistence that she find and record the phone number for P Paterson the handyman so she could steer callers to the person they really wanted. "The caller wanted someone to repair screens," she concluded, "and then I remembered my own screens."

Neither of them spoke for a minute. When Pete pushed back the sleeve of the woolly jacket to check his watch, Pamela took the hint.

"So anyway," she said, "thanks. Now I can cross screens off my to-do list. And I'll know who to call for . . . whatever." She picked up the receipt he had given her and quoted, "Jack of All Trades. No job too big or too small."

She gestured for him to precede her though the kitchen doorway and darted ahead to open the front door. As he was about to step over the threshold, he turned.

"I don't suppose you'd like to grab lunch with me at Hyler's in an hour or so?" he said. His lean face was hard to read, with its Roland-like intensity softened by melancholy eyes. "I've got another job nearby and I usually eat there when I'm working in town."

"Oh!" She seemed to be saying that a lot. "I can't today because I'm doing something with my friend"— she nodded toward the street and Bettina's house beyond—"but . . ."

But what? Asked a voice in her brain.

"But I'm free tomorrow." She said it almost without thinking.

"How about dinner then?"

Pamela suppressed the urge to respond with "oh" again, though she was surprised. A casual lunch was one thing—whereas dinner was like a real date. But she'd told him she was free without specifying a time frame. So she nodded and said, "Okay."

* * *

Bettina was absolutely pink with glee, and her laughter bubbled over the minute Pamela stepped across the threshold to join her on the porch.

"It's Friday," she sang, "and the *Advocate* is out and Clayborn said he'd have the case solved by now, but he hasn't solved it."

"I liked your article on the Wiccan," Pamela said.

Bettina had more to say on the topic of Detective Clayborn, however. "I called him this morning," she went on as they moved toward the steps. "I didn't gloat. I was very professional. I just said I was checking in to ask about progress on the case so the residents of Arborville, whose tax dollars support the police department, could be brought up to date."

"Is there anything to bring them up to date on?" Pamela asked. "I mean, anything he's done?"

"There actually is." Bettina smiled. Her lipstick today was a deep mauve, echoing the color of the scarf at her neck and, Pamela suspected, whatever outfit was beneath her pumpkin-colored down coat. The day was very chilly.

"There actually is," she repeated, "and I'm sure tomorrow's *Register* will have an article with Marcy Brewer's byline.

"And what will it say?"

"The report from the medical examiner is done, and Isobel Lister died as a result of striking her head on the corner of that metal desk as she fell."

"Nothing exactly new," Pamela commented.

"Not exactly. But it rules things out."

They had reached the end of Pamela's driveway,

where Bettina's faithful Toyota waited. Bettina unlocked the passenger-side door and Pamela slid into her seat.

"Like other possible murder weapons," Pamela murmured after Bettina had settled behind the steering wheel. "Like Siobhan O'Doul's shillelagh. I know you thought she could be a viable suspect."

"She *was* grumpy." Bettina turned her key in the ignition and the Toyota's engine came to life with a resentful snarl. "And she does have a motive, maybe not for premeditated murder, but I could certainly see her confronting Isobel and scolding her about trivializing Irish culture."

"I could see that." Pamela nodded. "And with that in mind, she could still be the killer. She brandishes the shillelagh and Isobel jumps back and loses her balance . . ."

That comment put the topic to rest, at least for the remainder of the short drive to the library. But there were other things to discuss, namely Pamela's realization that, like the caller who mistakenly telephoned her the previous Monday, she herself had been in need of a handyman to fix screens. She described her call to Pete Paterson, and the impressive speed with which he had carried out the task. For some reason, though, she didn't include the fact that she was having dinner with him the next night.

"What's he like?" Bettina asked.

"Oh, I don't know," Pamela said. "He seems nice."

They had reached the library by then. Bettina pulled into the parking lot, cruised past the kiddy playground, and coasted into a spot near the library's door. Upstairs on the library's main floor, they walked past the windows that looked out on the street, and the row of comfortable chairs where retirees dozed over newspapers or magazines. Bettina led the way down a narrow aisle between two tall bookshelves holding rows and rows of books. At the end of the aisle, small study desks were lined up against the library's side wall.

"You have to know the yearbooks are here," Bettina commented, "or you'd never find them."

She slipped off her coat, revealing mauve pants and a matching turtleneck, and draped it over the back of the chair that faced the nearest desk. Then she pulled the chair from the neighboring desk up next to it.

"Take off your coat and sit down," she told Pamela. "I'll fetch some books."

The covers of the Arborville High yearbooks were deep turquoise in color, with gold accents here and there, since turquoise and gold had always been the school colors. The typefaces spelling out "Arborville High School" varied from year to year, reflecting changing styles in graphic design. The particular issue of the yearbook that Bettina deposited in front of Pamela on the study desk featured swirly letters that seemed to melt into each other, as well as an image of the school's aardvark mascot depicted as a wily cartoon character.

"Nineteen sixty-eight," Bettina announced. "Let's start here." She settled into the chair next to Pamela and began paging through the yearbook.

Black-and-white photos, rather stiffly posed, documented the school band and the chess club and the photo club and many other clubs, as well as the school paper (the *Aardvarkian*) and the literary magazine. Many pages were devoted to sports, of course, including football and baseball and basketball and soccer.

And each class, freshmen, sophomores, juniors, and seniors, had its own section, with rows of tiny headshots arranged in alphabetical order.

"Let's check seniors first," Bettina suggested. She found that section, smoothed the first page flat, and bent toward it.

The variety of looks was entertaining. Many of the students still favored a clean-cut style, boys with well-trimmed hair and girls with coifs molded into improbable perfection. But here and there a wayward soul marched to a different drummer. Shaggy locks straggled below the ears in the case of boys, and long falls of impossibly straight hair framed the defiantly makeup-free faces of girls.

It was easy to locate Isobel Lister and Cheryl Radcliff in the grid of alphabetically arranged class pictures, and to discover that both had been seniors in 1968. It was also clear that they had been among the group that marched to a different drummer, Isobel with long blonde hair and an amused expression and Cheryl with a dark mass of frizzy curls and a pout that seemed designed to thwart a photographer's exhortation to smile. It wasn't clear, however, that Isobel and Cheryl had actually been friends. Arborville High enrolled a large number of students and had done so for decades.

"Maybe there's an index," Pamela suggested. "Yearbooks often have indexes that list all the pages each student's photo appears on."

"Good idea," Bettina responded as she flipped to the back of the yearbook. "Radcliff, Radcliff, Radcliff," she murmured, running a manicured finger down an alphabetical list.

"Here!" she exclaimed. "Remember these page numbers, and we'll cross reference with the page numbers for Isobel."

She called out a few numbers and then backtracked in search of "Lister, Isobel."

"Drama club," Pamela commented, as Bettina opened the yearbook to the page that Cheryl and Isobel had in common. There, black-and-white photos documented the drama club's production of *Bye Bye Birdie*, including several candid shots taken during rehearsals.

Neither Cheryl nor Isobel seemed to have had a major part. Rather, both were in the chorus, and one of the candid shots showed chorus members watching while the choreographer demonstrated a step. Isobel, however, was not watching. She was leaning toward Cheryl with an arm around Cheryl's shoulder and whispering something in her ear. Even then, Cheryl had been plump—though her plumpness had given her a voluptuous air. The photo's caption read, "Inseparable."

The aromas of fresh-baked cornbread and simmering chili combined to welcome them into the Frasers' kitchen. The kitchen table had been set with placemats and napkins in earthy tones that complemented Bettina's sage-green pottery, as well as small plates and Bettina's stainless flatware. Wilfred greeted them from his post at the stove, where he was tending to a large two-handled pot.

"Welcome, Pamela, and dear wife," he exclaimed. "Lunch will be served momentarily. Please make yourselves comfortable."

Coats had been shed in the living room. Murmuring

greetings and thanks in overlapping voices, Pamela
and Bettina settled into their chairs. Woofus looked up
from his spot against the wall and resumed his slumber.

From the cooking area of the kitchen came the sound
of dishes clattering as Wilfred set three pottery bowls
on the counter near the stove. Before filling them, though,
he inverted the pan containing the cornbread over a
wooden cutting board and divided the square loaf into
nine portions.

"Cornbread," he announced as he made his way toward the table. "Help yourselves," he added as he set
the cutting board down. "Butter is on its way."

Once the butter was delivered, he ladled a portion of
chili into each bowl and served Pamela and Bettina. A
few moments later, he joined them with his own bowl.
Flourishing his spoon, he bid them a hearty "Bon appétit!" and soon all three were lifting spoonfuls of the
thick, meat-and-bean-laden stew to their mouths.

Wilfred called his version of the dish "five-alarm
chili," but in fact it was more notable for the subtlety
of its flavors than for peppery heat. The hint of chiles
was present, smoky and complex, as well as tomatoes
mellowed through long cooking and the beefy broth
that tough meat yields when simmered for hours. The
meaty bits were tender and tasty, and the beans were
plump kidney beans that resisted the teeth just enough
to give each bite of chili a satisfying substance.

Wilfred accepted the compliments with a smile that
heightened his ruddy good cheer. As the bowls gradually emptied and the last bits of cornbread were buttered and eaten, the conversation turned to Pamela and
Bettina's library outing.

"How did your visit to the library go?" Wilfred inquired as his spoon pursued a few last beans around the bottom of his bowl. Before setting out to collect Pamela that morning, Bettina had described to her husband the curious encounter Pamela had witnessed at the Co-Op.

"The woman who insisted she was not Cheryl Radcliff was definitely Cheryl Radcliff in high school, though she's Cheryl Hagan now," Pamela said. "Of course she's older, a lot older, but she's still short and plump and her hair is still curly and she's kept it dark, so the resemblance comes through. And she and Isobel were definitely friends when they were at Arborville High together."

"Inseparable," Bettina chimed in. "They were in the drama club together, and from the looks of Cheryl back then, she was one of the ones who got up to rebellious things with Isobel."

"So"—Pamela set her spoon down—"Cheryl moves back to Arborville and is horrified to discover Isobel is back here too, and teasing about letting a more recent generation know about the wild times she and her old friend shared. And Cheryl decides she has to act fast if she's going to preserve the image of upstanding respectability she's cultivated."

"Yes." Bettina nodded. "Or she didn't plan to actually kill her, but after she slipped out while Isobel was singing, she circled around to the back of the rec center and waited in the green room to confront her with 'What did you mean by that weird comment?' or whatever."

"And they argued . . . et cetera, et cetera." Pamela nodded. "So now we've got three women, Liadan, Siobhan, and Cheryl, any one of which—we think—could have killed Isobel, though maybe not on purpose."

"Though in the case of Cheryl," Pamela went on, "it might have been on purpose. At the Co-Op she seemed awfully determined to deny any connection at all with Isobel. The other ones, I could see an argument getting out of hand. But Cheryl might have thought that the only way she could keep wild and embarrassing things from being revealed would be to kill the person capable of revealing them."

"My dear Pamela," Wilfred laughed. "I lived through the sixties too, and if all the wild and embarrassing things we all did back then were revealed, nobody's reputation would survive."

Looking at Wilfred seated at the kitchen table in his suburban home, still swathed in the capacious apron he wore while cooking and beaming contentedly at the woman he had married several decades ago, it was hard to imagine that he had ever done wild and embarrassing things. But Pamela herself had not lived through the sixties and to her the era was as far off and exotic as . . . well, as the era that had produced images of the Virgin Mary knitting.

"Maybe the wild and embarrassing things she did were *really* wild and embarrassing," Pamela said. "And here she is back in town, and her daughter is here . . ."

"I'd rather have it be her than Liadan." Bettina emphasized her statement by thumping the table with both hands, causing the spoons in the empty chili bowls to jingle.

"I know you don't think Liadan is a serious suspect," Pamela smiled at her friend. "Harm none. Do what you will."

"She seemed sincere. And she likes cats." Punkin,

the ginger-colored cat that the Frasers had adopted from Catrina's litter, had chosen that moment to join Woofus, who was still stretched out against the wall.

"I'm not convinced it wasn't her." Pamela shook her head.

"It could still be Siobhan." Bettina raised her carefully shaped brows. "The medical examiner's report ruled out the shillelagh as a possible murder weapon, but we had that other idea." Bettina plucked her spoon from her empty chili bowl and flourished it in the air. "Isobel thought Siobhan was threatening her with the shillelagh and she backed away and lost her balance."

Pamela nodded. "It has to be one of them"—she tightened her lips into a determined knot—"even maybe Liadan, because we know it can't be the men. Neither Nate Riddle or the old boyfriend left the luncheon room between when the concert ended and when Meg came out to say Isobel was dead."

Wilfred stood up and began to clear away. Pamela joined him, collecting the three spoons into one bowl and stacking the bowls. But before picking the bowls up, she exclaimed, "There's a person who might have seen the killer enter the back door of the rec center!"

"Who?" Bettina looked up.

"The florist delivery man." Pamela sat back down. "He was still in the parking lot behind the building when I followed you back to the green room. If he was paying attention he would have noticed a person who went in that door and then came dashing out again soon after."

"*If* he was paying attention." Bettina shrugged. "The proprietor of Beauteous Blooms said the delivery man was his nephew, taking what he called a 'nap year' before starting college. That doesn't speak well of the nephew's powers of observation."

"It's worth a try though," Pamela said, "talking to him. Otherwise we still have our three suspects and no progress." She gestured toward where the three spoons were nestled in the empty bowl.

"Maybe Wilfred would like to order me a surprise bouquet of flowers." Bettina was suddenly in favor of the idea.

CHAPTER 14

Wilfred had been on his way back to the table after delivering a few dishes to the counter by the sink, but he paused en route.

"Dear wife," he laughed. "Your wish is my command, and there's no time like the present." He picked up his phone from the counter. "I believe a particular florist was mentioned? Beauteous Blooms?"

"Of Timberley," Bettina supplied.

Wilfred stepped into the dining room with his phone, but Pamela and Bettina could overhear the conversation. Two dozen red roses were to be delivered as soon as possible to Bettina Fraser on Orchard Street in Arborville. Once he'd finished that task, Wilfred returned to the kitchen and busied himself at the counter.

Soon the tantalizing aroma of fresh-brewed coffee wafted toward the table, and then Wilfred appeared bearing a large plate of oatmeal cookies. Mugs and cookie plates were supplied, along with cream and sugar. Once the mugs had been filled with the steaming brew, Wilfred took his seat again.

Pamela had been so interested in the excursion to the library to look at the yearbooks, and then in the discussion that arose from the discovery of Cheryl and Isobel's friendship, that she'd forgotten all about the posts she'd happened upon the previous evening while checking AccessArborville for kittens in need of homes.

The reminiscences about Isobel's wild and crazy behavior had added nothing new to the portrait of Isobel she and Bettina were familiar with, so she mentioned them only in passing, as she watched Bettina calibrate the amount of sugar and cream necessary to prepare her coffee for consumption. But there had been that other thread, or two related threads actually.

"Someone in Arborville claims a knitting ghost is haunting the cemetery," she said, after sampling her own coffee and transferring an oatmeal cookie to her cookie plate.

"Really?" Bettina had been raising a cookie to her lips, but her hand paused in midair.

Pamela nodded. "The woman posting said she can see the cemetery from her kitchen window—probably one of those houses in Roland's neighborhood, where the Van Riper farm used to be. She said the ghost started appearing the night of St. Patrick's Day."

"Just after Isobel was killed," Bettina murmured, cookie forgotten.

"She did make that connection. And," Pamela added, "someone else near the cemetery thinks she's been hearing a banshee ever since then."

"Probably no connection with Isobel's death there,"

Wilfred commented. "Banshees only wail to foretell deaths. They don't wail afterwards."

Pamela laughed and said, "Someone—a male someone—on AccessArborville made that very point." She peered at Wilfred. "Or was that you?"

"Did he also say banshee means 'mound fairy'—as in a grave mound—in Gaelic?" Wilfred peered back in a teasing way.

It occurred to Pamela that even Wilfred was sometimes overpowered by the urge to make an authoritative pronouncement. She merely smiled to herself but Bettina suddenly looked stricken.

"I hope it's not really foretelling a death," she whispered. "That might mean there's going to be another murder."

But they were distracted from that grim thought by the ring of the doorbell.

"I'll get it." Bettina hopped up from her chair and scurried from the room.

Pamela turned to Wilfred. "That was very fast, if it's the flowers."

Wilfred winked. "I told the florist I'd just remembered it was my anniversary and I'd be spending my nights on the sofa with my dog for the foreseeable future if I didn't conjure up some flowers right away."

"I guess it worked," Pamela said, as Bettina's voice, cooing enthusiastically, reached them from around the corner. She rose and made her way toward the sounds.

Through the open doorway she could see the young man she recognized as the driver of the van in the rec center parking lot—though he was taller and thinner than the glimpse of his head through the van's window had led her to expect. He was wearing a brown poncho woven from wool so minimally processed that he might as well have been wearing an actual pelt. On his feet were rugged brown leather sandals and his shoulder-length hair was neatly tucked behind his ears. He was still holding the large flower arrangement that Bettina had been cooing over.

"It's so big," Bettina said, drawing out the vowels. "And it looks so heavy, but you're strong. Do you think you could . . . ?" She stepped back from the threshold and waved a hand in a hinting gesture toward a table near the staircase. "And of course"—she added a flirtatious glance from beneath a delicately shadowed eyelid—"I want to give you something for your trouble."

Wilfred entered at that moment, wallet in hand, and stood by as the young man deposited the arrangement on the table Bettina had indicated.

"Oh, my goodness!" Bettina raised a hand to her forehead, then darted toward the open door to peek out. "You are!" she said, turning back. "Beauteous Blooms! You're from the florist that delivered the funeral arrangement to the St. Patrick's Day luncheon."

"Yeah?" The young man's expression seemed to dare Bettina to go on. But she did.

"That was such a coincidence," she said, "because the very next thing that happened was—"

"I know what happened, and of course the cops tracked me down."

"They did?" Bettina's dramatic skills extended to amazing feats of feigned surprise, but this time her amazement was real.

"*Duh!* At first I said, 'Man are you going to arrest me for, like, going to the wrong address? Don't have a cow. It was an honest mistake. One eighty-two, one twenty-eight—anybody could get confused.' Then it turns out there was, like, a murder and did I see anything?"

"Did you?" Bettina was fairly trembling with excitement.

"Well, duh, like *nooo*." The young man's lips remained parted as he drew the word out, and he opened his eyes as wide as they would go for good measure. When he seemed convinced he'd made his point, he went on.

"I just dropped off the flowers at the front desk and then I went back to my van. So Claymore, Killmore, whatever, says what they mean is, did I see anybody go in or come out the back?"

"Why did you park in the back," Bettina interjected, "if you went in the front?"

"No spaces left at the curb, *duh!* Because the wrinklies showing up for the luncheon took them all. You don't think it was my choice to walk all the way around the building carrying ten pounds of Lasting Remembrance All-White Tribute, do you?"

"*Did* you see anybody go in or come out the back?" Bettina asked. She added a flirtatious smile. "Isobel Lister's murder is a big story here in Arborville and I'm a reporter for the town weekly."

"Like I told Killmore, how was I supposed to know I was looking at a murderer? It was just some, like, *normal* woman. And I was sleeping on and off. I didn't have any more deliveries till later and if I go back to the shop too soon he just puts me to work sweeping or something."

"You saw someone!" Again, Bettina's amazement wasn't feigned.

"Yeah?" The questioning tone implied surprise at Bettina's amazement.

Bettina turned her gaze toward Pamela, her expressive eyes eloquent, then she focused on the young man.

"Normal, you say? Was she carrying a big, knobby walking stick?"

He shook his head no.

"Did she have long curly gray hair?"

Again, no.

"Was she kind of . . . ?" Bettina patted her own ample waistline and hips. "Or more like . . . ?" She gestured at Pamela.

"I really only saw her from the back," the young man said, "because I must have been asleep when she came out again. But I'd say . . ." He nodded toward Pamela. "More like her. Yeah, much more like her."

Wilfred pulled a bill from his wallet and handed it to the young man, saying, "Many thanks for the prompt service."

"No problem." The young man nodded to the group and backed out onto the porch as Bettina stepped forward to close the door behind him.

"Well!" Bettina shook her head so energetically that her scarlet curls vibrated. "Well, well, well, and well! Clayborn has been smarter than I gave him credit for. Meg obviously told him about the ominous flower delivery and he tracked down Mr. Nap Year for an inter-

view. And"—with a few quick steps she joined her
husband, who was adjusting the position of the flower
arrangement—"speaking of flowers, this is absolutely
the most beautiful arrangement I have ever seen.
Thank you!"

She squeezed his hand and then leaned toward the
nearest rose and sniffed enthusiastically. The roses
were deep burgundy red, with enough petals unfurled
to advertise their rich color but not so open as to make
a blowsy display of their stamens. They contrasted
pleasingly with the dark green leaves that garnished
their long stems, and with the drifts of white baby's
breath that accented the arrangement.

"A happy wife is a happy life," Wilfred said, smiling delightedly. "You are quite welcome, my dearest."
He edged toward the arch that led to the dining room
and the kitchen beyond. "Shall we go back to the
kitchen? I can warm up the coffee left in the carafe and
there are definitely more cookies."

Seated again at the kitchen table, and with mugs
topped up with hot coffee before them, Pamela and
Bettina looked at each other, their foreheads creased
with matching frowns.

"All our suspects are gone," Pamela said, after sub-
jecting a bite of oatmeal cookie to a thoughtful session
of chewing.

"Seems like." Bettina nodded.

"Mr. Nap Year seemed pretty sure about what he
saw," Wilfred agreed. "No big knobby walking stick."

"That lets out Siobhan," Bettina murmured.

"No long curly gray hair."

"That lets out Liadan."

"And the woman he saw was clearly not a gorgeous, well-shaped woman like you." Wilfred beamed at his wife.

"Thinner, I guess," Pamela contributed. "So he didn't see Cheryl Hagan."

Pamela and Bettina frowned in concert again, and this time Wilfred joined them.

"Here's another idea," Pamela said suddenly. "We've eliminated Nate Riddle and the old boyfriend as the actual killers—but I don't know what to think about Nate Riddle. When the two men were arguing in the street outside Caleb's Table, the old boyfriend implied that Nate Riddle had come to the cemetery with a girlfriend in tow. He said he'd seen a woman hanging around in the cemetery parking lot waiting for Nate to, as he put it, 'finish pretending to be sad.'"

"Ohh!" Bettina clapped her hands. "A lovers' triangle within a lovers' triangle. Two men are . . . *involved* . . . with Isobel, but two women, one of whom is Isobel, are . . . *involved* . . . with one of the two men." Her eyes grew large, so large that Pamela could see white around her irises. "The girlfriend kills Isobel— out of jealousy! Tracks her down in the green room and fights with her, pushes her down, on purpose."

Excitement was making Pamela feel a bit breathless. She inhaled deeply before speaking. "Even if Nate Riddle just loved Isobel but didn't *love* her, the girlfriend could still be jealous. And a young woman is likely to be stronger, stronger and more vigorous than someone like Siobhan or Liadan or Cheryl, and anyway now we know they didn't do it."

Wilfred raised a finger. "You said you didn't know what to think about Nate Riddle, Pamela."

"The old boyfriend certainly didn't think much of him, and he said Isobel was too smart to take him seriously—whatever his actual feelings for Isobel were."

"Gold-digger?" Wilfred tilted his head as if considering the mystery from a different perspective. "I'm sure Isobel's share of the inherited Lister fortunes was substantial."

Bettina set her coffee mug down with a thump that was echoed by a disgusted snort. "What a weasel!" she exclaimed. "He knew she wouldn't live forever and he was sure he was in her will and if he was just patient . . ."

"But his girlfriend—his real girlfriend—gets impatient." Pamela's coffee sat untouched in front of her, along with most of an oatmeal cookie. She turned toward Wilfred and conjured up an imitation of a flirtatiously pleading smile. "Why should we wait for the old bat to die of natural causes, sweetums, when we could be enjoying your share of her fortune right now?"

Bettina joined the charade. In a wheedling voice, she crooned, "All we have to do is kill her, sweetums." Reverting to her normal tones, she added, "They plan it together, but he stays in the luncheon room so he has an alibi, and the girlfriend sneaks in the back door . . ."

She pushed her chair back, sprang to her feet, and darted toward the doorway that led to the dining room. In a few minutes she returned, carrying her phone.

"I found Nate Riddle online," she announced. "He plays gigs with local bands and he has a website. He also teaches at Haversack High. He directs the school's jazz band, and this term the practices are on Friday afternoon." She aimed her next words at Pamela. "So we'd better get moving."

"Why?" Pamela had rediscovered her coffee and partly eaten cookie, and her question was muffled by a mouthful of crumbs.

"To follow him, of course. And he'll lead us to the girlfriend. And then we'll figure out where she was between one thirty and one forty-five on St. Patrick's Day."

"He drives a red Fiat," Pamela said as Bettina pulled into the parking lot of Haversack High School.

The school sprawled over several acres at the western edge of Haversack, low buildings of dark brick in a modern style. Sports fields were visible from the parking lot, with football practice happening on a vast expanse of pallid grass and a few runners making their way around an oval track, oblivious to the early spring chill in shorts and sleeveless tee-shirts.

Classes had been out for a few hours by now and not many cars were to be seen. Bettina cruised past rows of empty spaces marked off with lines of white paint as Pamela swiveled this way and that, searching for a flash of bright red.

"Faculty and staff parking!" she exclaimed suddenly. "That way!" She had spotted a sign.

Faculty and staff parking was in the short leg of the L-shaped lot, hidden by the jutting wing of a building. Once Bettina turned the corner, they could see the school's main entrance, with a few wide steps leading to a set of wide glass doors. The faculty and staff lot contained more cars, presumably belonging to people who worked a regular eight-hour day, as well as faculty whose schedules involved after-school responsibilities.

Just as Pamela spotted the red Fiat, one of the glass doors at the head of the steps swung back and a girl carrying a black nylon case that looked like it housed a musical instrument emerged, followed by a few more students, some with instrument cases, some without.

"I think we're on the right track," Bettina commented as she cruised slowly past the Fiat and then slipped into an empty parking space a few rows away.

Soon their patience was rewarded. On the heels of another batch of students, a dashing middle-aged man strolled into the sunlight and descended the steps. He chatted with a few students, continued on across the asphalt until he reached the red Fiat, and climbed in. Bettina waited until the Fiat had disappeared around the corner of the building's jutting wing and then twisted her key in the ignition to bring the Toyota's engine to life.

Following at a discreet distance, she and Pamela trailed Nate Riddle through a neighborhood of humble houses situated on scruffy lawns, which gave way to a stretch of small apartment buildings interspersed with fast-food places, gas stations, and convenience stores. He turned onto the one-way street that ran through Haversack's main commercial district and they drove past restaurants offering takeout menus featuring everything from pizza to empanadas to stir-fry. Gradually, as they neared the north end of the commercial district, fancier restaurants took the place of takeout, as well as a photo studio, a jewelry store, an artisanal bakery, an antique shop, and other enterprises aimed at more upscale patrons.

The Fiat slowed as it neared a cross street, its turn signal began to blink, and it disappeared around the corner. Bettina followed. By the time she caught up with it, the Fiat was parked in front of a shop whose wide front window announced "Interiors by Alice" in an elegant script. Visible through the glass were a pair of wing chairs upholstered in a tasteful striped fabric. Nate Riddle was standing on the sidewalk.

The shop's door opened and a woman rushed out and into Nate Riddle's arms. She was dark-haired and willowy, dressed in a belted trench coat that seemed made of burgundy patent leather. Her striking features were accented with dramatic eye makeup and copious lipstick in the same burgundy shade as the coat—and as glossy. Despite the lipstick, they kissed, for a long time, after which Nate opened the passenger-side door of the Fiat and helped the woman in.

"I guess that answers that," Bettina commented. The Toyota had slowed to a crawl. Now it sped up and they were on their way again. "He had a real girl-friend."

"Do you think she's the person Mr. Nap Year saw?" Pamela asked. "The person who he thought looked like me?"

"Of course," Bettina said. "She's tall and thin and she has dark hair. And you could look just like that if you paid more attention to clothes and makeup."

Pamela wasn't sure she would like to look just like Nate Riddle's girlfriend—Alice?—though she had to admit the makeup and the dramatic coat made for a striking effect.

"What's the next step then?" she inquired as Bettina clicked on her turn signal and prepared to turn at the next corner. Their pursuit of the Fiat had led them quite a distance from Arborville.

"Figure out what the girlfriend was doing last Friday, of course," Bettina said, "specifically between one thirty and one forty-five."

Pamela laughed. "That satisfied smile tells me you have a plan."

"I do." Bettina nodded, and the smile became broader. She swung the steering wheel violently to the left and the Toyota careened around the corner.

Pamela suppressed a squeal.

"What are you doing tomorrow morning?" Bettina asked, bearing down on the next corner with turn signal still ticking.

"Shopping for new curtains?"

"Really?" Bettina took her eyes off the road and turned toward Pamela, a creased brow transforming her smile from satisfied to puzzled. "That's such a co-incidence—because I was just going to suggest—" From behind them came an insistent honking.

"Bettina . . ." Pamela laid a hand on her friend's arm. "Please just drive, or pull over, or something. Neither of us will be thinking about new curtains for quite a while if we end up in the hospital."

But once Bettina had made her second turn, they found themselves on a sparsely traveled residential street, and talking while driving became less challenging.

"I was going to suggest," Bettina continued, but her voice trailed off when Pamela began to laugh.

"I was teasing you," Pamela said. "I knew what you were going to suggest. We show up at Interiors by Alice tomorrow and see what we can find out about who was on duty in the shop last week."

"That *is* what I was going to suggest. I admit it's pretty obvious, but you didn't need to laugh."

"I'm sorry," Pamela said. "It's a good idea and I think we should do it. There's just one thing though . . . Detective Clayborn has turned out to be cleverer than we suspected—talking to Mr. Nap Year, for example. I'd be surprised if he hasn't already talked to the girl-friend—and since he hasn't arrested her, he must have dismissed her as a suspect. I'm sure he interviewed the old boyfriend, and the old boyfriend must have told him about her, based on the encounter I saw outside Caleb's Table. The old boyfriend saw the girlfriend at the cemetery and decided that Nate was a deceitful schemer. Of course he'd want to tattle to the police."

"Umm." Bettina tightened her lips into a thoughtful line. "Yes, yes, he would want to tattle. But Clayborn wouldn't follow up on the lovers' triangle within a lovers' triangle idea because the old boyfriend wouldn't have said that Nate was really in love with Isobel. So Clayborn wouldn't see the girlfriend having a reason to be jealous. And I don't think it would occur to him that Isobel could have been killed to liberate a hefty in-heritance that the girlfriend planned to share."

"But it occurred to us," Pamela said. "And given that the girlfriend was very likely the person Mr. Nap Year saw going into the back door of the rec center, I think we're definitely onto something."

They were silent then, as Bettina steered the Toyota back through Haversack's commercial district and then over the bridge that spanned the Haversack River. When they were cruising along County Road, Bettina spoke.

"So," she said, "tomorrow morning we go shopping for curtains at Interiors by Alice. Shall I pick you up at ten?"

"Tomorrow morning at ten." After a moment, Pamela added, "We need a plan. We can't just walk in, accost that woman, and ask her where she was last Friday afternoon."

"I'll think of something." Bettina sounded confident. "I always do."

Pamela smiled to herself, imagining Bettina preparing for the next morning's errand with the dedication of an actor preparing for a challenging role.

CHAPTER 15

It was nearly six p.m. by the time Pamela unlocked her door and stepped over her threshold. Catrina and Ginger, having responded to the sound of the key in the lock, were already sitting on the carpet, eyes lifted hopefully toward their mistress. Precious arrived as Pamela was slipping out of her coat.

Once the cats were contentedly hunched over their bowls in the corner that was their dining area, Pamela turned to the question of her own dinner. She set a pot of water to boil for pasta and sautéed chopped onion and garlic in a wide frying pan. When the onion was fragrant and translucent, she added the Italian sausage she had bought on her last trip to the Co-Op, breaking it up with a metal spoon as it browned. The last step, when the sausage was thoroughly cooked, was to pour in a jar of ready-made Italian spaghetti sauce.

When the water was bubbling vigorously, she slipped a generous fistful of spaghetti into the pot and nudged it with a wooden spoon until the strands separated and submerged. While the pasta was cooking she made a tomato and cucumber salad and set out a bowl of grated parmesan.

Fifteen minutes later, she was sitting at her kitchen table as contented with her own dinner as the cats had been with theirs.

Pamela knew her boss never slept. Saturday morning brought new evidence of that fact. Pamela herself had stayed up later than usual reading about the paradox of women's work in the Shaker communities, and thus it had been nearly midnight when she gave her email one last check before climbing into bed.

The only message in her inbox had been a note from her alma mater advising her that the New York City chapter would be holding a networking mixer on the last Friday in April. And yet here, at barely eight a.m. on Saturday morning, was an email from Celine Bramley requesting that she copyedit the article on Civil War quilts and return it by Tuesday morning, along with the review of *Shaker Communities and the Feminist Sensibility: The Paradox of Women's Work.*

Pamela opened her front door a few hours later to greet a smiling Bettina. "It's official," she announced. "I suppose you saw the article in the *Register* this morning—with Marcy Brewer's byline, and I suppose Miss Smarty Pants thinks she was the first to know."

"The medical examiner's report?" Pamela swung the door back and Bettina stepped inside.

During the night a warm front had arrived, and when Pamela fetched the newspaper she had noticed a springlike feel in the air. But Bettina's wardrobe was prepared for climatic vicissitudes. Today she was wearing a white canvas jacket in a military style, belted over a pale-pink turtleneck and matching skirt, with pink knee-high boots below. Chunky pink crystal earrings dangled from her earlobes, but her bright lipstick was the same scarlet as her hair.

"Nothing we weren't already aware of," Bettina said. "No evidence there was any weapon—except for the corner of the desk that her head hit on the way down."

As it turned out, Bettina didn't need to draw on her acting talents at Interiors by Alice.

"Good morning, ladies!" A statuesque woman with silvery hair coaxed into a smooth twist greeted them as they entered the shop. "What can I do for you?"

Bettina took the lead, gazing appreciatively at the window treatments displayed against the back wall: window shades of every kind and draperies ranging from elegant to austere. A round table held stacks of decorating magazines, and shelves at the far end of the room were crowded with bulky wallpaper sample books, identified by notations on their spines as "Classy Country," "Old-Fashioned Florals," "Modern Vibes," and the like.

Two women sat at the round table poring over an open magazine. One of them was the woman who had dashed out of the shop and into the arms of Nate Riddle. Her hair, dark and shoulder-length, was carefully waved, and her makeup was as dramatic as it had been the previous evening. She was wearing a form-fitting sheath in a streaky print that mingled black with tones of rose and burgundy.

"I'm in the market for some new curtains," Bettina said, focusing nonetheless on the woman who had greeted them. "It looks like I've come to the right place, and . . . are you Alice? Or maybe . . . ?" Her eyes strayed to the women at the table.

"Oh, no." The woman laughed. "I'm Alice. Linette Nesbitt is my assistant, when she's here."

"Bettina Fraser." Bettina held out her hand and Alice shook it. "Now what I was thinking . . ." Bettina fingered her chin. "My color scheme is basically green and brown, but that can get so dull . . ."

"What room are we talking about?" Alice inquired.

As Bettina responded, Pamela wandered toward the round table. She picked up a magazine, paged through it for a moment, and then eased herself into the nearest chair. Pamela had enjoyed furnishing and decorating her house, though her taste ran to refurbished thrift-store finds and do-it-yourself sewing projects rather than the conspicuously expensive effects documented in the glossy pages of the magazine she'd chosen. But it was tempting to imagine, just for a moment, what life would be like in one of these perfect dwellings— for example, the beachfront getaway featured in the magazine's lead article, which was decorated in sun-kissed tones that harmonized with the views of sea and sand offered by its huge windows.

But while Pamela was browsing through the maga-zine, she was also listening to the conversation going on across the table. The woman Linette was conferring with seemed in search of an upholstered chair, a wing chair, to replicate a look she admired in the magazine she and Linette were studying. Linette explained that such a chair could easily be supplied. A custom upholsterer was at the beck and call of Interiors by Alice. The woman needed merely to pick the exact chair shape from a catalogue and specify the fabric she wished.

"This sort of fabric," the woman said, pointing to the page. From where Pamela was sitting, the fabric looked like satiny pink and white stripes embellished with fleur-de-lis.

"I'll get a sample book," Linette said, standing up. She circled the table and headed for the counter where Bettina and Alice were huddled over a catalogue, leaving a drift of exotic perfume behind as her stiletto heels clicked across the floor.

"Alice?" she called as she got closer. "Did we get those new sample books from HomeFab yet?"

"Excuse me," Pamela heard Alice say. She met up with Linette halfway between where Pamela sat and where Bettina stood. Speaking in an undertone, she said, "The new HomeFab samples came a week ago, on Friday, which you'd know if you'd been here, and they're on the top shelf in the office. Come with me." She gripped Linette by the elbow and led her toward a door in the back wall.

With a smile and nod at the woman searching for the perfect wing chair, Pamela relinquished the seductive magazine and joined Bettina at the counter.

Bettina picked up the fabric sample book in front of her and, one by one, turned back the swatches of fabric until she reached one that blended peach tones with dark green in an abstract print.

"I think I really will replace the living room curtains," she said. "How do you like this? Something a little more modern than what I have now."

"Nice." Pamela nodded. "The green is darker than the green of the sofa, but the contrast could be interesting."

Alice emerged from the door through which she and Linette had vanished. Linette followed her out, carrying a large fabric sample book, and headed back to the round table.

"Honestly!" Alice exclaimed, but in a whisper. "If it weren't that she does so well with the clients, that woman would be off the payroll in an instant. Unpredictable might as well be her middle name."

Bettina allowed the swatches that preceded her favored one to fall back into place. They landed with a soft thud. "Really?" she said. "That must make it hard for you to run your business. Never knowing if your assistant is going to be on hand or not."

Alice leaned closer. She had the regular features and wide-set eyes of a woman who had probably been quite beautiful in her youth. Now her skin was lined but well-tended, and the hint of makeup she wore was flattering, as was the soft cornflower-blue shade of her sweater.

"She's in love, you know." Her tone implied a certain ironic detachment. "And nobody else has ever been in love or could possibly imagine what it's like." She raised her brows and the irony became more pronounced.

"Head in the clouds, I suppose." Bettina smiled a small, knowing smile. "Love does that to people."

"But, as I said, she does very well with the clients." Alice nodded toward where Linette was displaying a swatch from the sample book she had gone in quest of. The woman searching for the perfect wing chair was nodding rapturously. "And it doesn't hurt that she projects such a chic appearance."

"No, that wouldn't hurt," Bettina agreed. She consulted her watch, a gold bracelet watch with a pretty face. "This has been so helpful." She reached out to touch Alice's arm. "I'm going to consult my sweet husband—though I'm sure he'll have no objections—and I'll be back with some photos and measurements of the windows, and we can get to work."

Once they had settled back into the car, Bettina turned to Pamela. "It seems pretty clear," she said. "We have found our killer. Linette is desperately in love with Nate Riddle—as if the passionate kiss hadn't already established that, she fits the description of the woman Mr. Nap Year saw going into the back door of the rec center, and she was missing from her post at Interiors by Alice on St. Patrick's Day."

"What do we do now?" Pamela asked.

"I'll probably be meeting with Clayborn Monday or Tuesday. He likes to make sure something about what the police are up to goes into the *Advocate* every week, just to make people think the police are earning their tax-payer funded salaries. Sometimes it's nothing more than an update on street closings for sewer repairs."

"So you'll tell him you've solved Isobel's murder?"

"He wouldn't take kindly to that." Bettina laughed. "I'll just plant a seed in his mind."

"What kind of a seed?"

"I'm not sure yet." Bettina inserted her key in the Toyota's ignition and twisted. With a groan and a rumble the engine came to life.

As Bettina retraced the route that had brought them to Interiors by Alice, she mused about having her two living room armchairs reupholstered to coordinate with the new curtains.

"Maybe peach," she murmured. "Or rust."

"You're really going to get new curtains?" Pamela said. "I thought you just told Alice that so we could see what we could learn about Linette."

"At first that was my plan." Bettina nodded. "But I liked Alice and . . . why not? Those curtains have been up since Wilfred Jr. was a baby."

The conversation veered to other topics then—the book Pamela was reviewing for *Fiber Craft*, the surprising change in the weather, and plans for Easter. They had left Haversack's commercial district behind and were cruising past the park near the bridge that led to County Road, when Pamela twitched in her seat.

"I just thought of something!" she exclaimed, interrupting Bettina's description of the chocolate rabbits she had already bought for her grandsons' Easter baskets.

"What?" Bettina seemed startled but kept her eyes on the road, perhaps recalling the fright her driving had given Pamela the previous day.

"Linette might not really be the killer."

"Why?" Bettina sounded more skeptical than curious.

"Her perfume was very noticeable," Pamela said. "At least, I certainly noticed it."

"I did too. It smelled expensive." Bettina swung into the left turn that took them onto the bridge.

"Did you smell perfume when you were in the doorway of the green room taking those pictures?"

"No, I didn't." Bettina's lips tightened into an annoyed zigzag. "Maybe I won't plant that seed after all."

Work for the magazine awaited Pamela when she returned home. A Saturday afternoon might normally have been devoted to chores like housecleaning and laundry, but the deadline for the book review had been moved up to Tuesday morning, and the copyedited Civil War quilt article was due then as well. So, after a quick pot roast sandwich, Pamela settled down in her customary spot at the end of the sofa and picked up *Shaker Communities and the Feminist Sensibility: The Paradox of Women's Work.*

She read steadily, making notes for her review and standing up occasionally to stretch her legs, until a bit after five. Because of her date with Pete Paterson, the cats would be fed earlier than usual, but she didn't think they would mind. Indeed, they didn't. Leaving them engrossed in savoring chicken-fish medley, which they all seemed to like, Pamela went upstairs and opened her closet.

A casual date with a local handyman, albeit for dinner on a Saturday night, called for a casual outfit—not that Pamela's wardrobe yielded many outfits that weren't casual. From a stack of sweaters on the closet shelf she took one that had been a favorite knitting project some years earlier. The combination of extra-large needles and a fine alpaca blend yarn had created a loose, almost lacy texture that suited the yarn's deep forest-green hue and the style, cowl-necked with a blousy shape.

A fresh pair of jeans and brown loafers completed the ensemble. Downstairs, she took a lightweight jacket from the closet and stepped into the kitchen to check on the cats. Catrina and Ginger had emptied their bowl but Precious, whose manners were more genteel, was still lingering over her meal. The doorbell's chime drew Pamela back to the entry, where she opened her door to greet Pete Paterson.

CHAPTER 16

A sleek black Porsche was parked in front of Pamela's house. The man standing on Pamela's porch was wearing a sports jacket whose precise tailoring and luxurious fabric testified to its expense. Beneath the jacket, a dark-hued turtleneck that could only have been cashmere topped a pair of slim wool slacks.

"Hello!" Pamela tried to conceal her surprise.

"Ready?" Pete Paterson gestured toward the car waiting at the curb. Noticing the jacket she was holding, he reached for it, asking, "May I?"

"Yes, uh, sure." Pamela backed up, nearly losing her balance. As he joined her in the entry, she thrust the jacket at him, suddenly aware of its comparative shabbiness. He held it out and she slipped her arms into the sleeves, collected her purse and her keys, and stepped across the threshold as he stood aside to let her pass.

"I have a place in mind," he said as he maneuvered the Porsche away from the curb and steered it toward County Road. "If you don't mind a little drive—but it's a pretty drive, along the Hudson, and you like old buildings so I think you'll like the restaurant."

"Sure," Pamela said. "I don't mind a drive."

Despite clouds in the west stained red and gold with sunset, the sky overhead was clear, and lengthening days had drawn the evening into spring.

The route lay toward Timberley, tacking east then, until they were speeding along the parkway that skirted the Hudson heading north. The ride was smooth and quiet, and Pete drove with easy grace and obvious enjoyment. Headlights of cars headed south flashed by. The river, visible through the branches of trees not yet in leaf, was dark and still, beneath a blue evening haze. On the opposite bank pinpricks of light marked out scattered buildings.

"You know what I do for a living," Pete had said once the journey was underway. "What about you?"

So the conversation had been easy, with Pamela describing her work for *Fiber Craft* and some of the noteworthy articles she'd encountered.

"Did you know the Virgin Mary was a knitter?" she asked with a laugh.

"Really?" Pete laughed too. "Well, they did have sheep in the Holy Land."

"Yes," Pamela said. "They did, but I think mostly they wove the wool." And she described the painting in which Mary was depicted in a way that would encourage medieval viewers to identify with her.

"You must be constantly learning new things," Pete commented.

"Well, yes—and then there are the Shakers . . . I'm reviewing a book."

Pete, it turned out, was an admirer of Shaker craftsmanship, and for the next several minutes he described a visit he'd made to a restored Shaker village. As they neared an upcoming exit, he interrupted himself to say, "Here we are." He clicked on his turn signal and veered onto a narrow road that descended in hairpin curves to form the main street of a quaint town perched right on the riverbank.

As they drove past a sturdy pink sandstone building that faced the water, Pete said, "When we were still a colony, people crossing the river landed here and continued on their way to whatever." A long wooden pier not far from the house indicated that river activities were still a feature of the town. "Later the town was a summer getaway for rich people fleeing the Manhattan heat, so you'll see some Victorian houses too."

Pete steered the Porsche slowly past charming storefronts whose architecture reflected more recent eras, some with shop windows alight, others dark. There was more than one antique store, an art gallery, a cheese shop, a candle shop, a bakery offering artisanal bread. Clearly the town's inhabitants shopped elsewhere for most of their staples. Pete slowed down as the road surface disintegrated to gravel, and he turned left to steer the car up a slight incline.

"This is it," he said, and turned into a lot where several other cars had already parked.

Facing the lot, and looking out over the river from the vantage point of a small hill, was a splendid house with a wraparound porch, a steeply pitched roof, and a turret. It was built of wood, sheathed with a combination of clapboard and fish-scale shingles, and painted a shade of deep amber that seemed to glow in the twilight. A wooden sign hanging over the steps leading to the porch read "L'Auberge" in a flowing script that could have come from a penmanship manual.

Inside, the first impression was of dark paneled walls and an atmosphere that combined welcoming warmth with aromas promising delicious flavors to come. An attractive middle-aged woman stepped from behind a tall wooden hostess station and greeted them, Pete specifically, in French. He responded, also in French, and after a brief back-and-forth chat, he introduced Pamela to the hostess, and proprietress, Luce Chantilly.

A wide arch led from the dark entry to a larger, brighter room, crowded with tables and looking out toward the river.

"This one is noisy," Luce said, "but in here there are not so many people yet." She took a step toward another wide arch, accompanying it with a welcoming gesture.

They were seated, then, in a room where a low fire flickered in a fireplace surrounded by a carved wooden mantel. Wainscoting that seemed a continuation of the mantel covered the bottom third of the walls, with floral wallpaper above. A candle protected by a blown-glass chimney shed light on a white linen tablecloth starched to stiff perfection. Only one other table in the room was occupied.

Luce turned to leave then, after providing them with menus and assuring them that a waiter would arrive momentarily with the wine that Pete had requested. But she turned back before she'd retreated more than a few feet.

"We have those oysters you like," she said. "The ones from Long Island."

Pete had opened his menu but he looked up, not at Luce but at Pamela.

"I guess you're a regular here," Pamela commented.

Pete's expression was hard to read, but it featured a

teasing smile, half suppressed, that eased the melancholy of his eyes. "I was, once." He dipped his head in acknowledgment. "You're wondering, I suppose, how often a handyman can afford to splurge on oysters—from Long Island, or anywhere for that matter."

"I am wondering." Pamela lowered her menu and leaned forward.

"I wasn't always a handyman." Pete smiled. "Let's leave it at that for now. First things first: Do you like oysters? And I can recommend the coq au vin."

Wine arrived then, in a silvery ice bucket, on a stand pulled up to the side of the table.

The menu listed many dishes, most described in French terms that Pamela didn't recognize. She was happy to take Pete's advice and order oysters and coq au vin, though the number of times she'd eaten raw oysters could have been counted on the fingers of one hand.

"That's settled then," Pete said, as a waiter poured a splash of wine the color of pale straw for him to approve. The wine glasses were huge, their delicate bowls poised atop slender stems. Pete sipped judiciously and then nodded, and the waiter turned his attention to Pamela, tilting the bottle over her glass until the glass was a third full. The wine shimmered and glowed in the refracted candlelight.

Once the order had been placed and the waiter had departed, Pete raised his glass in a wordless toast and both drank. The wine was crisp but not unpleasantly so.

"Chosen with oysters in mind," Pete explained.

Pamela wasn't sure how to respond, never having contemplated the proper sort of wine to serve with oysters. So she introduced a new topic.

"You said your son is at college in Boston?" Pete nodded, and Pamela went on. "Do you get up there often?"

He nodded again. "Boston is a good town. I used to spend a lot of time there for work." With a small intake of breath that sounded like "oops," he compressed his lips and said, "No point in bringing that up though."

The oysters arrived then, nestled in beds of crushed ice on broad trays. Pamela contemplated the tray that had been set before her. Six raw oysters looked up at her, lying in their rugged bottom shells with a tiny fork nearby. The oysters were arranged in a circle around a few small cups containing sauces, and lemon quarters were tucked here and there.

Pamela picked up the tiny fork, which was cold to the touch from contact with the ice. She squeezed lemon juice on the closest oyster, speared it with the fork, and transported it to her mouth. It was cold too, and briny, and it slipped easily down her throat.

"Good?" Pete smiled at her from across the table.

The smile was sweetly attentive, but the candlelight lent his face an air of mystery, enhanced by the hint of melancholy in his eyes—or was the air of mystery merely her own projection, given that Pete Paterson now appeared to be something other than what he had initially seemed?

Yes, the oysters were good, but the appeal of raw oysters on the half shell was another, albeit more pedestrian, mystery to ponder. Perhaps it was the way they evoked the ocean, bringing to mind the fresh tang of salty ocean air. Or perhaps it was just that since they were generally served as a first course, a person dining on raw oysters was guaranteed to be very hungry and craving tidbits of concentrated protein.

"A penny for your thoughts," came a voice from across the table.

"Returning to the topic of Boston," Pamela said (for some reason she was unwilling to share her meditation on the appeal of raw oysters), "they certainly love their seafood up there."

"Indeed they do," Pete responded, and he seemed happy to elaborate on that theme as they both worked their way through their oysters.

By the time the waiter returned to claim the platters, littered with empty oyster shells and nubbins of squeezed lemon quarters, the conversation had veered north, to Maine and lobster territory, not to mention clambakes. Pete was happily describing a vacation with friends where he had been tasked with gathering seaweed for the project.

When the coq au vin arrived, Pamela wondered whether they should now discuss the best states in which to eat chicken. But first the dish itself deserved comment. The fowl had been braised with mushrooms and pearl onions in red wine. The result was a rich sauce the color of dark amber that mingled flavors of chicken and wine with the earthiness of mushrooms and the bouquet of thyme and parsley. The generous serving shared a plate with a small mound of rice and a leafy green vegetable.

"This is perfect!" Pamela exclaimed after her first bite.

"The chickens the chef uses are local," Pete said. "Running around outside just like they lived in a French farmyard."

A bottle of red wine had appeared with the main course, and the white wine had been whisked away, ice bucket and all. The combination of the sumptuous food, the second glass of wine, and the gracious surroundings had induced in Pamela a feeling of intense well-being. The fire, visible just past where Pete was sitting, maintained a steadily flickering glow, while murmured conversations and the subdued clink of cutlery against china provided a soothing backdrop to the conversation taking place over the coq au vin—currently focused on the surprising variety of food offered by the Co-Op.

"I only started doing my own grocery shopping recently," Pete said, after both had agreed that the bakery counter offered many temptations. "Before last year, my wife . . ." His voice trailed off and he suddenly became interested in freeing a bite of chicken from the bone it was attached to.

The conversations taking place at the surrounding tables only made Pete's abrupt silence more striking. As the silence threatened to stretch on, Pamela ransacked her brain for a new topic. Her plate was nearly empty by the time she looked up and observed brightly, "You must have seen the insides of a lot of houses in Arborville."

Pete looked up too, with a startled expression. Catching on that her motive was simply to ease an awkward interlude, he smiled.

"I haven't been at it—the handyman thing—that long, but I'm getting work. My customers seem pleased and they spread the word."

"Do you specialize in any particular sort of projects?" Pamela asked, pleased that her conversational gambit had been successful.

"No job too big or too small." The waiter was hovering nearby. Both plates were empty by now, Pete acknowledged him with a discreet nod, and he swept in to take the plates away. "Big is better though," Pete went on. "I've got two more years of my son's tuition to pay and my daughter starts college a year from this fall."

When Pamela didn't speak—she was unsure of an appropriate response—Pete laughed and added, "You're thinking I'm going to have to repair a lot of screens."

Penny's college expenses were being covered by money from Michael Paterson's life insurance policy. Pamela couldn't imagine how she would manage on her own income—though perhaps a handyman could make more than an associate editor of *Fiber Craft* magazine. Still . . .

Just then the waiter reappeared with menus, and the suggestion that madame and monsieur might like to finish their meal with coffee and dessert. Pamela stared at her menu, bemused by the realization that this meal would probably cost Pete all the money she had paid him for his work on her screens and then some.

"I can recommend the tarte Tatin," came his voice from across the table, "and would you like coffee?"

"Yes, yes." Pamela roused herself from her meditations. "That sounds good."

"The thing is," Pete said after the waiter took the order for two tarte Tatins and two coffees and departed, "I wasn't always a handyman. But I told you that." Though he wasn't exactly smiling, his expression hinted at suppressed amusement.

"What were you?"

"I was a Wall Street guy, playing around with money to the point that it became totally abstract—up so much today, down so much tomorrow, but there was always plenty. There still is, but I don't have my wife anymore because I was never home."

A silvery coffee pot appeared at the edge of Pamela's field of vision. A hand clutching its handle guided it toward a coffee cup that another hand had set in front of her. Dark, fragrant liquid filled the cup and the silvery pot retreated, only to repeat the motion on the other side of the table.

"I always liked to fix things," Pete explained. "And when we first bought the Arborville house I fixed things—just the way you described you and your husband doing. But the Wall Street money was so seductive, and I was good at my Wall Street job, and I got busier and busier . . ."

"And you're happier now?" Pamela said. "Being a handyman?"

"Yes." He nodded. "I'm happier now. I turned back into myself."

He looked up. The waiter was advancing with two plates.

The tarte Tatin proved to be basically an apple upside-down cake. Wilfred had made something like it once, Pamela thought. It was thin, just a buttery crust like a shortbread, with apple slices overlapping in concentric circles on top like the petals of a very large flower—a flower bathed in amber syrup. Each slice, elegantly narrow, was garnished with a ridge of thick, not too sweet, cream.

The meal ended pleasantly then, lingering before the fireplace in the welcoming room, sipping the coffee that was the perfect balance to the tarte, with its rich crust, caramelized apples, and cream.

*   *   *

Nearly an hour later, Pamela and Pete were standing on Pamela's porch, thanking each other for a wonderful evening, while the Porsche—which made more sense now that Pamela understood the handyman job to be Pete's second career—waited at the curb.

"I hope you'll remember me for all your home repair needs," Pete said in a half-joking tone.

"No job too big or too small," Pamela quoted back.

"And," he added, taking her hand, "maybe you'd like to do this again sometime, sometime soon?"

"I would," Pamela said.

The evening had left her with a lot to think about, but Pamela slept soundly, very soundly. She woke up staring into the amber eyes of Catrina, who had awakened first and made her way beneath the bedclothes to perch on Pamela's chest with just her head emerging from the sheet. Ginger soon followed, and the morning ritual of cat food, coffee, toast, and newspaper commenced.

The rest of the day looked to be equally predictable, since Pamela still had a quarter of *Shaker Communities and the Feminist Sensibility: The Paradox of Women's Work* to read and then the review to at least get started on. Before sitting down with the book, though, as soon as she was dressed she took her jacket from the closet, bade goodbye to the cats, and set out on a walk.

On this day, she walked down Orchard Street rather than up, and crossed County Road to ramble toward the nature preserve. There she spent an invigorating hour roaming over the remains of the leaves that had fallen the previous autumn, now decayed to a compost that gave off an earthy, organic aroma when disturbed. She zigzagged among trees whose branches formed a bare, cross-hatched canopy against the sky.

Back at home, she parked herself at the end of the sofa and took up the book.

The words stared back at Pamela from her computer screen: "Among utopian communities, perhaps the most . . ."

The most what? She asked herself. Reading the book about the Shakers had been an enjoyable experience, and it had even led to an interesting conversation with Pete Paterson. But writing the review was a different story. She had only positive things to say, but how to distill into five hundred or even fewer words the thoughts whirling about in her head? At least, given the fact that the book was nonfiction, she didn't have to worry about including details that might necessitate a spoiler alert!

Perhaps the most . . . contradictory? Shouldn't a true utopia erase rigid gender distinctions? She keyed in "contradictory" and pondered the effect.

Or maybe "traditional"?

She was just about to delete "contradictory" and replace it with "traditional" when she was startled by the shrill ring of the telephone on the table at her elbow.

"Are you busy right now?" Bettina asked, without waiting for Pamela to say hello.

"Sort of," Pamela said, "but I don't have to be." Sometimes it was better to let ideas percolate before trying to write them down. "Why?"

"I was browsing around on AccessArborville looking for people complaining about the ban on plastic bags—my editor wants a story on it." In the background Pamela could hear Wilfred announcing that he and Woofus were leaving for a walk.

"And?" Pamela's gaze wandered back to the words on the computer screen. Should she even refer to the Shakers as a utopian community? That hadn't been the author's main point.

"The woman who thinks a knitting ghost is haunting the cemetery posted again just a few minutes ago."

When Pamela didn't answer right away Bettina said, "Are you still there?"

"Yes, yes," Pamela said. "I was thinking about something else."

"Well, think about this," Bettina instructed. "The ghost finished what she was knitting and now it's draped over Isobel Lister's tombstone. Kind of like a shroud, according to the post, a white shroud."

"So I guess the ghost wasn't a ghost."

"Or the shroud is just a ghost shroud—a figment of this woman's imagination. She didn't go up to the cemetery to actually examine the shroud. She said she was too scared."

"A cemetery can be a spooky place," Pamela said. "I certainly wouldn't want to go up there alone to look at a ghost shroud."

"You won't be alone!" Bettina exclaimed. "There will be two of us. If the shroud is real, this is a much more interesting story than the town's reactions to the ban on plastic bags. And don't you see? The shroud is draped over Isobel Lister's tombstone. So it could be related to her murder. It could lead us to her killer."

"Why would her killer do something that obvious?" Pamela asked. "And a knitting ghost haunting the cemetery sounds like someone mourning her. Why would the person who killed her be mourning her?"

"Those are good questions," Bettina said, "and the first step in answering them is to see this shroud in person."

CHAPTER 17

"I'm ready for that gravel parking lot this time."
Standing on Pamela's porch, Bettina extended a foot
shod in a bright red sneaker. "Just as I predicted, my
good suede pumps were totally destroyed by that walk
from the car to Isobel's gravesite on Wednesday." She
headed for the steps leading down to Pamela's front
walk. "Come on," she urged. "I can't wait to see what
we're going to find."

Bettina had nosed the Toyota into Pamela's driveway and, carried away with excitement, had left its
motor running. She barely waited for Pamela to close
her door before shifting into reverse, jerking the steering wheel violently to the right, and backing out onto
Orchard Street. She shifted into drive and with a lurch
the Toyota took off for the corner. Wilfred and Woofus
were headed down Orchard Street on their way home
from their walk. Pamela saw them and waved but Bettina was oblivious.

"I just hope," she muttered as she waited for a break in the traffic that would allow the Toyota to make the turn onto Arborville Avenue, "I just hope that some busybody on AccessArborville hasn't beaten us to the cemetery."

"What would they do?" Pamela inquired.

"Why, take it, of course. Take the shroud as some kind of spooky souvenir, even though it doesn't belong to them." She pressed down on the gas and the Toyota sprinted into a perilous left turn that caused an oncoming van to honk.

"But aren't we going to take it?" Pamela inquired.

"No!" Bettina tossed her head vigorously, setting the scarlet tendrils of her coiffure in motion. "We're going to photograph it, just as it is. I picture a photograph with a moody feel, other tombstones in the background and one lonely tombstone in the foreground, with this . . . knitted shroud . . . draped over it, a touching tribute to a beloved daughter of a family with deep, deep roots in Arborville. The black sheep comes home . . . to tragedy, but she will never be forgotten." She paused. "That could be the headline."

They were passing the Co-Op now, and Bettina was silent. She didn't speak again until they had climbed the hill that formed the backside of the cliffs overlooking the Hudson and were approaching the cemetery's ancient iron gates. Beyond the gates lay the cemetery's gravel parking lot and the cemetery itself.

"The light looks good for a photo, don't you think?" she commented. "I'll have the sun behind me and it's late enough that the tombstones will cast long shadows. Very atmospheric." It was nearing five p.m. and a few hours remained until sunset.

The Toyota crunched over the gravel. No other cars were in the lot and Bettina was able to pull up right to the edge where the cemetery's grass began.

"We had to walk quite a ways to the gravesite, as I recall," Pamela commented as she climbed out of the car, "past those really old tombstones, and some of the graves where other Listers are buried."

"It's that way." Bettina pointed. "More or less straight ahead." She took a few steps and then stopped, frowning and squinting as she bobbed her head this way and that. "I'd think we'd be able to see the tombstone with the shroud from here though. That woman who posted on AccessArborville said she could see it from her kitchen window, and she lives way down on the edge of The Farm."

They set out over the ragged grass. The section of the cemetery where the Listers were buried was easy to recognize because the tombstones were so imposing, and they were clustered together as if even in death the family members were loath to mingle with people of uncertain pedigrees. Very soon, hurrying past humbler monuments as she tried to keep up with Bettina—who was usually the one struggling to keep up—Pamela caught sight of the polished granite slab engraved with the words "Isobel Elaine Lister" and the birth and death dates beneath.

And, clearly, no knitted white shroud was in evidence. Only a few wilted flower arrangements remained from the funeral ceremonies.

"There's nothing here," Bettina called over her shoulder.

"I can see that." Pamela had reached her friend's side.

Bettina had been staring bleakly at the unadorned

tombstone. Now she stared bleakly at Pamela. "What shall we do?" she asked.

"Go back home?" Pamela shrugged.

"It might be here, somewhere," Bettina said. "It might have blown away."

"But the point of your photo was going to be that someone placed it on Isobel's grave. If it's just lying in the grass, far from the grave, the connection with the Isobel Lister story is lost."

Pamela's words were wasted. Bettina was off again, scurrying toward a path that led up a slight incline. Pamela followed, but at some remove. The incline leveled off to a plateau bordering a wooded area that marked the cemetery's eastern boundary. Ancient tombstones worn to shapelessness by wind and weather shared the space with a few gnarled trees. Then the grass gave way to land claimed by a dense thicket of trees.

"I think I see something white," Bettina cried, plunging among the trees. "Yes, definitely," she added as she disappeared from view.

From the thicket came a wordless shriek.

"Bettina! What happened?" Pamela called, left panting and breathless the moment the words were uttered. Despite the evening chill, sweat prickled her brow. "Are you okay?"

"I am," Bettina called back. "But somebody isn't."

Stepping into the thicket, Pamela caught sight of Bettina kneeling near the base of an especially large tree. A twisted swath of white, like a knitted scarf or shawl, trailed over the composted leaves, but it was tethered at one end to the neck of a recumbent body. The body was that of a petite, dark-haired woman.

In a moment, Pamela was kneeling at Bettina's side, with one arm around her friend's shoulders.

"She looks so familiar," Bettina moaned. She transferred her gaze to Pamela's face. "I think she was at Caleb's Table after Isobel's funeral. She was wearing that black crepe suit with the tuxedo lapels and the little peplum."

"Bettina"—Pamela sighed—"this is Barb Lister, Isobel's sister-in-law. Of course she was at Caleb's Table after Isobel's funeral. We spoke to her there."

Bettina pointed at the swath of white knitting. "Do you think this is the shroud that the woman who posted on AccessArborville saw?" she asked.

"It could be." Pamela nodded. She was feeling calmer now that the cause of Bettina's shriek had been revealed. At least Bettina was okay. "It *is* white, and it *is* knitted."

She looked closer. The knitted object had been worked in a way that created an interesting pattern, but because of the twists in it and the way it was wrapped around Barb Lister's neck, the details of the pattern were hard to make out.

Pamela certainly didn't want to disturb a crime scene by touching the object, so she stared and stared. Near the lower edge, the part furthest from Barb Lister's neck, she thought she recognized something like a tree, roots reaching down, a sturdy trunk, and branches bearing leaves or fruit rendered in a stitch that looked like small knots.

"So the knitting ghost who was haunting the cemetery was knitting a murder weapon?" Bettina uttered the words in a horrified whisper.

* * *

As soon as Bettina completed her 911 call, Pamela retraced her steps down the incline and past the section of the cemetery where the Lister graves were clustered. Police would be pulling into the cemetery's lot, and someone would need to guide them to the thicket of trees.

It took only a very few minutes for flashing lights and the crunch of tires on gravel to announce the arrival of a police car. The car lurched to a stop and an officer sprang out of the passenger-side door, a burly man that Pamela didn't recognize. The driver's door opened next and Officer Sanchez swung her feet onto the gravel and stood up. She was clearly in charge, despite the delicacy implied by her sweet heart-shaped face, and she beckoned the burly officer to follow as Pamela pointed to indicate the route they would be taking. The three set off across the ragged grass.

They reached Bettina to find her sitting on the ground, leaning against a tree near the one that sheltered Barb Lister's body.

"I'm Pamela Paterson," Pamela said belatedly to the officers, "and this is my friend Bettina Fraser."

The nod of acknowledgment offered by Officer Sanchez was accompanied by the tiniest smile, hinting that the introductions had been unnecessary—at least as far as she was concerned. But in response she said, "I'm Officer Sanchez and"—she gestured toward the burly officer—"this is Officer Keenan."

"It's Barb Lister," Pamela said, "the wife of Isidore Lister. I recognized her from the funeral of Isobel Lister last week."

Meanwhile, Officer Keenan had stooped to peer more closely at Barb Lister. "The victim appears to have been murdered," he reported, "and the murder weapon appears to be a scarf or a shawl. One end is wrapped around her neck."

"Could be a shroud." Bettina spoke from her sitting position.

"How did you two happen to be here?" Officer Sanchez inquired.

"A woman who lives down at the edge of The Farm has been posting on AccessArborville about a supposed knitting ghost haunting the cemetery," Bettina said. She pulled herself to her feet with a grunt. "And this afternoon she posted to say that a knitted shroud had been draped over Isobel Lister's tombstone. So I thought I'd get a photo and do a little write-up for the *Advocate*. Pamela came with me."

As Bettina spoke, Officer Sanchez produced a small notebook and a pen and made a few notes, stopping at one point to double-check the spelling of "Lister."

Officer Keenan rocked back onto his heels and craned his neck to make eye contact with Officer Sanchez. "Call Clayborn?" he asked.

"I'll do it." Officer Sanchez tucked the notepad and pen away and pulled her phone from a pocket in her trousers. "And don't touch anything," she added. "This is a crime scene now." Speaking to Officer Keenan, she said, "Get the tape from the car." Turning her attention to Pamela and Bettina, she said, "Ladies, please move away from the immediate area. But don't *go* away."

Detective Clayborn came lumbering up the incline while the two officers were still stringing the crime-scene tape from tree to tree, its bright yellow creating a curiously decorative effect in contrast with the bleak landscape.

"We have an ID on the victim," Officer Sanchez said, pausing in her work for a moment. "Barb Lister, from town, if Ms. Paterson is correct."

The expression on the detective's homely face was noncommittal, though his glance flickered this way and that, finally landing on Pamela.

"You," he said. "Do I even want to know why you're here?"

It was Bettina who answered. "Whether you want to know or not, I'll tell you. She came up here with me."

"And you came because . . ."

Detective Clayborn too had produced a small notepad and a pen, and the pen moved busily while Bettina spoke. She repeated the explanation she had given to Officer Sanchez, and she added, "When we got to Isobel Lister's grave, nothing was there but some wilted flowers. I thought maybe the shroud blew away, so I went looking for it . . ."

The detective didn't exactly nod, but the explanation seemed to satisfy him, so Bettina let the sentence trail off. Next he turned his attention back to Pamela, but her description of events was no different from Bettina's and he soon tucked the notepad and pen back into the pocket of his shapeless overcoat.

"You two can go now." He shifted his gaze from Pamela to Bettina. "I guess that Toyota in the parking lot belongs to one of you, so you don't need a ride?"

"It's mine," Bettina said.

"We might be in touch again," he said as they started to leave. "So stick around Arborville." His next words were directed at Officer Sanchez. "Get the crime scene people from the county here."

* * *

The Frasers' house smelled of Cajun spices and roux and savory duck. Also cheese—the special aroma of cheese that has escaped the edges of a grilled cheese sandwich and become a crispy, dark golden tidbit to be scraped from a griddle.

"Dear wife! Pamela!" Wilfred, flushed from the stove and wrapped in his favorite apron, met them the moment they stepped through the front door. "I was beginning to worry! Did you get the photo you wanted?"

"Not exactly." Bettina dropped her handbag onto the end of the sofa and reached out her arms. Wilfred obliged with an all-enveloping embrace.

"Dear wife, dear wife," he repeated, breaking the embrace to back up and study Bettina's expression but gripping her arms tightly. "What on earth has happened?"

"We found a body," Bettina said, her voice mournful. "Up in the cemetery. The shroud wasn't on the tombstone but it had been used to strangle Barb Lister and she was lying under a tree."

Wilfred pulled her close once again. Over her shoulder he made eye contact with Pamela, who took up the story, describing the 911 call and the arrival of the officers and Detective Clayborn.

"Well," Wilfred said, loosening his arms from around his wife, "it sounds like you did all you could, and now the situation is in the hands of the redoubtable Lucas Clayborn. And you're both probably very hungry, and so I suggest we all proceed to the kitchen."

The tantalizing fried cheese aroma became more intense the closer they got to the kitchen. Once they entered, the source of the aroma became clear. Sitting in the middle of the scrubbed pine table was an oval basket lined with a linen napkin. Piled on the napkin were thin pastry rounds the color of cheddar cheese, but with a toasty tinge. Their irregular edges and varying sizes identified them as homemade.

"Cheese dibs," Wilfred announced. "That's what my new cookbook, *Great Recipes from Great Southern Chefs*, calls them, though the author says people have been making them in the South forever and there are as many names for them as there are recipes."

Pamela was happy to sink into one of the chairs that surrounded the table, to just sit and collect her thoughts for a few minutes before turning her attention to food. But Wilfred was eager for reactions to his creation.

"Try one, try one," he urged, leaning over to nudge the basket of cheese dibs several inches closer to Pamela. "And you'll want—we'll all want—" He interrupted himself to whirl around more quickly than his girth would suggest was possible. He hopped toward the refrigerator, opened it, and reached inside. "Beer!" he exclaimed, triumphantly displaying a frosty green bottle. "They're quite spicy. You'll see!"

Bettina, who had joined Pamela in a neighboring chair, was already nibbling, but Pamela waited until three tall glasses of beer had appeared on the table and Wilfred was seated too. Then she plucked a cheese dib from the basket and took a bite.

The aroma had not lied. The effect was crispy and intense, like fried melted cheddar, with more than a hint of cayenne. A long sip of the icy-cold beer was a welcome contrast. "Delicious," she breathed.

"Double delicious," Bettina added, not to be outdone.

"Mostly cheese." Wilfred was beaming, obviously pleased with the reaction. "And butter, and cayenne—I think you can taste it—and just the tiniest bit of flour to hold it all together."

He paused to pop a cheese dib whole into his mouth.

"Then you knead it all into a long roll, chill it, and slice it. The slices spread out a little bit while they bake so you can't put them too close together on the baking sheet."

They chatted for a while, avoiding the topic of the adventure at the cemetery, as Wilfred's imperturbable good cheer gradually restored Pamela and Bettina to themselves. He excused himself then, announcing that it was time to put the finishing touches on the evening's pièce de résistance, which was to be ... *Louisiana-style gumbo*.

Circling the end of the high counter, he approached the stove, where he lifted the cover off a large two-handled pot that had been simmering while they were talking, as well as for some time before. Once the cover was off, the distinctive aroma melded from spices, onion, green pepper, duck, and duck broth, with the deep, nearly burnt, undertone of Cajun roux, filled the kitchen.

"About twenty minutes," Wilfred declared from his post at the stove, raising a long-handled wooden spoon for emphasis.

Immediately Bettina was on her feet. "I'll set the dining room table," she said, stepping toward the kitchen doorway.

"Dear wife, dear wife," Wilfred called. "We can eat in the kitchen. Pamela is like family."

"Yes, yes, we can eat in the kitchen," Pamela echoed. "You don't need to be formal on my account."

"I like to be formal!" Bettina halted a few feet from the door and crossed her arms across her chest. "I like to use my pretty things, and after what we went through at the cemetery, sitting at a pretty table is just what we need."

"I'll help then." Pamela rose to her feet.

She could hear behind her the sound of rice cascading into a saucepan as Wilfred murmured, "One cup should do it, and two of water," followed by water rushing from a faucet.

In the dining room, Bettina was kneeling in front of the sideboard where she kept her table linens. Piled on the nearest chair was a tall stack of napkins, various sets in various solid colors and stripes. Sitting on the table was a smaller stack, of placemats, three of them, made of thick dark green velvet.

"I want to use these placemats," Bettina said, "and somewhere in this drawer I have some napkins that I bought when Wilfred and I went to New Orleans, green and purple and gold like those special cakes they make."

She lifted another stack of napkins and handed it up to Pamela, who transferred it to the table. "But they're just . . . they're just . . . I don't know what I did with them." She resumed burrowing in the drawer.

"I'll get the flatware," Pamela said, and retreated toward the kitchen.

"Shrimp is going in," Wilfred said, more to himself than to her as she collected knives, forks, and spoons.

When she returned, with three place settings of Bettina's sleek Scandinavian-inspired stainless, Bettina was still burrowing, and the carpet all around her was littered with napkins and placemats in disarray.

"Could they be upstairs?" Bettina wailed.

Pamela arranged the placemats, one at the head of the table, one at the foot, and one on the side of the table where she was accustomed to sit when it was just the three of them. She was laying out the flatware when she became aware of an unusual sound coming from where Bettina was still kneeling on the floor. It was a whimpering, snuffling sound, and she circled the table to find Bettina with her head nestled on her arms, which were crossed and balanced on the rim of the open drawer.

"What is it? What is it?" she whispered, depositing the rest of the flatware on the table and stooping at Bettina's side.

"I don't understand?" Bettina moaned. "I just don't understand."

Rubbing her friend's back, Pamela said, "They're here somewhere. Green and purple and gold, you said? There's no reason to get so upset about misplaced napkins."

"No, no, no." Bettina lifted her head. From the condition of her eye makeup, it appeared that she'd been crying. "The *murder*. *Murders*. I don't understand. Why would Nate Riddle's girlfriend want to kill Barb Lister?"

CHAPTER 18

"We weren't sure it was her." Pamela continued rubbing Bettina's back. "Remember? The perfume."

Bettina's head drooped forward and her face was hidden by wisps of scarlet hair. "So that means we hadn't actually figured anything out at all, even before we discovered Barb Lister's body. And now it seems we were barking up a blind alley anyway," she moaned, invoking Wilfred's tongue-in-cheek garbling of that old saying.

Wilfred stepped into the room. "Barking up a blind alley is nothing to be ashamed of," he said. "Nothing ventured, nothing gained."

But when Bettina climbed to her feet and turned to face him, his persona shifted from genial giver of advice to concerned husband. "Sweet wife!" he exclaimed. "You've been crying."

He edged around the table, held out his arms, and pulled Bettina close. She buried her head against the apron bib that covered his broad chest, and when she spoke, her voice emerged as a muffled squeak.

"Who killed Isobel Lister then?" she asked, near tears again. "And why did they decide to kill Barb Lister too? She's not even a blood relative."

"No problem was ever solved on an empty stomach," Wilfred declared—never mind that half an hour nibbling on cheese dibs had taken the edge off their hunger. "And so, dear wife"—he gently disentangled himself and looked into Bettina's eyes as he spoke—"why don't you freshen up while Pamela and I put the finishing touches on the table and prepare to serve dinner?"

Nodding in a resigned fashion—perhaps in acknowledgment that the New Orleans napkins were not going to make an appearance that night—Bettina headed for the stairs. Once she was out of sight, Pamela began gathering up the scattered napkins and placemats. She selected three napkins made of a green and cream striped fabric, folded them neatly, and arranged them on the green velvet placemats. Surely Bettina would approve. She then stepped toward the kitchen doorway.

Oval bowls from the sage-green pottery set had been lined up on the counter near the stove, ready to receive the gumbo and rice. Wilfred was standing nearby, slicing a long baguette and piling the slices into a basket lined with a napkin.

"This is an odd development," he observed when he became aware of Pamela's presence.

"Very odd," Pamela agreed. "Someone wanted both of those women dead." She paused for a moment. The bread-slicing was almost complete and then the basket, along with the butter waiting on the high counter, could be delivered to the dining room. "They were Listers, after all, though Barb was a Lister by marriage. So someone with a grudge against the family . . . ?"

"Blood is thicker than water." Wilfred handed her the basket.

Pamela picked up the butter and headed for the dining room. She'd never been quite sure what that saying meant, though she supposed it had to do with families sticking together. And people outside of a family could see the family as a united front, perhaps a threat to something or someone.

Wilfred had apparently been devoting further thought to the mystery while she was doing the bread and butter errand. He began to speak without preamble the moment she returned.

"What if there were two killers?" he said.

"Seems coincidental?" Pamela shrugged.

"Nate Riddle's girlfriend—Linette?—seemed such a likely candidate though. The motive made sense and she fits the description of the woman the florist delivery guy saw going in the back door of the rec center."

"The perfume?"

"Maybe she wasn't wearing any that day. I wouldn't get all fancied up if I was heading out to kill somebody. Would you?"

Pamela laughed. "I hardly ever get all fancied up." But suddenly she found herself staring straight ahead. "Oh, my gosh!" She raised a hand to her mouth. The room had seemed to tilt, and then tilt back, and things were the same but different.

"Maybe the person who killed Barb Lister thought they were killing Linette," she said slowly, "in revenge for Isobel's death. Barb Lister didn't look that different from Linette . . . though I think Linette might be taller."

But before Wilfred could respond, Bettina had reappeared—and as the version of herself that they were most familiar with. Her makeup was flawless and her hair framed her plump cheeks in artful scallops. She had changed into a wide-legged jumpsuit made of silky fabric in a print featuring leopards prowling among giant magenta orchids.

"I absolutely do not want to talk about the case—or *cases*—anymore tonight," she announced. "In fact, I do not want to talk about them ever again. Let Detective Clayborn blunder along as best he can. I want to have a nice, relaxing dinner with my husband and my best friend."

She reached out an arm and gave Pamela an affectionate squeeze. Wilfred, after bending to give Bettina a quick kiss, had returned to his post at the stove and was spooning rice into the bowls he had lined up.

"Salad is in the refrigerator," he said, "all ready except for a big splash of olive oil and a little sprinkle of vinegar. And salt and pepper, of course."

Pamela transferred the salad, which Wilfred had assembled in Bettina's hand-carved wooden salad bowl, from the refrigerator to the scrubbed pine table. The bowl was piled with bite-sized pieces of lettuce, red-leaf and green-leaf, with crisp ruffled edges. She was nearly as familiar with the Frasers' kitchen as they themselves were, and easily located the cruets containing olive oil and balsamic vinegar.

She was dribbling olive oil over the colorful contents of the bowl when the doorbell rang. Wilfred had reached the point of ladling gumbo over the rice in the bowls and Pamela was holding a cruet, so Bettina darted from the room. Pamela heard her feet on the wooden floor in the spot between where the dining room carpet left off and the living room carpet began. Then her footsteps were muffled again. There was the sound of the front door opening and a moment later Bettina's voice saying, "I suspect I know what you want."

Pamela set the cruet down and hurried through the doorway that led to the dining room. Standing in the arch between the dining room and the living room she had a perfect view out the windows that looked onto the street. A truck bearing the logo of the local TV station was parked at the curb. Pamela stepped further into the living room. Looking past Bettina's shoulder, she could see that the person Bettina was speaking to, the person on the porch, was Marcy Brewer from the *County Register*.

Pamela and Bettina had dealt in person with Marcy Brewer before. She was a diminutive young woman who made up for her small stature and her youthful prettiness with an exceptionally determined manner.

"Marcy Brewer from the *County Register*," she announced in a confident voice.

"I know who you are," Bettina responded.

Seeing the tilt of Bettina's head from the back, Pamela could picture the combative lift of her chin that likely accompanied the statement.

"And," Bettina continued, drawing the word out for emphasis, "please be informed that any interviews granted by Bettina Fraser concerning the unfortunate discovery at the cemetery this evening will be exclusive to the *Arborville Advocate*."

With that, she stepped back and closed the door. When she turned, Pamela could see that she was smiling a secret smile.

"Shall we eat?" she said, and a moment later, in the kitchen, answered Wilfred's curious look by saying, "It was Marcy Brewer. I sent her away."

A festive mood took hold as soon as they sat down at the table. Perhaps, Wilfred suggested, the gumbo itself conjured a Mardi Gras spirit—though with Easter two weeks away Mardi Gras was long over and technically they were deep in Lent. Nonetheless, with glasses of beer replenished and steaming bowls of gumbo ladled over hot rice before them, the memory of their recent experience at the cemetery began to fade.

The shrimp, which Wilfred had added only shortly before serving his gumbo, were tender and pink, their sweet flavor contrasting with the rich meatiness of the duck tidbits. Both shrimp and duck were bathed in the complex gravy-like sauce *conjured*—yes, that was the word!— from flour and oil stirred over high heat till the color resembled an old penny, and then blended with spices, onion, green pepper, duck, and duck broth.

No one spoke for the first few minutes, but it was clear from the nonverbal reactions that the gumbo was working its magic, a magic announced by the tingle of cayenne on the tongue. A bite of baguette, spread with a soothing layer of butter, was a welcome antidote to both the richness and the tingle.

"I'd say that new cookbook has earned its keep already," Pamela commented after she had temporarily set down her fork.

"It tastes so authentic," Bettina added, "just like the gumbo we ate on our trip." She took another bite, closed her eyes, and hummed with pleasure. The hum turned into words: "I could eat this every night."

* * *

The bowls had been cleared away and replaced with salad plates, and they were nibbling at the last bits of the refreshing oil and vinegar dressed lettuce when the doorbell rang again.

"I'll get it this time." Wilfred rose, leaning on the table to push himself to his feet.

Bettina watched, and as he passed her chair on his way to the living room, she said, "Tell them that any interviews Bettina Fraser grants will be exclusive to the *Advocate*."

"Will do" was the response, and Wilfred paused to give Bettina's shoulder an affectionate squeeze.

But as he stood in the open door, it became clear that the caller was not seeking an audience with Bettina Fraser—or at any rate, was not a reporter.

"Come in, come in," Wilfred boomed in his cheeriest tones. He stepped aside, and from her vantage point at the table, Pamela watched Richard Larkin cross the threshold, ducking slightly.

"I hope I'm not intruding . . ." Richard's glance wandered toward the dining room table. When he caught sight of Pamela, his eyes widened slightly.

"Of course not!" Wilfred seized his hand and shook it heartily. "Take your coat off and join us for some gumbo."

Richard protested again that he didn't want to intrude and added that he had already eaten, but he nonetheless shrugged his way out of his navy-blue pea coat, which Wilfred draped over the nearest armchair.

By this time, Bettina was on her feet too. "Neighbor!" she exclaimed, and reached out to tug Richard toward the chair that faced Pamela across the table.

"I . . . I . . ." Richard allowed her to seat him before he continued. "I just came over to see if you were okay," he said, focusing his attention on Bettina, who had sat back down. "I saw the truck from the TV station in front of your house, and the car with the *Register*'s logo on the side, and I wondered . . ."

"Well!" Bettina smiled a pleased smile. "I . . . *we* . . ."—she nodded toward Pamela—"are perfectly okay." She turned to face Richard and leaned forward. "*But*—you heard it here first—there's been another murder."

Pamela bit her tongue to keep from laughing. What had happened to Bettina's declaration, barely an hour ago, that she didn't want to talk about the murders of Isobel and Barb Lister ever again?

Bettina leaned even closer to Richard and described what she and Pamela had discovered as they searched the cemetery for what the woman posting on Access-Arborville had called a shroud. As she spoke, Richard glanced from time to time at Pamela, with a concerned expression that heightened the stern effect of his bony features.

When Bettina finished, his lips parted in a sympathetic smile and he said, "You're okay then." Shifting his gaze to Pamela, he added, "And you too."

"Fine." Bettina and Pamela spoke in unison. Pamela wanted to say more, but it was hard to put into words an appropriate response to his intense gaze. Wilfred, thankfully, filled the suddenly awkward silence.

"You'll stay for dessert, Rick." It was a statement, not a question, unanswerable, and Richard didn't try. He simply pulled his chair closer to the table and Wilfred headed for the kitchen.

Effortlessly shifting into hostess mode, Bettina offered Richard a coquettish head-tilt and said, "So, neighbor, what have *you* been doing?"

Chatting with Bettina seemed to come easily to everyone. Richard launched into a description of his gardening plans for the coming spring, agreeing with Bettina that pansies were the essential first step.

If dessert was to arrive—and coffee, judging by the tantalizing aroma beginning to waft through the kitchen doorway—the salad plates would need to be cleared away. Pamela was happy to have a distraction, and soon she was heading toward the Frasers' sink with a stack of three plates streaked with olive oil and bearing shreds of lettuce. Balanced across the top plate were three forks. On her way past the high counter she passed an oval platter containing the evening's dessert, chocolate éclairs, each one wearing a pleated paper ruff.

"I wish I could say I'd made them," Wilfred said, noticing her noticing, "but they're from the bakery in Timberley."

Pamela set the plates by the sink and returned to the dining room with four dessert plates, and Bettina's sage-green sugar bowl and cream pitcher. Richard and Bettina had moved on to the topic of mulch. Back in the kitchen, she collected four sage-green mugs from the cupboard and lined them up near the stove for Wilfred to fill with coffee.

A few minutes passed as more trips to and from the kitchen were made, but eventually they were all seated at the table. A plate at each place held an éclair, with a steaming and fragrant mug of coffee waiting nearby.

The éclairs were delicate elongated ovals of golden pastry, sliced horizontally to accommodate a custard filling that was visible in the narrow gap where top met bottom. Their tops were spread with chocolate icing. Pamela concentrated on the way the pastry, light but yeasty, and the creamy vanilla-accented filling, provided a backdrop to the intense icing, in which sweetness vanquished any hint of cocoa's bitterness.

Conversation ebbed and flowed around her, moving from garden plans to a new project Richard's architecture firm had embarked on, and thence to the firehouse Wilfred was building for his grandsons in his basement workshop.

From time to time Pamela found herself studying Richard's face as he bent attentively toward Wilfred or Bettina. He wasn't conventionally handsome, with his strong brow and bold nose, and the smiles that occasionally softened his stern expression came and went so quickly that it almost seemed he was aware of their incongruity.

"Take another one, Rick," Wilfred urged.

"Yes, yes, do." Bettina added her encouragement.

"Just one more," he agreed, after glancing across the table at Pamela, or more specifically at her plate, which still held half an éclair.

For the next few minutes, no one spoke, and the evening wound down of its own accord. A few muffled yawns, interspersed with coffee mugs tipped at angles guaranteed to drain the last dregs, signaled that the conviviality—welcome as it was after the cemetery adventure—had run its course.

Richard dispatched the last bite of his second éclair and eased his chair back from the table. "Tomorrow's a workday," he said, "but this has been . . ." His gaze drifted toward Pamela. "If you're ready to leave . . . I know it's not far, but . . . perhaps you'd like company?"

"Of course she would," Bettina exclaimed, hopping to her feet with an assist from the table, "especially with . . . a killer on the loose."

Pamela stifled the urge to squeal, and she managed to keep her voice calm when she said, "He doesn't seem to be targeting random people, given that the victims were both named Lister."

Bettina wasn't paying attention, however. She was already in the living room, plucking Richard's pea coat from the armchair where Wilfred had draped it and collecting Pamela's jacket from the sofa where it had been shed earlier.

Richard helped Pamela into her jacket as Bettina stood nearby, glowing with approval. Then he slipped his pea coat on, shook Wilfred's hand, and thanked both the Frasers. Bettina ushered them out the door, smiling a pleased smile, and they were on their way.

Neither spoke until they reached the steps that led up to Pamela's porch. Richard was on the point of turning away to head toward his own house when he seemed to change his mind.

"It was nice to see you and talk to you tonight," he blurted suddenly, looking not at Pamela but at the concrete surface of her front walk. Never mind that she had barely spoken and ninety percent of his conversation had been with Wilfred and Bettina.

"You were kind to drop by," Pamela responded. "Bettina was very shaken by our adventure at the cemetery, and having company really cheered her up."

"I like the Frasers." Richard continued to focus on the concrete. After a few moments, he raised his head and focused on Pamela. "I don't know if either of them mentioned it, but my . . . situation . . . has changed."

Was he alluding to the fact that Jocelyn was no longer in his life? She wasn't sure. But it was true that he had told Wilfred, who had told Bettina, that Jocelyn had gone back to an old boyfriend.

"Or maybe you already knew, anyway, because . . ." His back was to the streetlamp so his face was in shadow, but from the way his head dipped she could tell he was studying her face. "In fact, you must have known, unless he . . ."

He? Where was this going?

"He?" She said the word aloud.

"Brian Delano." His tone was flat, and in the dark it was impossible to read his expression. After a pause, he spoke again, this time sounding amazed. "Is he still seeing you too?"

"Brian Delano is Jocelyn's old boyfriend?" She felt like laughing, but wasn't sure why—maybe just amazement at the crazy way things had turned out, like a silly movie plot. Though silly movie plots like that always ended up with *two* couples at the altar.

"No, no," she said, sounding more amused than she intended. "He isn't still seeing me too."

"Are you okay?" His head dipped lower. In the silly movie, this would be the lead-up to a kiss, but she didn't raise her face to his.

"I'm fine."

He stepped back slightly and she blinked. He'd been blocking the light from the streetlamp and now it was shining full in her eyes. "You look fine," he said. "Keeping busy?"

"Work for the magazine." Pamela shrugged. "And there's the knitting group. How about you?"

"A college in upstate New York is looking to build a new student union. They liked our proposal and we're in the running to get the contract."

"I hope it works out," Pamela said.

"I do too." Silhouetted against the bright light,

Richard's shaggy head bobbed as he nodded. "It's good to be busy."

"Yes." Pamela nodded too. "It is."

On that note of agreement, they were both silent for a long minute.

"Well," Pamela said, after searching her mind for a new topic and coming up empty-handed, "tomorrow's a work day . . ."

"Yes," Richard said. "Yes, it is."

"So I'll say goodnight." Pamela turned and rested her hand on the railing that edged the steps. "Thanks for walking me home."

"You're welcome."

"I *will* find you a cat," she added over her shoulder. "There's one looking for a home out there somewhere."

CHAPTER 19

Though it was barely eight a.m., Bettina was already dressed for the day, in an ensemble that combined navy-blue corduroy trousers with a navy-and-white checked blouse and a short red leather jacket. When she caught sight of Pamela stooping to retrieve the *Register* from the sidewalk, she waved and then launched herself across the street.

"You'll see that Marcy Brewer got a story," she called as she drew near, "but not from talking to me. I suppose she latched onto Clayborn when he got back to the police station last night."

"You're up and about early," Pamela commented.

"I'm covering an event at the high school," Bettina said. She stepped back and surveyed Pamela. "You look rested. I guess your neighbor"—she nodded toward Richard Larkin's house—"didn't stick around after he walked you home?"

"No." Pamela felt a frown beginning to form. "He didn't stick around—and if you're going to talk about him, which I wish you wouldn't, you might as well just say 'Richard Larkin.' Calling him 'your neighbor' isn't the same thing as not talking about him."

"Well, anyway . . ." Bettina nodded contritely. "It was thoughtful of him to come by to check on me last night." She took a few steps toward the curb. "I guess I'll be off then?"

She peered at Pamela as if to assess her friend's mood. Pamela raised a finger and massaged between her brows, wondering if she was still frowning.

Bettina mustered a smile. "I'm going then." She stepped off the curb. "Oh, by the way, Wilfred is going to call Pete Paterson about replacing the treads on the basement steps. It sounded like you were happy with his work."

By the time Pamela returned to the kitchen, the kettle was hooting so furiously that the cats had abandoned their breakfast to stare at the stove. She quickly turned off the burner and made fast work of arranging the paper filter in the filter cone and grinding the coffee beans. As the boiling water, transformed into fragrant coffee, dripped into the carafe, she slipped a piece of whole-grain bread into the toaster.

A few minutes later, she was settled in her accustomed chair at the kitchen table with her breakfast before her: buttered toast on a wedding-china plate and steaming coffee in a wedding-china cup. She had slipped the *Register* from its flimsy plastic sleeve and it lay unfolded beside her plate. A bold headline on the front page read, "A Second Lister Killing Adds to Arborville Mystery." Marcy Brewer was credited with the article.

Already knowing what had happened, Pamela was in no rush to absorb the whole article, which continued on an inner page, so she nibbled her toast and sipped her coffee while skimming the first few paragraphs.

Bettina Fraser and Pamela Paterson, Arborville residents, were identified as having come upon the body of Barb Lister in the Arborville cemetery early Sunday evening. Ms. Fraser, reporter for the *Arborville Advocate*, had been following up on a listserv report of a mysterious white "shroud" that had appeared on the tombstone of Isobel Lister, whose murder the previous week was as yet unsolved.

Toast finished, Pamela set the plate aside and opened the *Register* to the page where the article resumed. Again, the article reported nothing that she didn't already know. Barb Lister, related by marriage to the Lister family, which had deep roots in Arborville, had apparently been strangled with a white knitted scarf or shawl—possibly the "shroud" mentioned in the listserv posting.

Marcy Brewer quoted Detective Lucas Clayborn, of the Arborville police, as saying the police had not yet determined whether they were seeking the same killer as the person who killed Isobel Lister. However, the fact that the two victims were related—though Barb Lister was an in-law—was suggestive.

Pamela poured herself a second cup of coffee and set Part 1 aside. Browsing through Lifestyle, she happily lost herself in a feature on a local woman who employed decorative painting techniques from the eighteenth century to rescue discarded wooden furniture.

Work for the magazine awaited. She had gotten no further with the review of *Shaker Communities and the Feminist Sensibility: The Paradox of Women's Work* than puzzling over whether to describe the Shakers as possibly the most contradictory or the most traditional of utopian communities. Then Bettina had called, they had driven up to the cemetery, and the Shakers had taken a back seat to the adventure that unfolded there.

Pamela rinsed her plate and cup at the sink and climbed the stairs. In her bedroom, she made her bed and arranged her vintage lace pillows against the brass headboard. She pulled on a fresh pair of jeans and a favorite, comfortable old sweater. Across the hall, seated at her computer, she checked her email and quickly responded to a message from Penny, who of course already knew all about Pamela and Bettina's cemetery adventure.

Assuring Penny that she and Bettina were fine and that they were both sure Detective Clayborn was nearing a solution to both mysteries, she opened the file labeled "Review—Shaker Book" and stared at the unfinished opening sentence.

Sometimes it was better to plunge ahead. Abandoning the unfinished sentence to be completed later, she plunged—and soon her fingers were moving quickly over the keys. Perhaps after she summed up the book's argument, she could circle back around and the opening sentence would write itself.

Three hours later, the review was complete, leading off with an opening sentence that simply declared the Shakers to be a utopian community perhaps best known for their influence on American design. Pamela's stomach reminded her, even before she glanced at the clock, that lunchtime had arrived, and she pushed her chair back from her desk and raised her arms over her head in a very welcome stretch.

Downstairs, she stepped out onto the porch to collect the mail. The day was springlike, again, as had been forecast by Bettina's outfit that morning, and she took a few moments to enjoy the sunlight and the mild breeze. As she stood on her porch, a familiar-looking truck came into view at the bottom of the block.

It was a metallic silver pickup truck, sleek and very new. It made its way slowly up Orchard Street and it pulled over to the curb in front of the Frasers' house. Pete Paterson climbed out. He obviously didn't notice her standing in the shadows of her wide porch as he circled the back of the vehicle and proceeded up the Frasers' driveway.

It would be silly to run across the street and accost him, she decided, and so she stepped back inside, sorted all but her credit card bill into the recycling basket, and headed for the kitchen. Cheese, she was thinking, grilled cheese.

Bettina was nearly breathless with excitement—but as it turned out, the news that she so breathlessly imparted wasn't news to Pamela at all. At least her arrival was well-timed though. Pamela had just finished checking through the copyedited manuscript of "To Make a Virtue of Necessity: Quilters and the War Effort, 1861–1865" when she heard the doorbell's chime. She clicked on "Save" and closed the Word file.

"Did you know," Bettina exclaimed before Pamela's front door was open even a few inches, "that Pete Paterson is not at all what we thought he was?"

Pamela swung the door open to its fullest extent and stood back. Fighting the urge to smile—she suspected she knew what was coming—she responded, "What did we think he was?"

"Some poor hardworking guy trying to piece together an income as a handyman."

"He's not hardworking?" Pamela said. "I thought he did a good job on my screens. He was very punctual too."

"He's not poor!"

Pamela felt a smile form despite her efforts to hold it back. "I'm sure a good handyman can make a decent living. People always need—"

"That's not what I mean." Bettina stamped her foot. It was shod in a trim red leather bootie that matched her jacket. "He came today to replace the basement stair treads and the minute he walked in the door, Wilfred recognized him. Of course the last time Wilfred saw him he was wearing a suit at a fancy dinner and being recognized for his contribution to the state's historical preservation initiative. He helped fund the restoration of the Cogglesworth Mansion in Newark."

"That was thoughtful of him."

"Pamela!" Bettina grabbed Pamela's arm. "He gave them half a million dollars!" She watched for a minute as if awaiting a suitably amazed reaction on Pamela's part. When it didn't come, she went on. "So, anyway, he told Wilfred that he left his big-deal Wall Street job and just wants to fix things now. I should have suspected he wasn't what he seemed when he showed up in that fancy and obviously brand-new pickup truck."

"He drives a Porsche too," Pamela said. "Like Roland's but black."

"What?" Bettina's grip on Pamela's arm tightened to the point that Pamela could feel her fingernails. "He told you that? He didn't seem like the bragging type to me. And he did do a nice job on the stair treads."

"I rode in it." Pamela made no attempt now to control the smile. In response to Bettina's speechless stare, she elaborated. "He took me to dinner Saturday night, at a charming French restaurant in a little town along the Hudson. We both had coq au vin."

"You went on a *date*? With *Pete Paterson*?" Bettina was nearly reeling.

"He's awfully nice looking," Pamela said.

"But what about . . . what about—"

"My neighbor?" Pamela interrupted. "He's nice looking too, but . . ."

"But?" Bettina felt behind her for the chair that was the entry's main piece of furniture and sank into it.

Pamela abandoned her playful tone. "I don't know what he thinks about . . . me . . . anymore. I suggested that maybe when Penny's here for spring break, if his daughters are here too, we could all do something together, and he kind of brushed it off. Though he did ask me if I knew of any cats he could adopt."

"It's probably too soon after Jocelyn." Bettina shook her head slowly and the large pearls dangling from her earlobes began to sway. "But if you think he could be the one, you don't want to get too involved with someone else." She fastened her gaze on Pamela with an intensity that was hard to ignore. "Do you?"

"The old boyfriend she went back to is Brian Delano," Pamela said. "Did you know that?"

"No, I did not." Bettina sighed. She consulted her watch. "I've got to get going. Don't tell me any more surprising things! I've had enough surprises for one day."

She stood up. When it came to hugging, Pamela wasn't usually the one to make the first move, but she reached out and pulled Bettina close. Bettina wrapped her arms around Pamela's waist, gave her a squeeze, and stepped back.

"Knit and Nibble tomorrow night," she said. "We're meeting here, I think." Pamela nodded. "What are you going to bake?"

"I'm not sure yet. I'll probably go up to the Co-Op in the morning to get whatever."

Bettina paused with her hand on the doorknob. "I'm seeing Clayborn so I might have news."

The first task for Tuesday morning, after three cats and one human had eaten breakfast, was to check over the review of *Shaker Communities and the Feminist Sensibility: The Paradox of Women's Work* one last time and email it, along with the copyedited article on Civil War quilts, to Celine Bramley at *Fiber Craft*.

Dressed, and back downstairs, Pamela studied her cookbook shelf. When she baked goodies, she liked to reflect the seasons by taking advantage of readily available and local fresh fruit. But mid-March was not a good month for readily available and local fresh fruit. She pulled out a few of her newer cookbooks and paged through them, only to return them to the shelf in favor of a truly vintage cookbook she had found at a tag sale.

Published in the 1950s, it reflected that era's fondness for convenience foods, as well as a postwar sense that life could be *fun* again—expressed in molded Jell-O salads and canned pear halves decorated to resemble bunny faces, and elegant dessert creations like . . . pineapple upside-down cake, made with canned pineapple slices and maraschino cherries.

Pamela collected her jacket and a canvas tote from

the closet, and soon she was strolling up Orchard Street en route to the Co-Op. As she approached the stately brick apartment building at the corner, she detoured through the building's parking lot. Sometimes cast-off treasures could be found along the back of the building behind the length of wooden fencing that hid the trash cans.

Today, however, there was nothing of note, and she paid for her curiosity by happening upon the super, Mr. Gilly, in an even more talkative mood than usual. Escaping ten minutes later, she continued to the corner and turned onto Arborville Avenue.

The bulletin board on the Co-Op's façade had attracted the usual knot of people, drawn first by interest in its offerings but lingering to chat with their fellow Arborvillians. Pamela nodded at Marlene Pepper, happy to see that Marlene was engaged in an absorbing conversation with two other women and was uninterested in including Pamela. As soon as a spot closer to the bulletin board opened up, Pamela stepped forward.

She quickly scanned the colorful collage of flyers, posters, business cards, and handwritten notices. A tricycle was for sale on Elm Street, local cleaning services were available mornings and some afternoons, a student was looking to carpool to the city three days a week, and free firewood was on offer to anyone who would haul it away.

But no one was seeking good homes for kittens. Into her mind there came a vision of Richard Larkin's curious expression when she assured him that she would find him a cat. Had he seemed grateful? Amused? Or something else?

Pamela needed only two things, a can of pineapple rings and a jar of maraschino cherries. So she bypassed the ranks of carts lined up on the sidewalk and took a basket from the stack just inside the automatic doors. Five minutes later, she was standing in the express line waiting to check out.

Back at home, she assembled the tools and equipment she would need for her creation: a small saucepan, a nine-inch cake pan, a good-sized mixing bowl, an electric mixer, a flour sifter, a rubber spatula, and a few big spoons.

The first step was to melt butter in the saucepan and stir in brown sugar to form a rich, dark amber syrup. The next step was to arrange the canned pineapple slices in the bottom of the cake pan. Pamela started by placing one slice exactly in the middle, then she placed six more slices in a ring around it. Finally, she cut the remaining slices in half and tucked them upright against the edges of the pan.

Each of the complete pineapple slices got a maraschino cherry tucked into the hole in its center, the red of the cherries, a hue like nothing found in nature, accenting the tropical brightness of the pineapple slices. She added a bit of the juice remaining in the can to the brown-sugar butter syrup and drizzled the syrup over the pineapple slices with their bright cherry accents.

Now it was time to make the cake batter. She melted more butter, beat in milk and an egg, and let the mixture rest while she sifted flour, salt, and baking soda into the mixing bowl. She stirred in sugar and then the butter-milk-egg mixture and beat until the batter was smooth.

Once the cake was in the oven, Pamela inspected the parts of her house that were likely to be seen by her guests that evening. She'd done a thorough cleaning just the past Thursday, but now she washed the kitchen floor and tidied the downstairs bathroom. By the time the cake began to announce that it was nearly done, with a sugary aroma bearing overtones of baked pineapple, the floor was dry and she was able to get access to the cupboard where she stored her wedding china.

Bettina was the first to arrive. "I know what it is! I know what it is!" she sang as she stepped across the threshold. She slipped off a lightweight coat in a soft shade of coral to reveal a fit-and-flare dress in tones of coral, orange, and chartreuse. Bobbing at her ears were large orange beads that matched a bold necklace.

"Pineapple upside-down cake!" she announced, draping her coat on the nearby chair. "I could smell it even before you opened the door. Yum." She closed her eyes and smiled, as if already savoring a taste. "Can I help?" she added.

"There's not much left to do." Pamela smiled. "I have the plates and cups and other things we'll need for the break set out in the dining room."

"Can I look at the cake?"

"Sure," Pamela said. "Come on into the kitchen."

"Oh, it's beautiful." Bettina sighed. The kitchen table was bare, except for the cake. Not having a round wedding-china plate large enough to accommodate it, Pamela had used a turquoise platter that was a recent tag sale find. The cake had been inverted onto the platter to display the top, which had been the bottom, and its pineapple circlets, now bathed in glistening syrup, with their cherry accents.

"What did Detective Clayborn have to say?" Pamela inquired, interrupting her task of measuring coffee beans into the grinder.

"Nothing that wasn't in the *Register* yesterday— and I suppose you noticed that Marcy Brewer quoted him in this morning's paper as saying there was nothing new to report."

Pamela pressed down on the cover of the coffee grinder and launched the beans into a whirling clatter. It subsided into a whine when the grinding was complete.

"So the status of things is that"—she paused for a moment as she tried to recall the details from Monday morning's article—"the person who killed Barb Lister might be the same person who killed Isobel Lister because the two victims were Listers, though not related by blood. But there might be two killers because the murder techniques were different."

"That's pretty much it." Bettina nodded. "But as I was walking back to my car it hit me. Maybe the murder techniques weren't so different after all. Maybe she was trying to strangle Isobel and they struggled and Isobel fell and was obviously dead. So the strangling didn't have to happen after all."

"She?" Pamela raised her eyebrows.

"Mr. Nap Year saw a woman going in that back door. Remember?"

"I do." Pamela took a paper coffee filter from the cupboard. "Could you strangle a person with a sweater?" she asked suddenly. When Bettina didn't respond, she added, "Though it seems like a lot of effort to peel a sweater off a live person to use as a murder weapon."

"Isobel could have already taken the sweater off," Bettina said. "We talked about that before. Her perfor-

mance was very energetic and maybe she peeled the
sweater off the minute she got back to the green room."

"And after it's clear that Isobel is dead, though not
with the sweater wrapped around her neck, the killer
runs off with the sweater? Just because?" Pamela
frowned and thought for a minute, raising a hand to
massage the wrinkle that she knew had appeared between her brows. "If I planned to strangle someone, I
think I'd bring my own weapon—something like a
rope or a piece of wire."

"But"—Bettina held up an index finger, carefully
manicured and with the nail painted orange to match
her ensemble—"it looks like the person who killed
Barb Lister used the knitted shroud."

Pamela had no answer to that—and, anyway, the
doorbell's chime indicated that more Knit and Nibblers
had arrived. With a last glance at the pineapple upside-
down cake, Bettina sang out, "I'll get it," and hurried
toward the entry.

CHAPTER 20

By the time Pamela joined her there a few moments later, Roland and Nell had stepped inside and Roland was helping Nell out of her jacket. Like the ancient gray wool coat she wore in the winter, the shapeless jacket that took its place in less chilly seasons had been a fixture in her wardrobe for decades. "No point in buying new clothes if the old ones will do just as well," she was known to say.

Once she'd been freed of the jacket, she directed her gaze first at Bettina and then at Pamela. The effect was all the more compelling given her pale eyes in their nests of wrinkles and her white hair, disarranged by the evening breezes and resembling a fibrous halo.

When she spoke, however, it was only to say, "I hope everyone's fine this evening."

She then walked directly to the comfortable armchair near the hearth that was always reserved for her. Roland echoed her greeting and followed her to the living room, where he perched on the hassock at the other end of the hearth.

The next Knit and Nibblers to arrive were more voluble. Bettina had barely closed the front door when footsteps echoed on the porch and Holly called, "Hello, hello! We're coming." Bettina pulled the door open again and Holly entered, with Karen right behind.

"You two have had quite an adventure!" Holly exclaimed, surveying Bettina and then Pamela. "But none the worse for wear, I see." She turned back to Bettina and added, "I love the dress! But you're always the fashionista."

Holly herself was looking quite stylish. She was wearing black leather pants and a matching jacket in a close-fitting style that emphasized her shapely figure. Her tousled hair hung loose to her shoulders, its raven hue accented tonight with an indigo streak.

"So, ladies," she went on, "how spooky was that? Coming upon a body—and so soon after the St. Patrick's Day murder, and right up there in the cemetery where Isobel Lister is *buried*!"

Karen, standing behind Holly, seemed a bit startled by Holly's levity, but it was Roland who spoke, half-rising from the hassock.

"I don't know about you," he said in a tone that had probably summoned more than one chatty professional colleague back to the task at hand, "but when I am at a Knit and Nibble meeting, I concentrate on my knitting."

Pamela had a good view of Nell from her spot near the arch between the entry and the living room. As Roland began to speak, an expression both surprised and pleased had softened Nell's aged features. But by the time he finished, all that was left was surprise.

"Roland!" Nell exclaimed, half-rising herself. "For heaven's sake! You're not disturbed by the notion of making someone's death the subject of lurid gossip—" She paused and puffed disgustedly, and then went on. "But just by the distracting effect the discussion has on the progress of your knitting?"

Roland lowered himself back onto the hassock looking more puzzled than chastened. But Holly darted from the entry to crouch at Nell's side.

"You're right, you're right, you're right!" she said. "A terrible thing has happened in our little town. No! *Two* terrible things. I won't say anything more about it—*them*—ever again. Poor Imogene, losing her aunt, and then her mother."

"She's not here tonight," Roland said, looking around as if to make sure this was indeed a fact. "I guess that means we didn't invite her to join."

"We didn't." Bettina had advanced into the living room and taken a seat on the sofa, where she had been joined by Karen. "I mean, *I* didn't." She leaned forward to make eye contact with Holly, who was still crouched by the armchair. "Did you, Holly?"

"No." Holly stood up. "Because you all didn't seem in favor."

"We weren't *against*." Bettina moved over so Holly could fit between her and Karen. "Were you *against*, Roland?"

"Certainly not." Roland had already taken out his knitting and launched a new row. A skein of pale yellow yarn shared the hassock with his lean body. He paused and looked up with a fierce expression that seemed designed ward off any further distraction. Confronted by five pairs of questioning eyes, however—with Nell's gaze especially probing—his expression softened, as did his voice.

"I never opposed inviting her to join," he said. "I only pointed out that we hadn't yet done so."

When there was no response, he continued. "And now, in fact, under the circumstances . . . that is . . . of course we all have to agree—but maybe we all do. She *does* like to knit . . . that would be a prerequisite. Cooking? I don't know. Sometimes people serve something they've bought, though I've enjoyed . . . uh . . . the things I've . . . uh . . ."

As he spoke, Pamela stepped through the arch and took a seat on the antique chair with the carved wooden back and needlepoint cushion. Roland's voice trailed off. He'd lowered his knitting to his lap, and now he took it up again, staring intently at the spot where he had left off.

"Purl or knit?" he murmured, lowered the knitting to his lap again, and bent over to retrieve the magazine that lay open atop his elegant briefcase.

"Are you trying to say you're in favor?" Bettina inquired, leaning forward on the sofa.

Roland set the magazine down. "I . . . well, yes," he said. "There's no need to be exclusive, and sometimes another viewpoint might be . . ."

"I'll ask her then!" Holly clapped her hands. "She might need a little time to grieve. Losing your mother is different from losing an aunt, but . . ." She paused as the attention of her listeners shifted to the porch, where footsteps could be heard. That sound was followed by the doorbell's chime.

"A package delivery maybe," Pamela commented as she rose, "though it's awfully late and I'm not expecting anything."

Even with the porch light on, it was hard to make out the shadowy figure on the other side of the lace that curtained the oval window in the front door. But the figure was small, most likely a woman. Pamela opened the door several inches and peered through the gap between door and doorframe.

"I know I'm late," ventured a hesitant voice.

The caller was Imogene Lister.

"Come in, come in." Pamela swung the door open wide.

Imogene stepped in. She was bundled in a kind of cape, in a dark fabric that blended with the dark pants and dark sweatshirt that were revealed when she cast the cape aside. The outfit was enlivened only slightly by her platinum hair.

"We didn't expect to see you tonight," Pamela said.

Imogen's wary expression suggested that she took the comment as a challenge, so Pamela quickly added, "You're very welcome though. Please have a seat." She gestured toward the living room, where in fact no seats were available except for the small wooden chair that Pamela had vacated to answer the door.

The next moment, though, Roland was on his feet, holding his knitting but leaving behind on the hassock the skein of pale yellow yarn to which it was tethered by a long strand.

"Sit here! Sit here!" he urged. "I'll get a chair from the dining room."

He set his knitting down and disappeared around the corner. Imogene advanced a few feet into the living room, where she halted uncertainly on the edge of the carpet as she faced a chorus of greetings. Not content with words alone, Holly leapt up from the sofa and pulled Imogene's tense body into a hug. Bettina rose too and wrapped her arms around both Holly and Imogene.

Holly disentangled herself and Bettina pulled Imogene toward the sofa.

"You'll be more comfortable here," she said. "I'll take the hassock." She waited until Imogene had settled herself and then added, "How are you doing, dear?"

The question was echoed by Nell from across the room.

"I'm okay, I guess." Imogene shrugged. Her expression was blank and her bold features immobile. Pamela was struck once again by the resemblance between aunt and niece, though in Isobel's case her looks—bold but by no means beautiful—had suited her dramatic personality. And she had used them to good effect as a performer.

"I didn't want to stay home and mope, so . . . I came out." She shrugged again. "You can all come to the funeral if you want. I don't know when it's going to be yet, but I'm sure the food will be good—though my mom won't be planning it."

She pulled her knitting bag onto her lap and rummaged around until she came up with a skein of pale yarn and a knitting needle with a few rows of knitting on it. More rummaging produced a second knitting needle. Bettina, seated on the hassock now, was back at work on the sleeve of the royal-blue sweater she was making for Wilfred Jr. Roland, sitting near her on a chair he had brought from the dining room, was absorbed in the lacy pattern required by his project, to the point that he was murmuring instructions to himself.

Pamela, Holly, and Karen were all empty-handed, except for crochet hooks.

"We're going to take you up on your awesome offer." Holly addressed Nell, with a smile that brought her dimples into play and displayed her perfect teeth. "Crochet lessons, with the goal of making nests for the Timberley Wildlife Center."

"Three eager students . . ." Nell looked up with a pleased smile. "I'll finish this later"—she held out a crocheted circle with edges just beginning to curve into the nest's sides—"and we'll all start new ones from scratch."

Pamela took out a partial skein of tawny brown yarn left from the sweater she had just finished. Brown seemed a comforting color for a nest to welcome a tiny orphaned creature. Karen, apparently thinking along similar lines, had produced a ball of yarn in a soft shade of tan. Holly, however, had chosen the same bright orange she'd used in her color-block afghan.

"Now," Nell said, "first we make a slip knot in our yarn." She demonstrated. "And then we crochet a chain of five stitches, like this."

She thrust the crochet hook through the loop of the slip knot, hooked it around the strand of yarn running from a ball of pale green yarn, and pulled the strand through the loop to form a new loop.

"Then we do it again and again until we have a tiny chain," she explained, and watched while her three students carried out that step.

They moved on to the next step, linking the beginning and end of the chain to form a tiny ring. Then Nell demonstrated the crochet stitch that would create the floor of the nest, spiraling around and around in a circle growing ever larger.

Pamela had soon lost herself in her work, as happy

plying a crochet hook as she was when busy with her knitting needles, and fascinated by the way a small tool could transform a single strand of fiber into a two-dimensional textile—not that the process of using two slender needles to accomplish a similar goal was any less magical.

Not everyone was as silent as Pamela. Imogene, at the end of the sofa closest to Pamela's chair, was engrossed in her knitting, but to Imogene's right, Holly and Karen were talking quietly, alternating between comparing progress on their nests and chatting about a visit Karen was expecting from her sister. Bettina had moved the hassock closer to Nell, and Nell was showing lively interest in Bettina's goal of eventually producing a sweater for each of her sons.

Imogene stirred slightly, rearranging her curious knitting bag, which sat in its open position on the floor near her feet, to allow easier access to the skein of pale yarn she was working with. Her movement dislodged the ball of orange yarn resting on the sofa between her and Holly, and the ball of yarn rolled onto the floor where it disappeared under the coffee table.

"I'll get it, I'll get it." Imogene and Holly both spoke in unison, and both stood up.

In the process, Imogene's knitting bag tipped over and some of its contents ended up on the carpet. Holly circled the coffee table and stooped to reach under it for the ball of yarn, while Imogene lowered herself back onto the sofa. She bent over to right her knitting bag and grab an errant skein of yarn and three mismatched needles.

Pamela bent over too. Among the things that had ended up on the carpet were a few of the swatches that Imogene had explained were test squares for various earlier knitting projects. One of them was the same lively shade of green as the sweater Isobel was wearing on St. Patrick's Day. And Pamela had seen that same shade of green on someone else recently too, perhaps outside the Co-Op. Yes, that was it . . .

Pamela handed Imogene the swatch.

"Did you make your aunt a sweater from this yarn?" she asked.

Imogene's face remained expressionless but she nodded, barely.

"And you made one for your mother too?"

Imogene stared as if she hadn't heard correctly, then her head tilted in a way that could have meant either assent or dissent.

From across the room came Roland's voice, announcing that eight p.m. had arrived. As he readjusted his immaculate shirt cuff, which had been disarranged when he pushed it back to consult his impressive watch, Holly and Karen sprang to their feet. Roland laid his knitting atop his briefcase, Bettina set hers on the hearth, and Nell balanced her crochet project on the broad arm of her chair. Imogene, with Pamela's eyes still on her, murmured something that sounded like, "Only one."

But as hostess for that evening's Knit and Nibble, Pamela couldn't linger to clarify. She climbed to her feet and hurried to the kitchen, where she quickly filled the kettle and set water to boil for coffee. Then she darted out through the doorway that connected the kitchen to the dining room. Bettina was already standing by the table, where wedding-china cups, saucers, and plates waited on the lace tablecloth, along with silverware and napkins and of course the pineapple upside-down cake in all its glory.

"There's going to be whipped cream," Pamela said, "and I'll bring it out in a few minutes."

She stepped toward the living room and addressed the group. "Please come in and get cake, and I'll serve coffee and tea."

As if she had read Pamela's mind, Bettina was already holding the knife and cake server Pamela had set out earlier. Without waiting another minute, she sliced the cake exactly in half and began to divide one of the halves into four pieces.

Back in the kitchen, Pamela poured heavy cream into a bowl, added a few tablespoons of sugar, and set to work with her electric mixer. The beaters whirred as the liquid bubbled and frothed and thickened. Just as it reached the perfect consistency to be spooned in soft drifts onto the cake slices, the hooting of the kettle summoned Pamela to the stove and she turned off the mixer and set it aside.

While the boiling water transformed the fresh grounds in the filter cone into the dark and fragrant brew filling the carafe, Pamela added a spoon to the bowl of whipped cream and carried the bowl to the dining room doorway. Bettina was just transferring the sixth slice of cake to a plate, but Holly was nearest to the doorway and she reached out for the bowl.

Leaning closer to Pamela, she whispered, "We need another plate."

"Of course! Imogene!" Pamela whispered it to herself as she retreated to the kitchen.

Once the plate was delivered, and another fork too, she launched another kettle of water to prepare the tea for the tea drinkers.

Several minutes later, everyone was back in the living room with cake and coffee or tea at hand. All but

Nell were clustered around the coffee table, with Bettina's hassock and Roland's dining room chair in new positions. Nell's cup of tea rested on the hearth and she held her plate of cake in her lap.

Holly was the first to comment on the cake, pronouncing it to be "Amazingly, amazingly delicious, and it looks like something right out of the 1950s!"

Others were not far behind. Bettina's enthusiasm for desserts was never a surprise, nor was Karen's, though expressed less dramatically given her shyness. But even Nell spoke out in favor, saying, "Very sweet, but it does contain fruit, and the servings aren't too large." And Roland, after his first bite, nodded in approval and noted that the cake was "very good indeed."

In a way it was a shame, Pamela thought, that the whipped cream hid so much of the cake's surface, obscuring the bright pattern of pineapple slices and strategically placed cherries. On the other hand, the airy topping was the perfect complement to the dense cake and the syrup-bathed fruit. A sip of coffee, with its pleasant bitterness, was a welcome contrast.

With almost everyone gathered in a congenial ring around the coffee table, conversation became general, launched by Bettina's observation that, based on the past few days' weather, spring seemed to really be upon them. Holly and Karen were happy to chime in with reports of a joint visit to the garden center, where pansies were already available. From her armchair, Nell described Harold Bascomb's perusal of seed catalogues, and even Roland contributed that he had signed and returned to his landscaping service the contract for the upcoming season.

Only Imogene was silent, nibbling at her pineapple upside-down cake with an abstracted air.

So lively had the discussion of spring gardening plans become that Pamela finally spoke up to ask if she could clear things away so they could get back to work. Unlike Roland, she wasn't usually the one to call people back to the task at hand, but just before the break her crocheted circle had become large enough to form the floor of a good-sized nest, and she was eager to learn from Nell how to make the edges curve up into sides.

"Yes, yes!" Holly was on her feet. "I do want to finish my nest tonight."

Before Pamela could move, Holly, Karen, and Bettina were busy gathering plates and silverware and napkins and cups and saucers. All that was left for Pamela to claim were the cut-glass cream and sugar set and a stray napkin that had ended up on the carpet.

Some minutes later, everyone was seated again and Nell was holding up her own completed circle with yarn still attached.

"Now," she said, "you keep using the same crochet stitch, but you don't increase. So you still go around and around, but now you're building upwards instead of outwards."

Picking up her crochet hook, she worked busily for a few moments and then displayed the result. Already a ridge had started to appear around the circumference of the circle. Pamela collected her own project from her knitting bag, where she had tucked it away, and launched a stitch.

She'd begun to see how omitting the increase caused the edges of the flat circle to curve up when she became aware that Imogene was stirring. She had paused in mid-row and was lowering her needles, with the small bit of knitting dangling from them, into her knitting bag, along with the skein of pale yarn. Imogene noticed Pamela observing her. A fleeting close-mouthed smile came and went, and she whispered, "I have to leave now."

"Oh! Oh, sure," Pamela said. She set her work aside, climbed to her feet, and stood aside as Imogen eased past her into the entry.

She joined Imogene in the entry and saw her out the door with a few cordial words. Imogene offered a quick, close-mouthed smile in return and she was gone.

Pamela returned to the living room to find everyone except Nell staring at her expectantly. When she settled back down on her chair without reacting, Holly spoke up.

"Imogene left?"

Since the answer seemed self-evident, Pamela merely nodded.

"Is she okay?" Holly continued.

"I think she just wanted to get home," Pamela said. "After all, she's been through a lot."

Holly turned to Karen then, and the conversation shifted to a comparison of the progress each was making in the transition from the floor of her nest to its sides. Pamela resumed her work, but silently, and no one else spoke for a bit.

Nine p.m. arrived, signaled by Roland's opening his elegant briefcase and carefully storing away knitting, needles, and yarn before lowering the lid and clicking the tongue of his briefcase latch into place.

Pamela held out her project at arm's length, trying to judge whether her nest's sides were high enough yet to guarantee that any creatures who had already endured one rescue would be safely contained therein.

"It looks good," Nell pronounced from across the

room. She stood up and took a few steps toward the sofa, where Holly and Karen were studying their own projects as well. "You're finished too," she told them. "You just have to make a knot, cut your yarn—but not too short, and hide the yarn tail."

She stepped closer and extended a hand. "Here, I'll demonstrate."

Karen held out her nest, as cozy a home for an orphaned creature as anyone could imagine. Nell perched on the edge of the sofa in the spot that had been vacated by Imogene and asked to borrow Pamela's scissors. A few moments later she handed Karen's completed project back and watched as Pamela and Holly performed the same operation.

"Keep them," Nell said, "to remind you what to do if you want to make more during the week, and at the next Knit and Nibble, I'll gather them all up to deliver to the Wildlife Center."

CHAPTER 21

Bettina had stayed after everyone else left, and now she and Pamela were in the kitchen finishing the cleanup from the evening's refreshments. The turquoise platter, with one remaining wedge of pineapple upside-down cake, had been returned to the kitchen table, and the dirty dishes had been stacked on the counter near the sink. Pamela was transferring the plates to the dishwasher's bottom rack, leaning over and slotting them in one by one.

"Sad—about Imogene," Bettina commented. "The way she left."

"Umm." Pamela responded. The sound echoed back at her from the dishwasher's metal interior.

"Didn't you think so?"

"About what?" Pamela inquired, standing up.

"Imogene." Bettina had returned the unused cream to the carton in the refrigerator and gathered up the napkins for the laundry. "Didn't you think it was sad?"

"Umm?"

"The way she left."

"What about it?"

"Aren't you listening?" Bettina's pleasant features did their best to express irritation. "It was sad that Imogene left early. She just packed up that—whatever it was—that she was knitting and was gone. The poor thing . . . She's really been through a lot."

"Bettina!" Fragments of an idea had been teasing at Pamela's mind ever since the Knit and Nibblers departed. Now, suddenly, the fragments had come together, and the image they presented left her so breathless that she could only gasp, again, "Bettina!"

"What? What?" Bettina looked up, startled, from her contemplation of the leftover piece of cake.

"We have to go to the cemetery right now!" Pamela tugged the dishcloth from its rack and dried her hands. "Don't ask why! Don't even talk! Just come!"

Pamela's tires crunched over the gravel as she steered her serviceable compact through the ancient iron gates that marked the entrance to the cemetery's parking lot. The night was dark but clear, the sky an expanse of black punctuated by a few constellations like random dots of light, and the moon a waxing crescent. One other car was visible, barely, pulled up close to where the gravel, which glowed slightly in the moonlight, gave way to grass, which didn't.

Pamela leaned across Bettina to take her flashlight from the glove compartment and stepped out onto the gravel. When Bettina didn't budge, she leaned back into the car to say, "Come on."

Bettina pushed the door on her side open and popped out to face Pamela over the roof of the car. At that moment, a keening wail arose from somewhere among the tombstones. Bettina immediately ducked back into the car and slammed the door. Pamela slid into the driver's seat and reached for Bettina's hand, which was trembling so violently that holding it sent a shudder through Pamela as well.

"It's not the banshee," Pamela said. "I know who it is—and you do too. Just think for a minute."

She climbed back out of the car and set out toward the dark grass with the pale tombstones sprouting here and there. *Like giant mushrooms in a lawn*, said a small voice in her head, but she had no time to ponder the comparison.

The crunch of gravel behind her told her that Bettina had overcome her fear and was following along, so she sped up and soon felt grass rather than gravel underfoot. As she got closer to the spot that was her destination, she switched on the flashlight, letting its beam guide her among the newer tombstones that constituted the Lister family plot.

The wailing had abated after that first startling outburst, but now it returned, up ahead and very close, nearly drowning out the horrified squeak coming from Bettina, who was about ten feet in the rear.

A dim shape came into view, huddled against a tombstone. Judging by its position, Pamela knew the tombstone to be Isobel Lister's, and she was not surprised that this huddled form was the source of the howling. She shifted the angle of the flashlight and its beam picked out, first, a skein of pale yarn and the beginnings of a knitted *something* dangling from a pair of knitting needles held by a pair of hands.

She let the flashlight's beam dance upwards and it illuminated the face of Imogene Lister, wet with tears. Behind her, Pamela heard Bettina whisper, "Imogene?" Imogene regarded Pamela with red-rimmed eyes that expressed no surprise.

"I wondered when somebody would hear me," she said in a hoarse squeak. She held up the knitting needles with the bit of pale knitting dangling from them. "She won't steal this from Isobel," she added. "She got the green sweater and the first shroud, but she won't get this one."

"She won't get it because she's dead." Pamela knelt on the grass and reached out a hand toward Imogene, who recoiled. "You killed your mother, didn't you?"

Imogene straightened her spine and lifted her chin. "Not on purpose," she said, and her voice became more forceful. "She was fighting with me. She took the shroud off the tombstone and wrapped it around her neck, like a scarf. It was the Tree of Life pattern, an old Celtic pattern that symbolizes immortality—because trees constantly renew themselves and they're gateways to the spirit world. I was trying to pull it off. She lost her balance and I lost my balance, and the shroud got all twisted up and then she bumped her head on Isobel's tombstone."

"How did she end up in the woods?" Pamela asked, and Bettina chimed in with, "And why did you leave the shroud wrapped around her neck?"

Imogene tilted her head up to focus on Bettina, who had remained on her feet. "I wasn't thinking straight," she said. "Would *you* have been?"

Bettina was standing behind Pamela, so Pamela had no idea what her friend's reaction had been, and in the dark Imogene probably couldn't see her either. But perhaps the question had been rhetorical and Imogene felt no need to wait for an answer.

"How did she end up in the woods? I put her there—though she didn't really deserve to be near trees, but I wanted her to be far away from Isobel. She'd already hurt Isobel enough."

"You said your mother got the sweater . . ." Pamela let the words trail off on a questioning note. "I think maybe she *took* the sweater. She was wearing it last Thursday when I ran into her outside the Co-Op."

"They were arguing the morning of the concert," Imogene said. "About me. They argued a lot about me, about Isobel's influence on me—but the truth was that I loved Isobel more than I loved my mother and she knew it and she was jealous. And she felt it was disloyal of me to knit gifts for Isobel but never knit gifts for her. She called Isobel a harlot and said she didn't deserve anyone's gifts."

"She tracked Isobel down in the green room after the concert to continue the argument," Pamela suggested. "And she wanted that sweater and she took it. And in the process, they struggled and Isobel fell and cracked her head against the corner of the desk."

Imogene laughed a curious laugh. "As if having the sweater would mean she had my love."

"Your mother's death was an accident." Pamela leaned forward to touch Imogene on the shoulder, and this time she didn't pull away. "And you can give the police the information they need to solve the mystery of Isobel's death. And Isobel would want that. She would rest more easily in her grave, though you should keep working on the new shroud of course." Pamela nodded at the knitting project Imogene still held in her hands.

She went on, "So I think—and I'm sure Bettina agrees with me—that the best thing for you to do would be to go to the police station right now and tell them what you know about Isobel's death, and then tell them what happened up here on Sunday night."

Pamela had turned the flashlight off, but in the faint moonlight she could see Imogene nodding.

The procession back to the parking lot was led by Pamela, with Imogene next and Bettina trailing behind. When they reached the gravel, Imogene cut off to the side and headed for the car they had noticed when they arrived.

A small caravan composed of two cars, but with Imogene in the lead, made its way through the iron gates and down the hill to the intersection with Arborville Avenue. Imogene turned left and Pamela followed, through Arborville's small commercial district with its streetlamps bright but shops shuttered for the night.

They made another turn, pulled into the parking lot that served the police station and the library, and nosed into spaces side by side. As Imogene, emerged from her car—which, reflecting the Lister family's social status, was revealed under the parking lot lights to be a Lexus—Pamela turned to Bettina.

"You could go in with her," she suggested. "You were determined to solve the Isobel Lister case before Clayborn did and now it's solved. Wouldn't you like him to know you had something to do with that?"

"He won't be here now."

"Probably not," Pamela agreed. "But word will get back to him. He'll probably even want to get your report of what happened tonight."

"He doesn't have to know I had anything to do with it," Bettina said. "Wouldn't things go better for Imogene if turning herself in was her idea?"

CHAPTER 22

Pamela was enjoying a leisurely morning, still in pajamas and robe at ten a.m. No new work assignment had been waiting in her inbox when she logged onto her computer, the house was clean, and laundry was up to date.

As she sipped her coffee, the phone rang and she picked it up to hear Penny's voice on the other end. Penny was glad, she said, that the Arborville murders had been solved, and that they had turned out to be not exactly murders after all. She had heard the news from her friend Lorie, and she was amazed and relieved that Pamela and Bettina had had nothing at all to do with their solution. Pamela bit her tongue to keep from laughing, happy that Penny couldn't see her face.

Penny's friend Lorie had also passed on another interesting bit of news. Lorie's grandmother, it seemed, had been inspired by seeing Isobel at the luncheon—despite the sad outcome—to dig out a box of souvenirs from her early life in Arborville. Among them she had found photos of the nude be-in, held—without permission from the authorities—in County Park in the summer of 1969.

"We were all there," she had emailed Lorie, along with a scan of one of the less revealing photos, "Isobel, yours truly, and Isobel's bestie, Cheryl. So maybe you'll change your mind about whether your grandma knows what it's like to be young."

Pamela was smiling when she hung up the phone. Maybe Wilfred was right. At this point who cared anymore what people got up to in the 1960s? Here was a grandma telling her granddaughter that she had paraded around nude in a public park all that long time ago.

Cheryl Hagan had been determined to keep that secret—though she hadn't killed Isobel in order to do so. Maybe she'd loosen up though. Maybe she'd even end up bragging to *her* granddaughter about the things she'd gotten up to.

The *Register* was still spread out on the kitchen table, though Part 1, with its blaring front-page headline, "Killer No Longer Sought in Lister Murders," had been set aside in favor of Lifestyle, which today featured ideas for Easter brunch menus.

The doorbell's chime pulled her away from contemplating a recipe for a Greek cheese pie. When she stepped into the entry and glanced toward the front door, she knew her caller could only be Bettina. A face topped by a crest of scarlet hair gazed back at her through the lace that curtained the door's oval window. A vibrant aqua ensemble completed the vision.

"I've been with Clayborn," Bettina announced as she crossed the threshold. "I was surprised he had time for me—but I reminded him that the *Advocate* comes out on Friday and today is Wednesday and we have a tight publication schedule and certainly he wants the taxpayers of Arborville to appreciate all that went into solving the Lister killings and to get that news in a timely manner."

She handed Pamela a white bakery box tied with string and took a deep breath.

"But the police didn't do anything at all," Pamela said. "Imogene turned herself in—and told them that her mother killed Isobel."

"He did have news for me though—and I've got an errand for us this afternoon if you're interested." Bettina tilted her head to look toward the doorway that led to the kitchen. "But first, is there any more coffee?"

"There can be." Pamela waved Bettina toward the kitchen and set out after her carrying the bakery box.

As Pamela set water to boil and arranged a fresh filter in the carafe's filter cone, Bettina described her meeting with Detective Clayborn.

"Imogene has been released pending trial," she said. "Bail was ten thousand dollars—not all that much, really, considering. And her father took care of it."

"What do you think will happen to her?" Pamela asked, pausing in the act of spooning beans into the coffee grinder.

"The medical examiner will have to determine whether Barb Lister died from being strangled or from striking her head on Isobel's tombstone—neither of which would be Imogene's fault. But forensics should be able to determine whether her head came in contact with the tombstone, and whether the struggle Imogene described really took place at the gravesite."

Bettina was silent for a moment and Pamela took

the opportunity to press down on the cover of the grinder, sending the beans into a clattering whirl.

"I suppose," she commented when the clattering subsided, "that establishing those things would support Imogene's version of what happened—Barb's visit to the cemetery and her attempt to claim the shroud. If Imogene planned ahead of time to murder her mother, why would she have done it there, and like that? How could she even have enticed Barb to go up there?"

"That's a good point," Bettina said, "and I think—I *hope*—that's how the case will be settled. A tragic, tragic accident. *Two* tragic, tragic accidents."

She loosened the string on the bakery box and folded the flap back to reveal a substantial piece of crumb cake.

"I know we just had this the other day," she said, "but it's my favorite thing from the Co-Op bakery—though I was thinking all night about that leftover piece of pineapple upside-down cake." She glanced around the kitchen as if searching for it.

"I ate it," Pamela said. "I ate it when I got home last night."

A whistle from the stove announced that the water had reached a boil. Pamela tipped the kettle over the filter cone and the tantalizing aroma of brewing coffee began to fill the little kitchen.

Pamela poured coffee into wedding-china cups as Bettina, sitting in her accustomed seat, transferred portions of crumb cake to wedding-china plates. Pamela took her seat then, after first providing Bettina with cream and sugar in the cut-glass set, and she watched as Bettina spooned and poured.

"There's one loose end that's still loose," Bettina

commented after she'd sampled her crumb cake and pronounced it as good as ever. "The person Mr. Nap Year saw going in the back door of the rec center."

"That was Barb Lister," Pamela said.

"Oh—of course!" Bettina tapped her forehead with a carefully manicured finger. "Not Liadan, not Siobhan, not Cheryl Hagan—but somebody who looked like you."

"She didn't really," Pamela pointed out. "She was quite petite, and . . ."

"You could look like that"—Bettina set down her fork and slapped the table for emphasis—"except taller of course, if you paid more attention to makeup and clothes. In fact, now that we've got this mystery all wrapped up, I'm going to the mall to celebrate. Do you want to come?"

"Is that the errand you mentioned?" Pamela laughed. "The errand you're doing this afternoon?"

"No, it's not." Bettina regarded Pamela over the rim of her coffee cup, then she put the cup down. "What I'm doing this afternoon—and you might really be interested—is that Liadan Percy called me this morning to say that she *loved* the story I did on her and that, though Ostara is long gone, her Ostara altar is still up. Since Easter will be here soon and Ostara and Easter are related, she thought I might like to get some photos of her Ostara eggs and do another story. And . . ." Bettina drew the word out with a teasing smile, then went on, "She has kittens now. Lots of them."

The long linen cloth still covered the piece of furniture that might once have been a sideboard, the star shaped from twisted vines still hung above it, and the vases containing pussy willow branches still anchored each end. But now there was more, much more. A rustic basket heaped with eggs dyed in shades of rose, sky blue, amethyst, soft yellow, and pale green had been placed in the center, with a vase of fresh daffodils on one side and a gleaming brass chalice on the other. Candle holders, some tall and some short, held candles in the same pastel shades, some flickering and some extinguished. A whole family of ceramic rabbits had been placed here and there, as if frolicking among the symbols of springtime.

"Shall we have some cider?" Liadan inquired after Bettina had admired the altar, asked a few questions about the significance of its decoration, and taken out her phone to photograph it from various angles.

As before, the cider was waiting on the ornate table that occupied the space between the sofa and the long wooden bench that faced it.

"Three," Liadan said with a smile as she waved a hand in a graceful gesture over the pottery mugs with their fragrant contents. "Three of us here today. A good omen. The number three was sacred to the ancient Celts. Please be seated." The graceful gesture enlarged to take in the sofa.

Pamela and Bettina obeyed and sank onto the welcoming velvety cushions, while Liadan lowered herself onto the wooden bench. She picked up the nearest mug, murmured a few words, and took a sip. Pamela and Bettina did likewise, but without the murmuring. As before, the cider was sweet but not cloying, and with the added flavor of some elusive spice.

"Tell me more," Bettina said after complimenting Liadan on the cider, "about how Ostara is celebrated. You have the eggs and even the rabbits—and Easter has them too. As a child I always wondered about that connection because rabbits can't lay eggs . . ."

"Oh, yes they can." Liadan laughed a merry laugh, pulled her shawl closer, and launched into a tale about an ancient Germanic goddess who turned a bird into a rabbit that laid colored eggs.

Bettina had her phone out again, recording, and Pamela was happy to listen. Liadan grew more and more animated as she talked about the lore that she believed reflected an ancient reverence for the natural world and an antidote to the woes of modernity. Her voice was soothing though, and the dim room, lit by barely more than the flickering candles, invited contemplation.

Pamela stared at the altar, her eyes drawn to the basket of eggs with the soft pastels appearing all the softer in the flickering light. Like Bettina, she had wondered about the egg and rabbit connection, so it seemed only right that someone, somewhere would invent an explanation . . .

Liadan had stopped speaking and the room was silent—only for a moment though. The soothing voice resumed, but now with an extra, crooning note.

"Here's my sweet girl," she was saying.

Pamela shifted her focus from the altar to Liadan, who was leaning to the side watching as the cat Pamela recalled from the previous visit made her slow way across the floor. She was white with dark markings on her tail and ears, and Pamela recalled that her name was Luna.

She came to within a few feet of the bench where Liadan was sitting and looked up at Liadan, who was making gentle welcoming sounds. But instead of going to her mistress, she veered to the side and approached

Pamela, settling back on her haunches right by Pamela's left foot. Then she reached out a delicate paw and rested it against Pamela's calf as she tilted her head and stared at Pamela with her curious mismatched eyes, one blue and one amber.

Not content with merely resting her paw, she began to knead, all the while staring.

"Kittens!" Pamela said suddenly, almost as if the cat was speaking through her. "You told Bettina there were kittens."

"Why, yes!" Liadan stood up. "There are kittens. Perhaps that's what Luna is trying to tell you." She took a few steps toward a doorway in the back wall. "Come!"

Pamela followed, with Bettina a few steps behind. They entered a bedroom, dim like the living room, with heavy curtains at the windows. A large bed with a carved wooden headboard took up most of the space, but in one corner a comfortable nest had been created from soft blankets.

Luna had scampered ahead. By the time they caught up with her, she was reclining there, amidst a squirming collection of tiny, tiny kittens, with eyes still closed and ears still folded. Two were tortoiseshell, three were calico, and one was black.

Still under the spell of the flickering candles and Liadan's soothing voice, Pamela felt tongue-tied, but yes, here were kittens, and she had been looking for kittens. They were too young for adoption now though, so perhaps she should wait a bit, though the black one might even be spoken for already . . .

Before she could speak, however, Liadan whispered, "Let's leave mother with her babies."

Back in the living room, Bettina thanked Liadan and

said that it was time for her and Pamela to be on their way. But as they were moving toward the door, Luna reappeared and headed straight for Pamela. She pawed at Pamela's calf and when Pamela glanced down she found a pair of eyes, one blue and one amber, staring up at her.

Liadan touched Pamela's hand, and added her own scrutiny to Luna's fixed stare.

"Luna is very intuitive," she said, "like me. She knows you want to ask a question, and you mustn't leave without doing so."

Pamela felt a shiver pass over her. Now Bettina was staring at her too, but at least Bettina's eyes were both the same color, and unlike Liadan, her face wasn't framed by a tangle of long gray curls that at the moment seemed to be vibrating with electricity. Pamela wanted to look at the floor, or the ceiling, or something other than all those eyes, but she was unable to break the spell. "The kitten," she said at last, in a small voice. "The black one. I know someone who wants to adopt a kitten."

"Adopt a kitten!" Liadan's face glowed, as if transfigured by joy. "Of course. Adopt a black kitten."

Pamela wasn't sure whether the "of course" meant that of course the kitten could be adopted, or whether it meant that Liadan had known all along what question she wanted to ask. But before she could inquire, Liadan spoke again.

"I don't think that question is the only question troubling you right now." She took Pamela by the arm. "Come," she said, and drew Pamela back toward the sofa. "Come and sit down."

Pamela allowed herself to be led across the floor, gently steered around the ornate table, and settled back down on one of the sofa's velvety cushions. Bettina joined her there, happily attentive as Liadan stepped toward the Ostara altar and returned with a deck of cards.

"Now . . ." The soothing voice seemed to emanate not from Liadan, who had resumed her seat on the wooden bench, but from somewhere inside Pamela's own mind. Liadan cut the cards with her right hand and began to shuffle them by holding half the deck loosely in her left hand and letting the cards in her right hand slip among them.

"I don't know the answer to your other question, but the Tarot will know."

Pamela felt herself squirm. "Oh, really, no," she murmured. "I don't think . . ."

But all those eyes were on her again, even Bettina's. Bettina leaned close and whispered, "Go ahead. Perhaps I could do a feature for the *Advocate* sometime."

Liadan was still shuffling the cards, and the soft whisper of card against card was almost as soothing as her voice.

She paused and said, "Now you must ask your question."

Pamela squirmed again, and said, "No, this is just too . . ."

"I know what her question is." Bettina spoke up. "It has to do with a certain—"

But Liadan silenced her with a commanding gesture. "The querent has to ask," she hissed. "Only the querent."

Pamela closed her eyes and sighed. "Can I just *think* the question?" she pleaded.

Liadan nodded, barely, and continued shuffling. After a bit—how long, Pamela would have been hard-pressed to say—she patted the cards into a compact pile and set the deck on the table between them. All that was visible was the back of the top card, glossy black with a scrolled border and a crest in the center.

"Now you cut the cards," Liadan instructed. Pamela reached out, but Liadan lifted and admonitory finger. "Uh, uh, uh—*left* hand. You want your unconscious to be in charge."

Once the cards had been cut and the top half of the deck set aside, Liadan took the top three cards from the remainder of the deck and laid them out in a row, images facing up. She was humming with pleasure as she seemed already to recognize a message forming.

The images faced Liadan, not Pamela, but studying them upside down, Pamela could nonetheless make them out. First, starting from her own right, was a queen, wearing a crown but dressed in a simple gown and cloak, sitting on a throne and holding a sprouting branch as if it were a scepter. In the middle was a knight in armor, charging forward on a horse and also holding a sprouting branch. To her left was a couple, male and female judging by their garb, though it was medieval, and the male was wearing a short tunic. They seemed to be toasting one another with large chalices.

"The Queen of Wands," Liadan announced, waving a hand over that card. "She is alone, and brooding, incubating an idea—yet her wand is alive, which shows that there is to be movement, movement and growth." She closed her eyes, inhaled deeply, and then expelled the breath.

"And in the center, the Knight of Wands." She raised her eyes from the card to Pamela. "This is significant," she whispered. "Two cards from the same suit, a knight and a queen. And he's moving toward her, whereas she's stationary, but both their wands are alive."

Pamela bent closer to the cards. The Queen of Wands had three sprouts on her . . . wand, she now realized, not a branch, while the Knight of Wands had five. Did that mean something too? she wondered. She could ask later, maybe. Liadan had turned her attention to the last card.

"The Two of Cups," she sighed. "So beautiful. A man and a woman, looking deep into each other's eyes, windows of the soul, and pledging their love."

She sat up straight and squared her shoulders against the back of the bench, as if working a crick out of her spine. "I'll leave you to decide how the cards have answered your question," she said, looking as deeply into Pamela's eyes as the people on the third card appeared to be looking into each other's. She remained in that pose and her gaze grew even more intense.

Then she bent forward and spun one of the cards around to face Pamela. "The images speak to everyone, if they listen," she whispered. "You don't need me." She aimed a finger at the card. It was the Queen of Wands, on her throne, beautifully detailed and complex with symbolism. And front and center in a scene heavy with mystical significance was a small black cat, staring straight at Pamela.

KNIT

Cozy Egg Cozy

Irish Knit Murder has a St. Patrick's Day theme, but since it takes place in early spring the plot also alludes to eggs. Egg cozies might not be common in American households but, according to a British friend, they are very much a thing in the UK. They look like tiny knitted hats and they serve to keep soft-boiled eggs, served in egg cups, warm until they are eaten. Egg cups are also not a common household item these days—one has to like soft-boiled eggs in order to want them—but they are delightful collectibles now and eBay is full of them.

Use fine- or medium-weight yarn and size 6 needles. One cozy requires only about 7 yards of yarn, so egg cozies are a good use for leftover odds and ends in your knitting basket.

If you're not already a knitter, watching a video is a great way to master the basics of knitting. Just search the internet for "How to Knit" and you'll have your choice of tutorials that show the process clearly. The egg cozy is worked in the stockinette stitch, the stitch you see in a typical sweater, for example. To create the stockinette stitch, you knit one row, then purl going back the other direction, then knit, then purl, knit, purl, back and forth. Again, it's easier to understand "purl" by viewing a video, but essentially when you purl you're creating the backside of "knit." To knit, you insert the right-hand needle front to back through the loop of yarn on the left-hand needle. To purl, you insert the needle back to front.

Cast on 20 stitches, using either the simple slip-knot cast-on method or the more complicated "long tail" method. It's easy to find instructions and videos for both methods on the internet.

First you will create 3 rows of ribbing to give your egg cozy a nice bottom edge. In order to create ribbing, you will alternate knit stitches with purl stitches. Classic ribbing is the basic knit 2, purl 2 concept, but the scale of the egg cozy is so small that knit 1, purl 1 creates a more pleasing effect. For your first row, knit 1 stitch, then purl 1, then knit 1 more, purl 1 more and continue like that to the end of the row. On the way back, knit 1, purl 1 and so on again. If you've cast on an even number of stitches (which 20 is), you'll see that now you're doing a knit where you did a purl, and vice versa. This is what creates the effect of ribs. After you do a few rows, you will see the ribs starting to form and this concept will become clearer.

One important note: After you knit the first stitch, you must shift the yarn you're working with to the front of your work by passing it between the needles. After the purl stitch, you must shift it to the back, and so on back and forth. If you don't do this, extra loops of yarn will accumulate on your needles and you will have a mess.

After you complete the three rows of ribbing, work five rows using the stockinette stitch, starting with a knit row. On the sixth row, which will be a purl row, begin to decrease by purling every 2 stitches together for the whole row. You will now have 10 stitches. On the next row, knit every 2 stitches together for the whole row. You will now have 5 stitches. There's a photo of this step on my website. (See below for URL.)

Cut the yarn, leaving a tail of at least 8 inches. Thread a yarn needle (a large needle with a large eye and a blunt end) with the tail, transfer the 5 stitches from the knitting needle to the yarn needle, and pull the tail through the loops, pulling up tight to gather the loops in a circle. There are photos of these steps on my website. Make a knot to hold the circle tight.

Use the tail to sew the two edges of the egg cozy together. To make a neat seam, use a whip stitch and catch only the outer loops along each side. When you finish the seam, make a knot and work the needle in and out of the seam for half an inch or so to hide the tail. Cut off what's left. Hide the tail from when you cast on too.

For pictures of a few Cozy Egg Cozies, including in-progress photos and some just-for-fun photos, visit the Knit & Nibble Mysteries page at PeggyEhrhart.com. Click on the cover for *Irish Knit Murder* and scroll down on the page that opens.

NIBBLE

Wilfred's Irish Coffee Trifle

I thought Irish Coffee Trifle would make a nice, and very original, St. Patrick's Day dessert, but one can scarcely conceive of a recipe idea anymore without discovering that someone has posted a version of that very thing on the internet. This version, however, is my own invention, which I arrived at after studying online recipes for tiramisu and consulting Fannie Farmer's recipe for "Tipsy Pudding."

Trifles of all sorts are traditionally prepared and served in footed clear-glass compotes, rather like large versions of the wide and shallow glasses used for champagne before champagne flutes came into fashion. The clear glass allows the various layers to be seen.

A mixture of strong espresso and Irish whiskey is drizzled over sliced pound cake, and layers of vanilla pudding and whipped cream are added, with shavings of bittersweet chocolate sprinkled on top. I used store-bought pound cake—Entenmann's "All Butter Loaf Cake" is a good version. I made vanilla pudding from scratch, but you can use a boxed vanilla pudding mix instead.

Ingredients
½ cup plus 2 tbsp sugar, divided
3 tbsp cornstarch
¼ tsp salt
2 cups milk
2 egg yolks, slightly beaten
1 tsp vanilla
1 cup heavy cream
4 tbsp Irish whiskey
½ cup strong espresso coffee
1 loaf-type pound cake, sliced
A few ounces bittersweet chocolate, grated

Make the pudding

Mix ½ cup sugar with the cornstarch and salt in the top half of double boiler. If you don't have a double boiler, you can improvise one with a larger pot and a smaller pot. I include a photo of my improvised double boiler with the photos for this recipe on my website. (See below for URL.) Add the milk and blend well.

Bring water to a boil in the bottom half of the double boiler, put the top half in place, and cook the mixture over boiling water, stirring frequently, until it starts to thicken, 10 to 15 minutes.

Add a few spoonfuls of the milk mixture to the egg yolks and stir, then add the egg yolks to the milk mixture and blend well. Continue cooking and stirring until the mixture is thick enough to coat a metal spoon. There's a photo of this step on my website. Turn off the heat and stir in the vanilla. Transfer the pudding to a bowl, let it cool, and then refrigerate it.

Assemble your trifle

Add 2 tbsp sugar to the heavy cream and beat until it forms soft peaks.

Stir the whiskey into the coffee.

Arrange half the pound cake slices to cover the bottom of your trifle bowl or compote; more than one layer is fine. Drizzle half the coffee-whiskey mixture over the pound cake. Spread half the pudding over the pound cake and top the pudding with half the whipped cream. Repeat the process, starting with the rest of the pound cake slices. Sprinkle the chocolate shavings over the top. Chill until ready to serve. To serve, use a large spoon to scoop portions into bowls.

For a picture of Irish Coffee Trifle, as well as some in-progress photos, visit the Knit & Nibble Mysteries page at PeggyEhrhart.com. Click on the cover for *Irish Knit Murder* and scroll down on the page that opens.

Visit our website at
KensingtonBooks.com
to sign up for our newsletters, read
more from your favorite authors, see
books by series, view reading group
guides, and more!

Become a Part of Our
Between the Chapters Book Club
Community and Join the Conversation

Betweenthechapters.net

Submit your book review for a chance to win exclusive
Between the Chapters swag you can't get anywhere else!
https://www.kensingtonbooks.com/pages/review/